SUICIDE TEST

Professor Samuel Langley ushered Jules Kincaid into his office.

"On Wednesday morning, Jules, you will become the first man in history to make a powered flight in a heavier-than-air machine."

Jules was shocked. "Surely you don't expect me to attempt a flight in the *Langley Flyer* already! It's absurd—I could easily be killed!"

Langley smiled contemptuously. "Losing your nerve, Jules?"

"It's not a question of nerve, and you know it! I've made many glider flights, and I fully intend to fly this machine—but tests must be made to ensure the safety of the aviator."

"There is *no time*, Jules. You know as well as I that the Wrights are on the verge of making their own powered flight. We must move now or they will certainly beat us."

"This is no horse race, Professor. If someone were to die testing the *Langley Flyer* it would not only make you the laughing-stock of the entire scientific community, but it would set back progress in aeronautics by at least five years!"

"Jules, son-in-law or not, you are not indispensable, and you *will* make that flight as scheduled."

"And if I were to expose you—your recklessness and financial trickery?"

"You wouldn't do that, Jules. You are much too involved in this project to see it scrapped. You *must* know if our aeroplane will fly, and you are going to find out—firsthand—on Wednesday."

The
Skymasters
Series

SEEKERS
OF
THE
SKY

Richard Hale Curtis

A DELL/JAMES A. BRYANS BOOK

Published by
Dell Publishing Co., Inc.
1 Dag Hammarskjold Plaza
New York, New York 10017

Dell ® TM 681510, Dell Publishing Co., Inc.

ISBN: 0-440-07868-7

Printed in the United States of America
First printing—June 1982

1

HE stood alone at the bow of the packet Eagle as it crashed through the choppy wind-blown waves of Fall River harbor. A cold summer sun threw arcs of flashing rainbows to glint on the salt spray that chilled him as he pulled his tweed cape closer around his thin shoulders. He was seventeen, an orphan, with two younger brothers in his charge; and he was seeing the land of his fathers for the first time.

He was seventeen, but he was not young. Already he had traveled to England and to Berlin with his father. He had seen his parents die. He had shepherded his brothers from the Paris apartment that had been their home—survived tearful *adieus* from their French grandparents, and herded them and all their trunks from the boat train to the *paquebot* at Le Havre, to the harbor in New York, to the Fall River line with the help of the French consul, and now he was to meet his American grandparents for the first time.

He was Jules Kincaid, he was seventeen, and he knew French, English, German, and Latin, and stress engineering, internal combustion, electrical circuitry, and other fragments of his father's expertise. And he knew one more thing, for he had a secret: *he had flown.*

In the Year of Our Lord 1893, few men had flown through the air. Oh, there were hot air balloons, and fools jumping off roofs in ridiculous flapping contraptions. There was even Maxim's steam-powered aerodream that never got off the ground. But Jules Kincaid had flown in a monoplane hang-glider that he could guide. He had flown thirty-five yards from a cliffside, over a sunlit field near Steglitz, Germany. And he knew that he would fly again. It was a burning ambition with his Gallic soul. He would fly again one day, in his own machine, with an engine for power. He would fly *above* fifty feet, *above* the fields and forests, *above* the trees and rivers, *above* the world that laughed at his dreams! He would fly one day as free as the wind, and the world would know of Jules Kincaid.

They had laughed at his father. They had laughed at poor Uncle Penaud. They had laughed at Lilienthal. But powered, guided flight was inevitable, Jules knew, and he would master it.

"Jules, où sont-ils? Est-ce-que ça c'est Grandpère?"

"Tais-toi, François." Jules took his youngest brother under his cloak, the nine-year-old's pinched features peering out from below the frogged fastening

as he warmed his squirming body against his bigger brother.

"Is it?" The middle brother, reserved and proud as his Scottish crofter forebears, peered into the cold sunshine from beneath his shock of bushy red hair at the old couple standing to one side of the little crowd that waited on the Fall River dock.

Jules looked, and he thought he saw a resemblance. The man with the furled umbrella—"*Oui, je crois . . .*" the same red hair, the same erect stance. It had to be his grandfather; it had to be Henry Kincaid. And the woman beside him—emotion rose to Jules' gorge as he looked—he saw something of his father there, his father now gone, now dead.

"Hi, you stupid frogs, clear out of there!" Shouting Irish sailors pushed the boys to one side. "Get that line out, you blockheads! Single her up!"

Jules walked his brothers to the gangway where their five huge trunks and three valises were glistening in the salt spray. Pompous businessmen already flushed with port and puffing great cigars pushed ahead of them down the gangway.

"You come back again, young fellow." The chief engineer was touching his grimy cap in goodbye. "Anybody who knows steam like you do is welcome in my boiler room any time."

The old couple was standing to one side. Jules took Francis by the hand, but Henry resolutely kept his hands to his sides.

"Gran'pa?"

"Jules?" The two older boys extended their hands, taking off their hats. "Henry, and Francis." Henry extended his hand stiffly to his namesake and to his Great-Aunt Prudence, and they were all very correct until Prudence Kincaid leaned over timidly to kiss Francis on the cheek.

"*Grandmère, grandmère!*" The nine-year-old threw his arms around her as she tried to hold back her tears, and Jules dabbed at his face with his deer-stalker hat while old Henry, clearing his throat, put his arms around the shoulders of the two older boys. "Welcome," he said. "Welcome home. I have a hackney waiting." They had to engage another carter for the trunks alone.

Old Henry Kincaid was a Harvard man, class of '44, and a proper Bostonian. His grandfather had crossed the ocean to a new land, and his knowledge of weaving had stood him in a good stead. Henry's father became an accountant in the wool mills. His parsimony had put Henry through Harvard college and his foresight had hoarded enough mill stocks so that the War between the States, which Henry bought himself out of, had made him moderately wealthy.

Henry could afford his town house; he could afford his little summer place. He could have afforded even a coach-and-four, but ingrained thrift led him to hoard his patrimony, and the habit of hard work kept him to his humble but respectable job as a mathematics instructor at Harvard. Timidity kept him from rising above the world of shabby gentility. To be sure, after his son Carl had made such a brulliant record at the college, then had wanted to go on to Berlin, and after his son Carl had made such a brilliant record at the monthly remittances; he was appalled at year after year of payments for the boy, but, after all, his father's fortune had yet increased.

His other son, Stephen, was independent; too independent. After graduating from college, he had gone out West, and he seldom even wrote home. The family had, in effect, broken up following the death of Henry's first wife, after which he had married her sister, Prudence. Henry had never regretted doing so.

"What is in all those chests?" he asked as the carriage lurched along toward the railway that would take them to Boston.

"He wouldn't let me take my *Tour Eiffel*," young Henry said indignantly.

"*Mais alors*, it was two meters tall!"

"What can be in those big trunks!"

Jules regarded the two Henrys, alike as two peas—erect and straight, reserved and correct. "All of my father's papers," he said. "All of them. One day they will be *'istorique*."

Jules sat to one side of his Aunt Prudence, little Francis on the other. The little boy was watching wide-eyed as they clip-clopped through the village. "*Voilà! Un negre, tu vois?*" "*Tais-toi.*"

"What is he saying?" Prudence took his hand. Francis smiled winningly and buried his head in the white ruffles of her dress. Francis couldn't seem to understand that his grandfather's wife was not his grandmother.

"Doesn't he speak English at all?" she asked.

"I do." Henry answered primly. He had learned English more at school than at home, but his very British accent with its French overlay was soon to disappear into prim Bostonian. Jules, on the other hand, having travelled with his father in his fruitless quest for powered flight, spoke rough and ready French, English and German.

"*Gran'mère! Où sont les cowboys?*"

"What did he say?"

"He wants to see cowboys. Like Boofalo Beel."

"Oh, there are no cowboys." Prudence let out a delicate whoop and made an Indian sign. "And no Indians." Francis was disappointed. "But we have a horse every summer."

"*Un 'orse?*"

"And maybe a pony this year?" She peered timidly at her husband. "Humph!" he exclaimed.

"We will go to the seaside," old Henry said, "as soon as we get you some suitable clothes. I have a place at Plymouth." He might have been describing a mansion, but he wasn't.

The ride to Boston was a revelation to the boys. It was all so different, not Parisian at all. The verdant parks of the city reminded Jules of England. His grandfather's house on Brattle Street seemed dissappointingly austere until they discovered the comforts within.

When the boys got outside the next day, they found themselves the objects of animosity and ridicule. Pinafored girls pushing hoops with sticks gawked and gazed. Correct boys in caps and knickers looked down their noses at the three foreigners. "We'll take you to Kurman's," their Aunt said.

In that vast emporium, with its string trio playing tea-time music beside a babbling fountain, there were all the accoutrements of a Boston childhood: plus-fours, high-collared shirts, Buster Browns, and brogans, as well as striped knit bathing suits that hung from their thin shoulders like empty meal bags.

Before the week was over, Jules was registered at Harvard College for the fall term, taking physics and math as had his father and grandfather before him.

Henry and Francis were accepted grudgingly into Boston Latin School, although their placement was to be dependent on their mastery of English.

Grandfather Kincaid did not object to taking all the heavy trunks to Plymouth. He had no intention of bringing them back. Indeed, there was no more room even in the tiny farmhouse he had purchased years before as a summer retreat. Upon their arrival at the farm, the trunks were hoisted on the hay loft to the top of the barn. After Jules saw the hay loft and compared it with the tiny bedroom under the eaves in the old farmhouse, he asked permission to make his bedroom in the barn. It was spacious, and he already had ideas for it.

Once it had been swept out and scrubbed, it became a haven for the pallet bed he constructed. Using his own money, he built shelves for his many papers, and a water-proof cover for them, and a makeshift drafting table for himself. All the plans, all the tracings from Lilienthal's gliders in Germany, all of his father's many successes and failures—all the old plans had their appointed places, including the plans for the Eiffel Tower.

"*Henri, j'ai promis . . .*"

"English, speak English!"

"I have promised to make you a new tower. Grandpa, can we buy some wood in town?"

Jules paid for the materials, and they built yet another replica of the famous new landmark. Henry was helpful, and enjoyed making the precise scale rendering with its tiny figures on the terrace and its working elevator suspended from tiny wires.

As the summer wore on and Francis rode his rented pony or went to the beach with Grandma to

study his English in the sun, it was only one step to
reproducing a model of one of Lilienthal's gliders,
and finding that it always crashed. They tried moving
the center of balance forward and backward, flying
the model from the upper door of the barn, only to
see it glide for a moment, and then nose over into the
mud.

"What we need is colored air," Jules complained.
"Colored air we could blow over the wings to see
what it actually does."

"There is no such thing," young Henry would reply primly. "What's the matter with you? Colored air!
Humph."

One evening they sat in the tiny farmhouse living
room, while old Henry smoked his customary after-
dinner pipe and riffled the stock-market report pages
of the *Boston Evening Transcript*, which was delivered each day for them at the Plymouth Post Office.
The younger Henry was reading *The Rover Boys in
Africa* by the fireplace, while Francis, seated at the
cleared dining table with its smelly kerosene lamp,
worked with Aunt Prudence on his English grammar.
Jules was struggling with a letter to Thomas Edison.

Dear Mr. Edison,
*I am a young research man who has worked with
Herr Otto Lilienthal in Berlin on problems of aero-
dynamical engineering with my late father. Could
you guide me to experimenters working with the
effects of air flowing over fixed wings? I know your
wonderful work with sound waves is not like air
waves, but . . .*

"More flying machines?" his grandfather grunted. "Man will never fly. Look at your father. You just settle down and take some pedagogy courses. With your background, you could be a full professor before you were forty."

"But you don't understand, Gran'papa. I 'ave flown!"

"*Have,* Jules, not *'ave*! Aspirate!" Old Henry rattled his paper and went back to making surreptitious notes on the margin. He, too, had a secret.

When the nip of cold air from Canada began to chill the sand dunes, they closed up the house, returned the horse to the livery stable (the pony went back followed by the copious tears of Francis), and returned to Brattle Street to prepare for the school year.

Without his dreams, his plans and models to work on, Jules was lost. He paced the quiet streets of Cambridge, or he crossed the river into Boston and walked its cobbled thoroughfares. It was now that he missed his father, not only as a parent and friend, but also as a companion in the quest for flight. He was alone, and he missed the opportunity to test his wild ideas against his father's practical experience—the opportunity to launch a Montgolfier balloon of conjecture only to have it punctured and sunk by his father's arrows of common sense.

Of course, his grandfather did not approve. His brother Henry could not understand the technical criticisms of gull wings or articulated rudders, but then, Henry seemed to care only about becoming the perfect Bostonian as soon as possible.

So Jules walked the streets of Boston, watching

the gulls soaring over the masts of the harbor, and the pigeons alighting on the tower of Faneuil Hall. He wasked past the fish houses, the haberdasheries, the saddleries, the blacksmith shops, he watched the horse-drawn drays and the open shays, and marveled at the sights of his father's native city.

It was one afternoon in the basement of Kurman's Department Store that he found the dusty bookshop that was to become so familiar to him. The shop was musty and unkempt, and presided over by a sallow-faced old Jew in shiny gabardine, but it had foreign books, many of them in French.

The manager of the book department would regard Jules with suspicion as he asked for scientific works, or the latest volumes of Rénan, or some Dumas thriller, and give monosyllabic answers. Jules tried to draw him out in French or German, but the old man seemed to despise all of his customers with democratic impartiality.

One Saturday evening just before the store closed, Jules asked the girl who was apparently in charge of the book department that evening if she could import for him the latest proceedings of the British Aeronautical Society.

"Yes, but it will be costly."

Jules listened to her French accent, and replied in the quick argot of the Eighth Arrondissement. "Perhaps so, but I need it to keep up to date."

Her sallow face brightened visibly as she continued the conversation in French. "You have a lot of money for such a young man."

"I am nineteen," he lied. "And I have the best aeronautical library in the world."

"We import a lot of aeronautical works for a man

in Chicago. A Frenchman. Would you like to see his order list?" She took him back to her little desk and opened up an account book. Jules' hand touched her arm as he leaned over her to read the page. He couldn't concentrate.

"You speak French rather well for an indigenous American," he stammered, smiling.

"And so do you—like a *boulevardier*," she said, giving him a sidelong glance and shaking her wavy black hair aside with a toss of her head. She pointed out the name at the top of the ledger page. "Octave Chanute, Chicago." "Proceedings of the British Aeronautical Society, *Revue de l'Aeronautique, Der Vogelflug als Grundlage der Fliegekunst,* by Lilienthal . . .

"He was my mentor," Jules said. "You speak good German, too."

"Yiddish," she giggled nervously.

"*I' bin 'n kosherer Goy.*"

"*Plus royaliste que le roi?*"

They continued the conversation as she made out a ledger page for him. The free and fluent French found them both starved for conversation with a sensible person of the right age. It was like opening a floodgate of vowels as the young lady took his name and Brattle Street address and led him to tell more about himself.

Jules was finding out about her, too. Her name was Leah Dreifuss, and she watched him carefully as she said it, but Jules had no reaction to the name that had figured so prominently in recent headlines. As she supervised the young girl who was closing up the register and counting the cash, Leah gradually told more of herself.

Her father was the proprietor of the book department. Like Jules, she had recently lost her mother, and immigrated to Boston. She was twenty, and Jewish, though not very Orthodox, as he could see from the fact that she was working on the Sabbath, rather than staying at home to be with her father.

"He spends the whole day at the temple anyway," she said, "and we have a little Irish girl who comes in to light the stove and heat up the pork chops." She smiled for the first time, delighted with her little joke. Her smile, her ivory complexion, her large and limpid dark eyes were fascinating to Jules.

"May I escort you home?" he asked, hardly knowing how to phrase it.

"It's only two squares away," she said with a nervous smile. "But, yes." She kept glancing at him as she told the girl how to pull down the metal lattice-work and lock up with the padlock.

On the sidewalk outside, the steet lamps cast dappled shadows through the leaves of trees as they strolled slowly in order to prolong the conversation. "We live almost on top of the shop," she said. "In Paris, we lived upstairs."

"What happened to the Paris shop?"

"The Christians sacked it," she said, watching his expression. "We are distant cousins of Captain Dreyfus. It's the same name."

Jules tried to remember what he could of the French army officer who had been convicted of treason and sent to Devil's Island. "I don't read the newspapers much," he said.

"It was like a pogrom," Leah said, "when they wrecked our bookshop. They came down the street like a flood — big, ham-fisted army sergeants half-disguised in working-men's smocks, big blond Bretons, roaring drunk with cheap wine. They tore down the gates, broke the doors and windows, threw the books out into the gutter and did unmentionable things to them. They started a fire. We had a Caxton—apocrypha on parchment—irreplaceable things." She stopped and withdrew her hand from his to run it nervously through her hair. "My mother was terrified, trembling!"

Jules put his arm around her shoulders, instinctively, lightly.

"They went away," she continued. "We put the fires out and salvaged what we could, and then my mother went upstairs. And then she died." They both walked on, heads down, looking at the sidewalk. "It was quick. One minute she was there, the next minute she wasn't." Leah looked up at him. "It's strange," she said. "I've never told anyone about it."

"Terrible," he said, for want of anything else to say. After more than an hour of rapid-fire French, they were talked out. They walked slowly, in silence. Jules was very aware of the warmth of her arm as he held it pressed against his body, and of her hand within his.

"I live here," she said. "Four flights up. You needn't walk up."

"I insist."

They paused to rest on the second landing.

"Kurman lives next door," she said, "with his whole family. But they're on *premier étage*." They kept climbing, and he admired her little feet in their black cotton stockings. "They get a good rent from us," she said.

They paused outside the door of her apartment, and Jules could hear a strange sing-song whining within, interrupted as Leah knocked on the paneled door. Two chain-locks and a tumbler lock rattled before the door opened a crack to reveal a nearsighted little man, now be-hatted, wearing a strange shawl and holding a prayer book.

"It's about time," Leah's father grumbled, unfastening a last chain-lock on the door.

"Papa, this is Mr. Jules Kincaid."

The old man grunted, gesturing them inside. Wine and a warm dinner waited in heated covered dishes on a candle-lit table. The room was small, but it was brightened by a warm Oriental carpet on the polished wooden floor.

"*Der is kein Yid,*" the old man muttered, and turned away.

Jules was embarrassed. "Well," he said, "good night."

"I'll see you again soon," Leah smiled tentatively as she walked him to the door. "At least when your books come in."

"Yes." Jules smiled thinly, and he heard the locks click into place as he went down the hall. "Going out with Christians?" he could hear the old man start. "Aren't Jewish boys good enough for you?"

"Father, I'm not a child . . ."

Jules hurried down the stairs. He didn't want to listen.

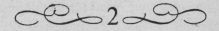

2

THERE was a lot of studying to be done, for Jules had to take special examinations for advanced standing, and he had to be sure that he knew the correct English terminology in physics and math. His technical vocabulary was a mish-mash of German, French, and English. Then there was the strangeness of it all. Jules was used to being an outsider, in and out of Lycee, in and out of London and Berlin, usually talking with no one of his own age, but Cambridge was different. The townies detested the students, and the students seemed to look down their noses at anyone who hadn't gone to Groton or Middlesex.

The professors were cordial. Many had known Jules' father and uncle, and they respected Jules' grandfather. But they didn't really understand how such a brilliant student as Carl Kincaid could have wasted years in gay Paree, trying to flap his wings like a bird. Most of them thought he must have played the dilettante, dabbling at science while enjoying the capitals of Europe.

Jules had been thinking of Leah. She excited him. He remembered the touch of her hand on his arm. He remembered the strange feeling that seemed to come from the middle of his being, a mixture of fear and excitement unlike anything he had ever felt before. Never had he talked to anyone the way he had talked to her in their brief hours together. She had seemed immediately close, an instant confidante; and then, she was a girl.

As he walked through Kurman's and down to the basement that following Saturday, he couldn't identify what it was he felt. He didn't know the word "love." It was not a word he had ever used to win a pretty girl.

Leah was there, with her employee, and she saw him all the way down the long and crowded aisle. She smiled uncertainly, and his pace quickened. "Oh, hello, Mr. Kincaid," she said as she turned her head aside. "Your periodicals didn't arrive yet." He didn't know what to say to her. "But I found something that may interest you." She took him back to her desk, away from the salesgirl.

"Hello, Jules."

"Hello, Leah." She felt it too. They smiled tentatively at each other, and couldn't say a thing.

"I did find something. It's by Cayley."

"Oh, yes." He picked up the old volume. "*On Aerial Navigation.* I've heard about it, but I've never seen a copy. Where did you find it?"

"In Cambridge, where all the used textbook stores are."

"That's wonderful. What do I owe you?"

"Oh, nothing. It was part of a big purchase."

Again he didn't know what to say. "Do you go there often?" They started toward the front of the shop.

"I'd never been there before," she admitted.

"I'll take you to see the college." They stood together, very correct and proper, watching the well-dressed Bostonians, all so much alike and so untroubled, bustling through the aisles in search of bargains.

"Can you leave early tonight?" he asked. "I thought we might have a soda or something."

"Yes," she agreed instantly, as if she had been waiting for him to ask. "Patricia, I'm going now." She turned back to Jules. "First let me get my hat."

They paused on the sidewalk outside the store. "It's such a beautiful night," she said, "and there won't be many more. It's too nice out to go inside."

"Would you rather take a walk?" he responded to her lead with a lack of obtuseness unusual for him. He felt alert and alive as never before.

As they walked toward the Common they spoke of Paris, and of the schools they had attended; she told him of the cold winters in Boston, and he told her of the London fog. Only when they sat down in the park on a bench overlooking a little lake did he take her hand. It was cool this time. Trembling, but cool. They could hardly see each other's faces in the gloom. Bushes rustled behind them and a yellow moon rippled in effigy from the placid surface of the pond.

"I've been thinking of you," Jules said.

"I've been thinking of *you*, too," Leah replied softly.

Jules clumsily tried to kiss her cheek and Leah

turned her head aside and began chattering nervously. She asked him about his father and mother, and how they had died. She asked about his grandparents, too, and his little brothers.

"But how did you live?" she asked. "You must be very rich."

"No. Papa spent his capital on blueprints, on models, on us. Oh, sometimes he would take a job designing an electrical system or a lightweight steam engine, and he once taught at the *École Polytechnique*, but he never spent a franc on himself. He never had an extra suit. He never owned a house, or a horse and carriage, or a piece of land big enough to take his coffin.

"But I don't mind. I understand. Uncle Penaud was the same way. I'm the same way. And I want to build a flying machine! There have been so many failures. And yet, we keep trying."

"And you keep dying."

"You sound like my Grandfather. But yes, they keep dying. *Opfer müssen gebracht werden . . .*"— that's what Lilienthal used to say.

"That's not Yiddish," she changed the subject. "Where did you learn Yiddish?"

"In Paris, not Berlin. Even the Mendelssohns don't speak Yiddish in Berlin."

"Moses Mendelssohn is practically a prophet to my father, and to many others."

The moon shone golden white as they lapsed into silence. Then Jules raised her hand to his lips, and Leah turned to him, and looked him in the eyes, and they kissed.

* * *

Cold fall followed Indian summer just as a caress follows a kiss. The boys were enrolled in Boston Latin School, coming home every day with wonders to tell. Francis, with his charm and outstanding athletic ability, immediately made friends. Henry came home with stories of boys whose fathers owned railroads or steamship lines, boys who spent their summers at Newport and their winters in vast, drafty mansions.

Jules had to study for hours each evening to keep up with the advanced classes in which he had been placed. One physics professor allowed him to do a special paper based on Lilienthal's new book *"Der Vogelfug als Grundlage der Fliegkunst"*, and Jules sent a copy of it to Lilienthal in Berlin.

Also that fall, Jules took Leah to show her the buildings of Harvard, although he didn't take her to his grandparents' home. At Leah's suggestion, he offered to help her and her father with their translation of a new work, Herzl's *The Jewish State*.

On warm weekends he had to go with the family to Plymouth, taking huge baskets of food and sitting on the beach watching the gulls fly. He and Francis made another glider, using waxed paper and the lightest of woods.

As the fall wore on, they spent more weekends in town, and Jules got into the habit of spending his Sunday afternoon at Leah's apartment. Old Mr. Dreifuss had somehow been made to tolerate the goyish Jules, and had even asked for his help in translating Herzl's book.

"Do you believe all this?" Jules would ask.

"With all of this hatred—" the old man would reply testily, "—the only way the Jews can survive is with a homeland. It must happen. It will happen. And I've made a promise to Baron Rothschild to open an office for the Zionist cause."

"But surely, Mr. Dreifuss, French Jews should be French and American Jews should be American, not each serving some foreign country they've never seen."

"Captain Dreyfus is a French patriot. They sent him to Devil's Island. My wife was French. They murdered her."

"I mean, being in the service of a foreign country would only serve to isolate the Jews even more."

"When they kill us and drive us out, where are we to go? We must have a safe home, a refuge."

Jules' frequent trips to Boston in the evenings or on Sunday afternoons led Prudence Kincaid to suspect what might be happening, but she said nothing. Jules seldom took Leah out in public places where they might be seen by his Harvard classmates or members of the Jewish community. If Leah resented never having been to the Kincaid home, she never let on. Even though her father was a very liberal Jew, Leah felt it would do him no good if his daughter were seen out with such an obvious gentile as the blond Jules. Yet she could not help herself. Jules attracted her as a moth to the flame, and she found herself again and again trying to find ways to be with him. It was Leah who gave him the idea of taking her for a beach picnic, and she knew well where they would end up spending the day.

"Mr. Dreifuss, Leah says she has never been to the beach. Uh, with your permission, I'd like to take her for a picnic some Sunday. We could leave early and take a lunch and . . ."

"In this climate? You're crazy!"

"Oh, Papa, don't say no. I've never been. And if it's too cold, we'll just bundle up."

"*Ach,* so you've made your mind up. Just like your mother . . ."

"Oh, Papa—" Leah kissed her father on the cheek with an unusual demonstration of girlish glee.

It was a brilliant and cold Sunday morning when they caught the inter-urban to Plymouth with their blankets and overcoats and two huge wicker baskets. They stared out of the sparkling clean windows of the rattling unheated trolley as it zipped through the countryside, its electric arm overhead making a hissing sound, and the steel wheels clicking on the rails.

Like all good Frenchmen, they had two bottles of wine in their basket, and it helped to warm them as they huddled together under the plaid blanket, their faces turning red with the sun and the wind. It was some time before Jules worked up the courage to present his little plot as a *fait accompli.*

"We'll go to our country house first," he said. "The house is all closed up for the winter but I want you to see our models and plans, and the Eiffel Tower. It's two meters tall."

"The Eiffel Tower?"

Flushed with the wind and the wine and the mid-morning sun, they went striding along the road from the trolley station to the house, swinging their baskets and laughing into the breeze, their bodies singing with the vibrance of their young years. Forgotten were their cares, their duties and work. They were revelling in the joy of youth. They felt free and alive.

They put their baskets down when they got to the house. It was shuttered and locked. Jules helped

Leah peek in through a chink in the shutters to see the white-shrouded furniture, the fireplace and the paneling. They were quiet, like children peeking over a banister at the grown-ups, ready to break into giggles at any moment.

"It's the barn you have to see." Jules said as they picked up their baskets and stole away. "Race you!"

They ran across the yard and arrived panting and laughing. Jules showed her the stalls, now swept and empty, and the feed boxes with residues of wheat. "And upstairs! Here, let me take the basket." As she climbed the ladder ahead of him, Jules caught a glimpse of white petticoats. "Here," she said. "Give me those baskets. You'll fall." She helped him up.

"It's lovely," she murmured when he opened the huge haymow doors to let the warm fall sun shine on the smooth, gleaming floor. "It's like a little house!"

The haymow was fragrant, half full of fresh shocks of hay. It was sheltered from the wind and warmed by the sun.

"Leah . . ." Jules lifted her to her tiptoes. "Over the dunes you can see the sea." Leah turned and put her arm around him, and then broke away.

"We can have our picnic right here." Gleefully, she opened the blanket on the floor, and they took off their coats to use as pillows and spread out their victuals: fresh pumpernickel bread baked by Leah, gooseberry preserves canned by Jules' great-aunt, rich patés, cold roast chicken, and fragrant herb wine.

After they ate and drank, Jules sighed and stretched out in the sun, and Leah lay down beside him. They fell asleep there, and awoke together, warm and close. As if in a trance, slowly and silently, they stood up, touching, looking each other in the eyes—

Jules' sky-blue eyes burning, her dark eyes wide with expectation and yet some little fear. He led her to his little pallet bed in the corner and helped her to undress. "It's all right. It's the safe time." she murmured reassuringly. Jules had on idea what she meant.

They made love slowly, touching, caressing, each worshipping the other's body. Laughing, they almost fell from the narrow bed, but it only served to bring them closer. They lay together, silent and content, and Jules drew her petticoats over her as he saw her shudder with chill.

"Oh—" he looked over at a shelf. "Uncle Penaud's planophore." He jumped out of bed, and picking up the model, wound up the rubber band attached to its propellor.

"You must see it fly! Come."

He ran over to the open barn door, ignoring the cold. "Come on!" Leah giggled, scampered over to stand behind him, and put her arms around him. The blond hair on his chest glinted in the sunlight.

"Isn't it lovely?" he said with a smile, watching as he launched the gull-winged glider out the door.

Leah pressed herself to him, shuddering in the cold and running her hands down his hard chest to his lean flanks.

"Lovely . . ." she said, and he turned to embrace her as they sank to the polished sunlit floor and made the fall season sing with their youth.

The wind was chilly when Jules kissed Leah goodnight at the door in Boston. They kissed, and touched, and kissed again—gently, lovingly, regretfully, gratefully. But they knew that they had to say goodnight.

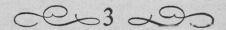

3

In December, Jules received a letter from Otto Lilienthal. It was postmarked from Cross Lichterfelde/Berlin.

> *My dear Jules,*
>
> *It gave me great pleasure to read your school paper on my "Principles of Flight". It gives me even more pleasure to know that my work is being understood and carried on by others across the sea, because one day I will be gone, as your father is gone, and your Uncle Penaud.*
>
> *We have been extending our efforts of late to the production of a carbonic gas motor for our gliders. The principles remain unchanged from Gayley's day: we must build a machine that can*

be guided, and is powered, and has a fixed wing. While I know you are interested in screw-type propulsion, I am pursuing the idea of designing a wing tip which will function like a bird's outer-most feathers.

We are still fashioning our new gliders with willow and muslin covered with wax. How like Icarus that sounds.

I enclose photographs of our latest flights. Control surfaces are still a problem, but trial and error alone can be our teachers. The wind and the weather must have their say. How ironic it is that with all our science, and designs, and risking our lives, we are still outdone by the lowliest of birds, the smallest of God's creatures. Yet we will con-quer. With paternal sentiment, I remain,

> *Most sincerely yours,*
> *Otto Lilienthal.*

In all innocence, Jules let his youthful enthusiasm for aeronautical research become known to one of his professors and several of the students. They were fas-cinated by his Uncle Penaud's planophore, regarding it as a marvelous toy.

One of them, resplendent with a figured tie and a club jacket, said, "Penaud—that's the chap who shot himself?"

"We don't talk about it much," Jules felt forced to answer. "He was very despondent. It's easy to laugh, but hard to make progress."

Jules forgot about it, but in the next issue of the Harvard Crimson, an unsigned column appeared.

"Beyond the blue seas some strange geniuses have recently invented machines that fly through the air—not unlike a setting hen falling from a haystack. Some of these 'great men' even agreed to rise on them themselves, and came down most precipitously. Some came down on top of their machines, while others preceeded them by a few feet. One even survived his fall from the sky only to experiment with a pistol bullet through the head some days later—out of sheer birdie envy, no doubt.

The mechanical birds, invented in order to skim through the ether blue, have not skum. The machines were built with sophomoric enthusiasm and a throbbing heart, but the aforesaid ether still remains unskum. The Milky Way is yet in the same condition, awaiting the arrival of the fearless skimmer.

Now it seems that the evil Atlantic winds have blown one of these genii to Harvard Square. We trust that wiser heads will prevail before the weather vane atop Faneuil Hall is decorated with the gizzards of flying freshmen, and the Common is furbished with floating fluff."

It was no secret who the column was about. Jules was embarrassed, some of his professors even more so. It caused a crisis for Grandpa Kincaid.

"Jules," he took him aside to say, "Jules, you must give up this foolishness. Man was not made to fly any more than the elephant to swim. Your father gave the whole of his short life to it. Now you're trying to do the same. You're making a laughing stock out of me, and squandering good money on imported books and model aeroflyers."

"But Grandpa, Hiram Maxim was just knighted for his research."

"That was for his mechanical rifle, not for his attempt to fly."

"Better I should invent a machine to kill people than a machine to fly, is that it?"

"What a Semitic turn of phrase."

"Grandpa, this is the age of inventions. Look at Edison, and Graham Bell, and Pullman."

"And look at your so-called flyers. They all end up as beggars, or dead, or both. There is not a government in the world that will invest a shilling in flying contraptions."

"Grandpa, I know you mean well, but I have flown, and I will fly again, as surely as I sit here before you."

"Be that as it may, Jules, I cannot let you spend money that rightly belongs to Henry and Francis, and if you continue to do so I will cut you from my will, and they will inherit what little I have. I'm not getting any younger."

"Gran'pa . . ."

"I have reached my threescore and ten."

"Gran'pa, you're a wonderful man." Jules embraced him. It was a rare happening. But he could not change.

There was a small hotel overlooking the Charles River in one of the poorer sections of Boston. Sometimes Jules would take Leah there for an afternoon. They would tell each other of their hopes and dreams, of their frustrations and little victories over life, and they would make love.

There, looking out the grimy window at the gray passers-by and the leaden river, Jules in his shirt and Leah in her camisole and petticoat, they would speak of their lives, Jules' trim blondness contrasting with her black wavy hair as he stood behind her, arms around her, looking over her shoulder.

"*Ah Jules, mon cher, mon tout petit oiseau . . .*" she said as she caressed him. "If only we could run off

together. I'd live in a cave, just to be with you, *cheri*." He pulled her hair aside and kissed the curve of her neck.

"If only we could," she murmured. "But father would never let me. He's so dependent on me. And he'd never let me marry a gentile."

"I wish we could," Jules sighed. "But I have less and less money, and most of it has to go for the boys' tuition. And what are they teaching them? To look down on the Micks and the Jews and the frogs and the wogs."

"The Cabots speak only to the Lowells, and the Lowells speak only to God."

Jules went over to sit on the bed, his naked legs crossed. "What is it?" Leah asked. "Did I make you sad with all my complaining?"

"No, it's not that. It's my grandfather. He wants me to stop my research and turn into a college professor like him. He mentioned Maxim. He'd rather have me invent guns than flying machines. Can you imagine that? He'd sooner have me helping to kill people than helping them to fly nearer the stars, nearer to God."

"The Lord your God is a jealous God,
So Sayeth the Lord."

"That Maxim. Now he's 'Sir Hiram,' and he affects a British accent. Great God! He had this huge steam engine he wanted to mount on a machine built of hickory and canvas. How does he think those balloon fires started? Best way to get killed you can imagine. And he had it tethered! It went two feet up and then crashed at twenty miles an hour. That pompous ass!"

"Pauvre Jules!"

"And Grandpa! He wants me to quit, just when we're so close. He's like the rest of them—he has no imagination, no dreams. Why, only a generation ago, when he was a boy, people traveled the way they did four hundred years ago. And now we can get to New York in a matter of hours on the steam cars, and travel to Europe in less than two weeks."

"Man is so small and God is so great,
The waves of fate break around God's knees
In an endless flow.
Yet men are small and the waves mount high
And engulf our souls—engulf our mortal souls.
The limits to our lives here are many,
But others will come.
And climb through the starbursts . . ."

"What's that?" Jules asked. "The Torah?"

"Goethe. A Christian poet."

"Then maybe there's some hope. If we Christians can be that smart . . ."

Hope there was, in the form of a letter from Octave Chanute. It came in care of the Dreifuss bookstore.

> *May 2nd, 1894*
> *Chicago, Illinois*

My Dear Mr. Kincaid,

I have heard of your experience and aeronautical works through the kind offices of Miss Leah Dreifuss. I am putting together a collection of writings on this subject and would welcome a copy of your paper on Herr Lilienthal's new book. I have the book, but unfortunately I cannot read German.

I am advised also that you are, like myself, a

Frenchman, in spite of your very difficult name, so hard to pronounce in French, and that you are a nephew of the late Alphonse Penaud, whose great efforts, in my humble opinion, are vastly under-rated.

I have been basing my latest efforts to make an air vehicle upon the designs in Herr Lilienthal's book. Since I am an experienced builder of bridges, I venture to say I have made some improvements on the bracing of the wing structure.

If you could spare the time from your studies, I would like very much to avail myself of your expertise. May I, without offending you, offer to send you the railway fare for a journey out to the dunes of Michigan, where I hope to make my gliding experiments this summer? You would be my guest, of course, and may I say that the cuisine of our rough camp is worthy of that greatest of French artists, Maxim of Paris.

In the sincere hope that I may hear from you in the near future, I am,

> *Most respectfully yours,*
> *Octave Chanute.*

For Jules, it was good to know that there was someone in the United States who took him and his work seriously. While he began a voluminous correspondence with Chanute by sending him photographs of Lilienthal's flights, he had to decline the invitation. His Aunt Prudence, at sixty-seven, was in steadily worsening health.

Francis had become very attached to her. When summer came and they moved out to Plymouth, the two of them would sit on the beach for hours—talking, singing songs of the Civil War period, and sleeping in the sun. Jules and Henry had to keep their eyes on them, for when Francis went to curry his pony or take a swim, Aunt Prudence would awaken with a start, complaining of assorted aches and pains.

The boys had to pitch in the keep the house clean, to hitch up for a drive to the village for supplies, even to prepare the vegetables and build the fire; for old Henry, well aware of Prudence's condition, was withdrawing into a world of his own invention. He set up a little table in the corner of the room and began making records of the stock market fluctuations of the previous fifty years. Consulting volumes from the public library, he would make averages of prices, adjusting them for the season and then charting them on a great sheet. He would sit in his lamp-lit corner making calculations in the evenings while Francis read Jane Austen aloud to Prudence, and Jules and Henry lay on the floor in front of the fireplace making plans for the new flyer. It was to have a wingspan of ten feet, just wide enough to go through the haymow door.

"Henry, you can figure the wing-lifting area so it can hold up its own weight plus the weight of a man, can't you?"

"Of course. We've got that from Ader's figures. But they always flip over. We have to make some sort of vertical wing that we can adjust for the side wind."

"The thing is, I think, that we're looking at three dimensions. It's not like flat surfaces. We've got up and down, and left and right, and rolling on its own axis. That's the thing we have to think of." They would go on and on, making sketches, comparing them with older designs, and making new calculations.

On one of Grandpa's trips into Boston to visit his brokerage house, Jules went along to see Leah.

"You must find an excuse to come out to Plymouth," he told her. "I can't get away. My aunt is failing fast. I've seen it before with my mother. Come out and spend the day. Deliver some books or something."

Leah's almond-shaped eyes gave him a sidelong glance. "I'd like to. *I will.* It's been so long, Jules." Glancing around to see that no one was watching, she put her hand over his. "You look so brown! Like an Indian!"

"Come. Come next Tuesday. I'll meet the 10:01 and you can go back after supper."

"I will, I will. I'll tell papa something. Another beach picnic."

By nine o'clock on Tuesday, Jules had already curried down their rented horse and harnessed him to the carriage. Aunt Prudence was preparing a picnic lunch. Her husband was planning to stay at home to work in the garden.

"Jules, I want to go with you to town," Francis insisted.

"No, Francis. I'm just going to pick up this girl with the books and come right back. You have to stay and help Aunt Prudence. And Henry—you get the beach chair and the blanket ready."

"Don't boss me around, Jules. Just because you're bigger . . ."

"I'll make it up to you. Be a good fellow."

"All right," Henry said grudgingly.

Jules drove off on the Plymouth road, slowing down to a walk after he checked his pocket watch. At the station, he tethered the horse in the shade of a tree and waited impatiently for the "ding-ding" of the trolley as it rounded the last turn from Boston and crossed the Plymouth road.

And then she was there, wearing a straw hat with a ribbon down her neck, fresh in white and black.

"Hello!"

"Hello." Jules took off his boater with a sweeping gesture and smiled as he took her hamper. "My, what's in there?"

"Books. And the last of the Passover wine. Are you glad to see me?"

"I can't tell you how glad." He helped her into the carriage and off they went at a trot. When they reached the first grove of trees, just outside the village, he stopped and kissed her. "That's how glad I am, Miss Dreifuss. Welcome to Plymouth."

"Do I get to see the Plymouth Rock this time?" she asked.

"See it? You get to touch it!" He smiled, putting her hand just where she had wanted to put it.

"Oh, you're terrible. What if someone saw us? Drive on, MacDuff." She moved primly to her own side of the carriage as he wryly picked up the reins.

"Goethe?"

"Shakespeare, a Jewish poet." She couldn't help smiling as she watched him from the corners of her eyes. The sun glinted on the trim line of blond hairs on the backs of Jules' hands, and almost made her forget to be nervous about meeting his family.

"Oh, are we there already?"

"A long walk, or a short ride." He handed her out as the boys came running from the barn, barefoot and already in their bathing suits.

"Henry, this is Miss Dreifuss." Henry blushed as

red as his hair, and tried to keep his voice down in its new and very masculine lower register.

"And this is Francis."

"How do you do, Francis?" Leah said with a smile.

Prudence was coming out of the house. "Aunt Prudence, this is Miss Dreifuss. Isn't it nice of her to come all the way out here just to deliver some books?"

"How do you do, Miss Dreifuss? You must be tired after that long trip. Come in and let me give you a cup of tea." She had a very good idea why a young lady would travel so far to deliver books to a handsome young man.

"Come in; I'll introduce you to my husband."

"Henry, you go load up the carriage for the beach. Francis, take these books up to the haymow."

"Aw gee. You do it."

"Where are you learning language like that?"

"Aw heck, everybody says it."

"Never mind, just go ahead and do it."

Jules hurried after the two women. Prudence was just introducing Leah.

"Henry, this is Miss Dreifuss from Kurman's. She brought some books out for Jules all the way from Boston. Wasn't that nice of her?"

Henry Kincaid stood up from his desk and eyed the girl with polite suspicion. "How do you do," he said.

"Your grandson has quite a library."

"Well, nice to meet you." He sat down again and continued making notes from a library book.

"Well, Miss Dreifuss . . ." Prudence took Leah by the arm.

"Call me Leah, Ma'am."

"All right, Leah. My husband is staying home. Would you like to wash up at the sink, or . . . " She gestured at the two-holer "facility" visible through the back window.

"Oh no, I'll wait 'till we get to the beach. I'm looking forward to it so much! I've never been there."

"Ah, yes. Well, we have some fresh rhubarb pie and cold ham. Oh—I don't suppose you eat that."

"That's all right."

"Well, I'll bring some cold chicken and the potato salad Francis made, and . . ."

"All right. Let's go!" Jules was impatient.

"Well, I'm—all right. Are the baskets all loaded? And the unbrella?"

The three of them sat in the front, the ladies with their parasols, and Henry and Francis sat in back on the tops of the wicker baskets. It was only a short drive to the beach and they were able to put the horse up by the club bath-house. Other families that summered nearby were not out yet, or had gone home for their heavy Victorian mid-day meals, but there were enough on the beach so that Prudence had to greet several family groups.

The two younger boys were cavorting in the surf even before their lunch was spread out. Prudence sat in her heavy beach chair and supervised. Leah murmured to Jules in French. "Where can I change? I've got my bathing suit on under these, and I'm all hot and sticky."

"Behind the dunes. At the bath house. Wherever you want to."

When they finally sat down to eat, the boys were already over their first exuberance, but they ate heartily. Prudence seemed very tired. Leah just nibbled at her food.

"*Jules, que est-ce-que c'est que c'est* rhu-bar-be?"

Henry and Francis looked at each other.

"You don't know rhubarb?" Francis laughed, his shock of hair bleached gold-blonde by the sun.

"*Adorable,*" Leah said, reaching out to touch him.

"You didn't say she was French," Francis accused Jules.

"Well, she is," Jules answered.

After they had finished their heavy luncheon and poured more iced tea from the thermos jugs (Leah hadn't unpacked the wine), Prudence relaxed in her chair under the big parasol while the boys stood up eagerly. They weren't to be allowed to swim for an hour, but they kept watching for their aunt to fall asleep.

Leah's ankles and feet were tiny and trim, and very white. She waded gingerly into the surf until it was up to the knees of her pantaloon bathing costume. Jules got himself wet, his hair dark and plastered to his head, and then kept her company.

"Now you look like a Frenchman," she smiled.

"Well, I am, I guess," Jules smiled. "Let's take a walk."

"*Et les gossons?*"

"Oh, we can watch them over the tops of the dunes."

After speaking to the boys, they strolled away from the beach, Leah picking her way carefully on delicate feet. Behind the first line of dunes they sat down, brushing sand from their feet. They could see the boys running and playing with a piece of driftwood. Jules lay down and closed his eyes.

"Feel that breeze?" he asked. "Perfect for gliding. I wish I were in Michigan. Or Berlin."

"Could you leave me so easily?" Leah asked.

Jules squinted up at her face, now delicately pink and somehow sad in repose.

"*Baise-moi*," he said, reaching up, and a tear came to his eye.

They kissed, at first gently, and then more insistently as the sun beat down on them, warming them, giving life where there was none before.

"*Jules, non*! What if they see us?" He put his arms around her from the back and they looked over the top of the dunes, but soon they could not see what they were seeing, so far gone were they in sensations of love. The sound of the surf became thunderous, and then faded; the warmth of the sun became as nothing, and then soothed them as they came to.

"Let's go into the water." Jules stood up and brushed himself off.

"I don't know how to swim."

"Neither do I."

They laughed and went down to the beach, into the surf.

It was late as they packed up everything they could without disturbing Prudence. They even brought the horse-and-carriage down the slanted shingle.

"Oh, I'm stiff," Prudence said when they woke her up. "Oh, you should have gotten me up. You're all dressed!"

They helped her into the carriage and packed her big chair into the back.

"There's just time to take Leah to the trolley," Jules said.

"I'm so sorry I fell asleep. We didn't get a chance to talk." Prudence put her hand over Leah's.

"I had a lovely day, Mrs. Kincaid. Thank you so much."

"You must come out and see us again. I'm sure there's so much we could learn from you."

Prudence didn't get out of the carriage when they got to the station. "Boys, you take Aunt Prudence home. I'll wait and walk," Jules said.

He stood close to Leah as they waited.

"I'm worried about my aunt," he said. "She overdid it."

"How old is she?"

"Sixty-eight, I think.

"That's not old."

He helped her put her things on the car when it arrived, and then, after a quick look around, leaned over to kiss her.

"Thank you for coming out, Leah," he murmured softly.

"Goodbye, Jules," she called to him as the car pulled away.

"Goodbye, Leah," he called back.

Dusk was falling as he walked back to the farm. The lamps were lit. "Aunt Prudence was so tired she didn't want any supper," Henry explained when Jules came in. "She went right to bed."

"Where's Grandpa? Did you eat?"

"He's outside, hoeing the weeds."

"In this light? We'd better get him in. And I'd better get some food on the table for you."

They ate in silence.

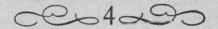

4

"Jules! Wake up. Wake up!" It was a brilliant morning. Sunshine flooded the hayloft.

"What? What is it?"

"It's her. Aunt Prudence. She's still in bed."

"All right, Francis. I'm coming." Jules brushed the sleep out of his eyes and pulled his clothes on. "Where's Grandpa?" he asked as he splashed water on his face from the stone horse-trough. "Have you had your breakfast?"

"Grandpa's just sitting at his desk. Henry's trying to build a fire in the stove. It went out. I'm hungry." Jules thought he looked scared as well.

"Everything is going to be all right," Jules tried to reassure his brother as they went into the house.

"Good morning, Henry. Got the fire going? Make

45

some toast, will you? You know how." He went to his Grandfather, who appeared to be occupied with a slide rule.

"Good morning. How are you, Grandpa?"

"Mmm . . ." The old man quickly covered up his scratch paper. "It's getting hot," he said. Jules patted him gently on the back. "Have some breakfast, Grandpa."

He knocked gently at the door to the bedroom. "It's me, Aunt Prudence." She looked pale even though her cheeks were pink with fresh sunburn.

"Oh, Carl. You came back."

"It's me, Jules. You've got to eat something." Francis was peeking in from the doorway, and the odor of burning toast pervaded the house.

"Aunt Prue, are you all right?" Francis came to the bedside hesitantly, and took her hand.

"Good morning, Francis. Of course. I was just dreaming."

Jules kept himself busy, making sure that his aunt got up long enough to clean herself up, and he made sure that everyone had some breakfast before he went out to harness the horse to drive to town for a doctor. He didn't want to think. Too easily, his mind returned to Paris and his mother's lingering death, his father's sudden demise, chattering relatives trooping in and out, taking care of the boys, and writing to Lilienthal, and getting passports. . . .

The village doctor interrupted his morning office hours to drive out to the farm. After spending twenty minutes in the room with Prudence, he came out and stood by Henry's desk. But he addressed himself to Jules.

"She's fine. Just a little overtired. She worries too

much. I'm going to send you some medicine for her. You must all make sure that she gets plenty of rest, and make sure she eats enough. Now, there's nothing to worry about." Henry looked relieved.

"Thank you for coming out, Doctor." Jules tried to smile. "You made us all feel much better." He turned to his brothers. "Henry, why don't you put our horse in the barn, and Francis, wash up the dishes by the pump. I'll take care of the doctor."

He accompanied him out to the yard. "Is she really all right?" he asked.

"Well, young man," the doctor spoke seriously, "I think she had a very mild heart attack. I understand she's had a strenuous time of it lately."

"Yes. It was just her and Grandpa all those years after my father went back to Europe. And now—three noisy boys all of a sudden. Schools and clothes and two houses to keep up . . ."

"Your grandfather seems to be very preoccupied. That happens sometimes. All those years of depending on her . . ." The doctor peered more closely at Jules. "You seem to be a responsible young man. You're going to have to make sure she doesn't overdo it. She must have plenty of rest and quiet. Do you think you can see to that?"

"Yes, sir."

"Then I'll leave it to you. Now, about my bill . . ."

Jules quietly reorganized their lives around his aunt. Henry would do the cooking while Jules kept the house and barn clean. Francis washed all the dishes, breaking one occasionally. Old Henry tended to his garden, and kept making his mysterious trips into Boston every week, coming back laden with books and charts and stock market reports as well as his lesson plans for the fall.

In the mornings Francis would sit by his aunt's bed reading to her from the Victorian novelists or the New England poets she loved so much, and Prudence would gently correct his pronunciation.

At mid-day, they would put a table under the trees in the yard and eat their luncheon *al fresco*. In the afternoon Francis would be riding his pony while Jules and young Henry worked together in the barn, constructing a large glider.

They had built a single-wing model with tiny slivers of wood and waxed paper. When it seemed to fly well enough from the haymow door, they tried to duplicate it on a larger scale, using flexible willow covered with cotton, sewing the fabric, and coating it with wax mixed with kerosene.

"Stability, control, and then finally power. That's what we have to look for, Henry."

"It still looks like the same old plans from Cayley," Henry said.

"Sure, after sixty years of experimenting and all those deaths and all that money lost, that still looks like the conformation that will have to be used to make a flyable, guidable powered aeroplane."

"It's something like Lilienthal's gliders, and you actually flew them. Why is he still experimenting if they fly so well?"

"He keeps detailed records of every flight. He says we have to gain flight experience, even if it's only sixty seconds at a time, before we'll be able to make any progress. Man has to learn about the winds and air-currents. It's like a new ocean, with uncharted currents, and once man has learned to float in it he must learn to swim."

"Well," Henry said, "If I have to do all your figuring for you, why don't you translate all of Lilienthal's notes; the ones you have from your trip to Germany. That way I can get some idea of what actually happened."

"That's a good idea. And I can get some of the new material he has accumulated. I think I'll write to him."

Jules sat down that very night to write a letter in his labored German to Lilienthal in Berlin, asking for copies of his latest experimental records. As the summer went on, and he found himself spending more and more time at the bedside of Aunt Prudence, he made a complete translation of all the notes of Lilienthal's many flights.

"Henry," he would say as they sat on the dunes overlooking the beach at Plymouth, "Henry, the real problem is control. We're gaining flight experience of course, or at least Lilienthal is, but this business of working the wings or shifting the weight from side to side—it will work with small gliders. As soon as we get something big enough, though, to have a motor on it, we're going to have to have mechanical controls."

"And then you're going to start to add weight. It's like Maxim all over again."

"And we're going to have to make lighter metals or use wires. Or steel rods." Francis came riding by on the sand, kicking his pony in the ribs and whooping like a wild Indian. Jules and Henry tried to signal him to be quiet so that he wouldn't wake up Aunt Prudence, but they couldn't help laughing.

"At least one of us doesn't have his head up in the clouds," Henry said.

As the summer wore gently on, Aunt Prudence seemed to drift slowly away. She ate less and less. She slept more and more. She spoke of her childhood, of spinning wheels, of carding wool, of cooking in a pot suspended over an open fireplace. She spoke of her sister, and how proud she had been of Carl.

"Your grandmother—my sister—loved your father so. He was as blond as you are, Francis. But his hair got darker as he grew taller. We all adored him. So long ago . . ."

Grandpa seemed to withdraw more and more into himself, working on his lesson plans for the fall, although they'd been the same for twenty years, and making his weekly trips into the city to visit his brokerage house or the public library. Although the younger boys had come to depend more and more upon Jules, he did manage to break away one weekend and go into town with Grandpa to register for the fall term—and to get away from it all.

It was a perfect summer day when Jules strolled through Kurman's Department Store, feeling agreeably correct and proper in his high collar and stiff suit. He could see Leah all the way across the crowded basement sitting at her desk, working hard on pages of figures. The serious look on her face and her ivory complexion made her seem more desirable than ever.

"Oh, hello Jules. What a surprise."

"Leah, I came here the moment I got into town," Jules said glibly.

"I thought you had forgotten me." Leah's smile was cool and reserved. Jules sat down on the corner of her desk with the studied casualness that he had learned in Harvard.

"My Aunt Prudence has been so ill, I felt I couldn't leave."

"That's too bad. Give her my regards."

"Leah."

"What? . . ."

He tried to take her hand, but she stood up quickly and smiled. "Aren't you afraid someone will see us?"

"Don't be that way. Take the afternoon off. Let's go over by the Charles—"

"Oh, I couldn't. I have so much to do. My father's going to Switzerland."

"What for?"

"He's a delegate to the World Zionist Conference."

"What in heaven's name is that?"

"You remember. The Jewish state."

"It'll never work." Jules smiled in a superior manner.

"We have to start somewhere."

"Leah, leave that to old men with beards. You're young, you're beautiful," he leaned over and whispered into her ear. "I need you."

"No," Leah took a step back. "No more of that. I have some new books for you. How's Francis?"

Jules toyed with his straw hat. This was a new sensation to him, and he didn't quite know what to make of it.

Prudence Kincaid got weaker and weaker as the summer went on. Everything was neglected for the long, gentle deathwatch. The huge glider, almost completed, gathered dust by the haymow door. Francis' childish voice, reading the poets in the accents of New England, echoed trembling in the cooling August air. Henry, tall and straight, and now with the deep voice of manhood, paced alone, or did his chores in silence. Only Grandpa seemed unaffected.

And then the day came when she drifted away. Now so thin, so pale, so light, white against the coverlet, she dreamed no more.

With careful foresight Grandpa Kincaid had long since made provision for Prudence to be laid to rest next to her sister, his first wife. It fell to Jules to make the funeral arrangements. Together, the four Kincaid men stood side by side at the gravesite to hear the stern words of the Puritan ethic. After losing so many who were so close in such a few years, death had become a way of life for the Kincaids.

It was Jules who had to hire a local farmer to cut the hay and store it in the barn that fall, and it was Jules who closed up the house at Plymouth. It was Jules who made sure that the boys were properly registered in school, and who opened up the house on Brattle Street, removing the white dust covers from the furniture like exorcising ghosts of the past.

When he finally made it to Kurman's to see Leah, he discovered that the book store had been sold and that Leah was preparing to go to Basel with her father as his assistant at the World Zionist Conference. Somehow Jules' conversation with Leah never seemed to become personal again. He was able to hire her maid to come in and cook dinner for the Kincaids. When he saw Leah off on the steam-cars to New York to take ship for Europe, he was but one among many. Jules stood alone to one side.

Like his grandfather, Jules withdrew into his studies. If for a while Leah had drawn him out of himself, and if for a few years he had found new warmth in his Aunt Prudence, a woman who had loved him, now they had left him, as his mother had left him. They had all left him.

Young Henry, too, had found his own way of withdrawing from the family life he had enjoyed for such a brief period. He excelled in his schoolwork, he excelled in sports, he excelled at making important friends; yet he was cold: cold, objective, reserved.

Francis—ah, Francis; he accepted death as a part of life. He smiled and moved on to other things. Everyone loved Francis. His teachers patted his golden head. His schoolmates laughed at his ready smile. The girls soon noticed his twinkling eyes. Francis, the youngest of the Kincaid boys, was beloved.

Octave Chanute wrote Jules from Chicago saying that his new book reviewing the available literature on flight had brought him many friends who were devotees of this new science, which had for so long been a popular sport for crazy people.

"Instead of putting a dihedral on the wings," he wrote, "some of my new friends, particularly two avid young bicycle manufacturers from Ohio, have in mind adding a vertical structure to the airfoil plane or planes in order to achieve stability. This avoids the very complicated structural problems of angling the wings and I have made new plans for a double-plane structure with extremely light but strong bracing of sitka spruce, a local wood. Control will be achieved by shifting the body weight of the flyer who will be at the point of balance at the center of the craft.

"I repeat my invitation to you to come gliding this summer on the dunes of Michigan. From what you tell me of your as yet untested glider, you sound like a very practical young man. I look forward to meeting you."

Jules advised Mr. Chanute that he did indeed want to make the trip that year and proposed to come out for the month of July. In order to earn his keep he suggested that he make various translations from the German.

The year flew by on gull wings. The boys were happy at school, and Grandpa seemed unchanged—teaching his classes as if by rote, the same from year to year. Grandpa seemed to spend more and more time at his borkerage office in downtown Boston, as if it were a private club. Jules found it irksome to have to hire the maid and make sure that the house was kept clean and neat, but housework did at least give him some exercise.

At the end of the school year they all went out together to open up the country place at Plymouth. They shared the cooking and cleaning, and Jules made arrangements for them to eat at the beach club when Grandpa went into Boston for the day.

Francis had a full-sized horse of his own to ride this year, which gave him two horses to curry and exercise. With his equitation classes in Plymouth and his swimming, he kept himself busy. Henry and Jules put the finishing touches on their gull-winged glider and built a long ramp down from the upper hawmow door. The local farmer who cut their hay for them put strategically located stacks of spring wheat around the barnyard so that their glider might have soft landings.

With its ten-foot wingspan, the glider was designed to carry the simulated weight of a pilot. The first flights, however, without such a weight, went far beyond the end of their ramp and caused great damage to the glider as gusts of wind flipped it over every time. Constant repairs had to be made and within weeks practically all of the angled-plane structures had been reconstructed at one time or another.

"What we should do, Henry, is to angle the wing-tips and pre-set them before every flight to counter the prevailing winds," Jules said.

They were able to buy a used anemometer from the nearby Coast Guard station and they installed a windsock on top of the barn. Then, when Henry had devised a method for pre-setting the wing-tips, they began to make flights with a simulated pilot weight, tying bags of grain to the center of the aeroplane and flying into the wind. They found that they could direct the flights with considerable precision, and guide the glider to land on the haystacks.

Henry kept a running record of his wing-tip settings, and became engrossed in making mathematical calculations of the air pressure at the various settings. He coined the Anglo-French word "aileron", meaning "big wing", to describe the movable tips.

It was toward the end of June, on a grey day when the winds blew in steadily from the ocean, that Jules and Henry made their best flight. Using only a token ten-pound bag of wheat in the pilot's position, they launched their glider down the ramp into the face of the wind. It took off before it was even half-way down the ramp, flew past the haystacks, past the road, past the fence, and on to a long grassy meadow—six hundred yards of flight. All three of the boys were yelling with excitement as they chased it. Earthbound it was not.

It landed undamaged. As they gleefully walked it back across the road and the field, they shouted that their time had come.

"Imagine a pilot," Jules laughed, "with the wings set at zero, and shifting his weight the way Chanute does."

"All we have to do is find a fifty-pound pilot," Henry said with a straight face. "Or build a bigger glider," Jules laughed.

"Can I be the first flyer?" Francis' eyes lit up.

"Not on your tintype," Jules said as they prepared to hoist the model on the haylift rope and position it on the ramp for its next flight.

The next morning was cold and blustery. Old Henry Kincaid got up early to catch a trolley to Boston to go to the office of Morgan and Company, where he did his banking and brokerage. When Jules returned from taking him to the station, he asked Francis to rub down the horse and stable him, while he went in to assist Henry in cleaning up the house and washing the breakfast dishes.

Things were very quiet in the barn; too quiet. The stillness of the windy morning came to an abrupt halt when they heard Francis yell, "Jules! Henry! Come on. Do you want to see me fly?" Jules glanced out of the window, and then ran out into the yard.

"Francis, no! You'll hurt yourself," he shouted. Henry, still holding a dish-towel in his hand, was yelling too. "Don't do it. You'll ruin it! You'll kill yourself." Francis was spread-eagled in the center of the glider as it sat at the top of the ramp. Only his twelve-year-old arms held it back. As they watched, he let go

and put his arms out on the wings, and the glider began to descend the ramp, picking up speed in the face
of the wind and then taking off in a gentle glide,
about six feet above the level of the field. They
watched Francis raise his shoulders, and his blond
hair blew in the wind while a smile as wide as the
heavens crossed his face. Then the aeroplane just
seemed to stop, and the tail dropped, and it slid onto
the earth with a sickening crash.

"Francis, Francis!" The boys ran across the barnyard, Henry still holding his dish-towel in his hand.
But Francis was already standing up, shaken, and
muttering "I flew—I flew it!"

They stopped and stared at him. "You could have
been killed," Jules said.

"I flew! I flew!" Francis began to get a silly smile
on his face. Then Henry started to turn as red as his
hair.

"You wrecked our beautiful aeroplane. You—you
cad. You snivelling little fool, I'll kill you!" Henry was
actually jumping up and down with anger, and then
he started beating Francis with the dish-towel until
Francis ran away laughing, with Henry running after
him as hard as he could, screaming sophomoric impre-
cations.

Jules sat down in a heap and watched his brothers until they were out of sight behind the barn. He
looked at the wreckage of his aeroplane and laughed
wryly. And then, after some time, his eyes began to
measure the distance from the barn, and the angle of
the wind, and the course of the flight. *Francis had
flown.*

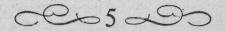 5

THIS time the glider was beyond all salvation. They swept up the remnants and saved a few scraps, but the rest made a glorious fire in the fireplace. Henry was depressed; Jules preoccupied.

The Saturday dances at the Plymouth Beach Club, swimming, and boating had begun to occupy Henry. Francis, of course, had his horses. And Grandpa was busy with his mysterious charting, so Jules felt no guilt as he contemplated the tickets that unfolded in accordion pleats: Boston to Albany; Albany to Gary, Indiana; and from Gary north to the deserted dunes of Michigan.

Jules had never travelled alone. The prospect was exciting. He packed and repacked his dictionaries, his plans, the plans of the glider, a letter of credit; cotton collars, celluloid collars and his boater and his cap. Then came the day to say good-bye at the station and

59

to go to Boston to spend the long night. Then came the steam-cars and the long voyage across a vast wilderness—which to his Gallic mind was still peopled with red Indians, hard-riding cowboys, and fast-talking railway candy butchers who went on to make great fortunes.

The world was his apple as he sat by the train window, hot summer winds blowing cinders in his face. The world was all his—his dreams, his future, and someday a woman to love him again, to kindle that spark that had burned and gone out. But that was the future and this was the present, and the world was all his, to live and to learn.

The hamlet of Gary in the state of Indiana was hardly more than a one-horse town. Jules was exhausted as he stood at the station with his valises, perspiring under the July sun, still astounded at the vastness of his father's United States. From the station he could see the one paved street in the town of Gary, and though he could not spot the famous one horse, it was presumably stabled on one of the dusty side streets. Also perplexing was the whereabouts of the Indians in this famed state named for them.

Finally the huffing, puffing locomotive from Chicago came around the lower bend of Lake Michigan. Jules stumbled aboard, his seersucker suit now crumpled, his high collar wet, and his white galluses now grimy with dirt. He fell asleep promptly, only to be shaken awake by the conductor as they arrived at the village of Saugatuck. He stood alone on the unpainted station platform until he was hailed in thoroughly incomprehensible French by a huge Negro, brilliantly handsome in a white suit and broad Panama hat, who was holding the reins of a mettlesome

horse that was harnessed to a carriage, the back of
which seemed to be filled with crates of squawking
chickens and baskets of green, fresh vegetables. En-
throned on the polished black leather front seat of the
carriage was a tiny princess in white, holding a diminutive parasol above her sun-tanned face and long,
wavy gold ringlets.

"*Bonjour, Monsieur Kincaid,*" the fairy apparition
piped improbably. "*Vous êtes Monsieur Jules Kincaid?*" she asked, giving his name the absurd pronunciation he had last heard from Leah Dreifuss.

Jules was stricken dumb at this miniature vision
of Parisian elegance in the middle of the wilds of
Michigan.

"*Moi, je suis Ariel Chanute,*" the little girl said.
"*Et ça, ça c'est le Prince d'Orleans.*"

"That's right, and welcome to Michigan," the
huge Negro said, picking up Jules' heavy valises with
a wave of the hand and plunking them down on the
back of the carriage. "Step right this way, sir," the
man continued in his peculiar patois.

Jules sat down next to the little girl and she began chattering away as they turned out of the station
and trotted along a dusty country road. "My father
sent me to get you but we had to stop on the way to
purchase supplies," the child said. "It's such a pleasure
to be able to speak French. It's only my father and
Mademoiselle and Monsieur Sam I can talk to. All the
rest of them talk like cowboys. I'm learning English,
though.

"Monsieur Sam is the prince of New Orleans. He
runs the camp. We have four tents. One of them blew
down last week but we put it right up again."

"Are you from Paris?"

"My daddy was born in Paris. We built a great bridge last year. The Mayor of Chicago came to our house. I was in my nightgown," she giggled. "We gave him *Poulet à la Reine*. My daddy knows Prince Napoleon. He's a bad man. Prince Sam is my friend."

"Ahem—" the huge black man smiled down at the little girl. "Did you have a good voyage?" he asked Jules. "That's a very long trip, all the way from Massachusetts."

"I'm exhausted, hot, and dirty," Jules replied as they drove up to the camp. "And astounded!"

"*Ah, tout ça!*" the black prince smiled. "We try to retain some vestiges of civilization here in the wilderness."

The four tents were in a sandy valley surrounded by dunes waving with green dune grass. Jules held the reins while the big Negro unharnessed the horse and hobbled him near a tent.

"Mademoiselle! This is Mademoiselle." A French maid, frilly in black and white from neck to toe, and rubbing sleep from her eyes, curtsied and said, "*Bonjour, Monsieur.*"

"Over there's the cook-tent," Sam said with a smile, gesturing at a tent with rolled-up side curtains. A young boy sat inside it, peeling potatoes.

"And over here is your tent," the big man said, carrying Jules' luggage inside one of the tents and putting it down beside a canvas cot. "All the men are out gliding."

Jules, dazed, put his straw hat down on the bed.

"You can take a nap if you wish," the Negro said, "or come over to the cook tent if you're hungry; and if you need anything else, Lake Michigan is just behind the dunes."

After he had been left alone, Jules unpacked his two suits and hung them up on a hook screwed into a tent pole. He changed into his striped bathing suit, took a towel from another hook in the corner, and walked through the grass up a twelve-foot dune from which he saw for the first time the great inland sea of Lake Michigan. He waded into the surf and out again, and as he stood drying in the sun, he looked again, marvelling at the vast expanse. For miles to the north, miles to the south, there was nothing but deserted sand and dunes just barely demarked by a few lines of trees inland. To the west was a vast green sea topped with whitecaps; to the east only the red, white and blue pennant of Napoleon III that surmounted Mr. Chanute's tent gave evidence that there were other human beings still alive on the face of the earth. Despite his long voyage over plains and farmlands waving with bright grains and untouched copses of trees, Jules now realized for the first time the vastness of this great country which had been bequeathed to him by his father.

Above him, strong winds swept in invisible currents, and a chicken-hawk soared so high that it was nearly invisible. Jules knew that that soaring hawk was seeing something that had never been seen by man. He breathed deeply and then stumbled back to his tent, where he fell asleep between fresh cotton sheets.

Jules woke up to the sound of a silver bell. The sun was setting behind the dunes as he pulled on his stiff dark suit and searched his luggage for a collar button. He looked at his shirt sleeves where Aunt Prudence had lengthened them and noticed how his sun-browned hands contrasted with the white of the cotton, and he reminded himself that he would have to get some lemon soap to bleach himself out. Otherwise he would go back to Harvard in the fall looking like a red Indian. He examined himself in the steel shaving mirror he had hung up on a tent pole, and approved of what he saw: a very correct Bostonian. He looked like Francis trudging unwillingly to Boston Latin School. "*Quelle blague!*" he muttered.

His polished brogans sank into soft sand as he walked up to the door of the lamplit mess tent. "*Papa, c'est Monsieur Jules. M. Jules, ça c'est mon Papa.*" The little princess was fairly skipping with joy. The heavenly odor of fresh fish pervaded the air. Four men sitting at a long trestled table rose to their feet.

"*Bienvenue à Camp Chanute.* I am Octave Chanute." The eyes of the genial white-haired man crinkled with a smile as he extended his hand and then gestured toward the others. "This is Dr. Spratt, and Mr. E.O. Huffaker. Jules Kincaid. Have some wine. It's chilled to perfection."

"This is what we call roughing it," Mr. Spratt said as he poured wine for Jules and for Mademoiselle, who was trying to quiet her little charge. "Mr. Spratt is our medical expert, "Chanute said with a smile," just in case any of us should fall out of the sky. He also does a little bridge building on the side. Mr. Huffaker, of course, built our models. Did you see them as you came in?"

"No, I . . ."

"Of course you didn't. We just brought them back. They're tethered behind the tent. You'll have to look at them after dinner. And this, of course, is Will

Wright, the famous bicycle salesman. He designs them, builds them, sells them, repairs them . . ."

"—and wrecks 'em."

"Mr. Wright brought one of his velocipedes all the way from Ohio only to discover that you can't ride a bicycle in loose sand. Like yourself he has read and done everything in the way of heavier-than-air experiments."

"Here you are!" The huge Negro placed a great silver platter in the center of the table and began to serve them "—fresh Michagan perch, caught today by the Mayor's son."

Jules concentrated on the fish course, peering shyly at the others as they talked, and watched Mademoiselle expertly fillet the fish for the little girl, who was squirming impatiently. Professor Chanute, with his red face and his white hair, seemed the very picture of the successful engineer and bridge builder, which of course he was. The two middle-aged men were probably employees of his, out for a pleasant and luxurious camping trip to play with the huge toys they called gliders. Mr. Wright, although balding and of a more serious mien than the others, appeared to be younger than they were. He was angular and gawky, his forehead red-bronzed by the sun below a line of demarcation, dead white above. The lamp-light gleamed through the sparse hairs of his balding head.

"I understand you knew Penaud?" Wright said in a drawling Midwestern accent.

"We called him Uncle Penaud," Jules smiled thinly. "Actually he was my mother's cousin." Will Wright said nothing. "I was only five when he—died," Jules ended lamely.

"He knew more than any of them," Wilbur Wright

drawled. "More than Cayley, more than Ader, more than any of 'em."

"I have some of his original sketches with me, if you'd like to see them." Jules smiled rather more comfortably. The dinner-table conversation disintegrated into a technical discussion of theories of flight punctuated by the delightful digressions of Ariel Chanute.

"My Mama said she couldn't come out this time because the new fashions are just coming in from Paris to Marshall Field's *grand magasin*, but we are supposed to go ahead and have a good time without her, although I don't know who's going to cook dinner for her. Do you think Mama will go hungry?"

"I doubt it, my dear," Chanute smiled.

"My Mama is the best-dressed woman in Chicago," the little girl said.

"And the most beautiful woman in Chicago," Huffaker managed to interject.

"Don't let Mrs. Field hear you say that," Spratt chimed in.

After the main course and a chocolate mousse, Mademoiselle took Ariel away to get her ready for bed, and the men took Jules outside to show off their tethered gliders. "Don't get that lamp too close," Spratt warned. "They'll burn like kindling."

The biggest one was a great box-like affair with two wings and spars of sitka spruce, but another one had three wings, and looked like Lilienthal's recent efforts, except that the flexible wings were straight rather than curved. "It must have a terrible tendency to turn over," Jules commented.

"You'll see tomorrow. We made almost twenty flights today. One of them was twenty-two seconds!"

"It's the only way to learn," Wilbur Wright said.

As he lay on his cot that night listening to his tent-mate's snores, Jules stared at the fabric above him and looked forward to the dawn. This was action, not sitting in some dreary office someplace designing wing spars. This was gliding, the way God's own creatures flew—instinctively, without thinking about it. And Jules Kincaid and Wilbur Wright, like Lilienthal in Berlin, would be among the first human beings ever to learn those instinctive reactions; the first human beings ever to fly.

The day shone brilliantly clear. The early morning sun brought a fresh breeze off Lake Michigan. It lacked only the salty tang of the sea. They were out on the dunes, the five men, and from the beach, not a tree could be seen above the dune line.

Chanute and Spratt sat at the top of a great dune at a wooden table with an anemometer and a stop watch. They took notes recording the details of each flight, while Wilbur and Jules, assisted by Huffaker took turns gliding down over the beach on the great bi-plane glider. At the end of each flight they would pick up the craft, one on each wing, and slog back up through the sand. Panting, Wilbur would say, "Hot air rises above the heated sand. Try to ride it up, like that eagle there. He isn't moving a muscle, he's just soaring higher and higher."

Often, they would touch a wing-tip and crash down—"digging a well," Wilbur called it. Then there would be spars to repair or replace, and fabric to be sewn, and dope to be applied. Chanute always sat at his table. The two older men would try a flight only under the best of circumstances. But Jules and Wilbur, both in their twenties, were resilient, and paid no attention to bruises or minor pains.

As the days went on, they made scores of flights, shifting their bodies and trying different methods of control. The bi-plane was stable, but hard to control. The triple-decker, however, had all the airworthy qualities of a locomotive. They would laugh about it, but not when Huffaker was around.

At lunch, at dinner, and far into the night, they would discuss their short flights; what went wrong, and what went right. They would speak of the angle of incidence, and the shape of the leading edge. And sometimes they would go in theory beyond gliders, to the next step: powered, controlled flight. "You could fly a barn door, consarn it," Wilbur would ejaculate, staring with the burning eyes of a religious fanatic. "You could fly a barn door if you put it at the right angle and had enough power on it."

On Sundays, in deference to Bishop Wright's son, they did not work. They would take a picnic lunch down to the beach in the morning while Wilbur went to town for church, and they would lie on the sand in the sparkling sun or under the umbrellas, while Ariel scampered up and down the beach chasing birds. They would sit in the sun, drinking champagne from the bottles, chilled in silver buckets, that Big Sam had brought down from the camp, and talking of Paris, or of Chicago and San Francisco, fabled cities Jules had never seen.

Ariel was a revelation to Jules, her blond ringlets always tied up with a satin bow, her eyes sparkling with joy, her flashing white teeth punctuating endless chatter. Jules had never known anyone quite like her. All the women in his life—his mother, his aunt, Mrs.

Ader—had been older. Even Leah Dreifuss, young as she was, had seemed to be old with the wisdom of centuries. This shining child, like a faceted jewel sparkling in the sunlight, continually delighted him with her feminity, her sudden sharp desires as changeable as the wind off Lake Michigan, and her sudden kisses as she ran to jump into his arms, almost knocking him over on the sand. And old Octave Chanute, incredibly *soigné* in his immaculate white suit and gray silk cravat, was delighted to see the two of them run shrieking down the beach, or come dripping out of the surf exhausted with laughter, plunking themselves down on the sand at his feet.

"She reminds me of my little brother," Jules would pant. "Except that he sometimes stops talking."

"I imported an *enfant savant*," Chanute would smile at his older friends, shrugging, and the two of them would nod sagely. "Not only a scientist, but a Roman Deity, in striped bathing suit, flying by on winged foot."

The summer days went by, and Jules often wondered what he was there for. They didn't seem to learn very much from their flights, but in years to come Jules would often recall word for word the laconic but pungent and pointed remarks that Wilbur Wright made. The three older men with their cigars and fine wines often seemed to be on a summer vacation, and Octave Chanute could well afford it. Yet it was a serious game, and one at which young men would surely triumph. Away from the beach and the child and the sunlight, Jules felt strongly the invisible mantel that cloaked his young shoulders with vague authority. The heritage of Penaud, of Ader, of Lilienthal, and the genial authority of Chanute pervaded the camp. They discussed and digested the flights and the failures, the lives and the deaths of men gone before. If their limited understanding was still veiled with misapprehension, it was there in their psyches, one day to come forth. Strange oceans of air swirled high above them, and now—now at last—they would begin to conquer the sky.

The brilliant sunlit August days wore into cool September. "Jules," Chanute said, "you're almost like a member of the family. Come to Chicago for a few days. Let me be your host." Jules decided to see what life was like among the very rich.

Their camp was struck, the tents pulled down. A flurry of telegrams had been exchanged, and now as they went in their carriages to the little station at Saugatuck, Jules could see why. Because of Chanute's pre-eminence in railroad building, the private car of the president of the Erie Railroad had been sent for them, and another car had been sent to take their carriages and luggage. Jules couldn't believe the luxury of the great walnut-paneled private car into which he and the rest of the summer campers stepped. It had a private galley, which was immediately taken over by big Sam for the preparation of their lunch, as well as a private bedroom suite for Ariel and for Mademoiselle. Jules sat with Wilbur Wright as the cars were joined to a local train that rattled down to Gary, Indiana, where it hooked up with the Chicago train. Wilbur got off there. He had to return to his bicycle shop. Just before they arrived he showed Jules a little news story he had found in a Chicago paper.

"It's from Rear Admiral George Melville, the Navy's chief engineer. 'A calm survey of certain natural phenomena,'" Wilbur read with a pompous accent, "'leads the engineer to pronounce all confident prophecies . . . for future success of heavier-than-air machines as wholly unwarranted, if not absurd."

"That's quite a statement," Jules said with a smile.

"Wal," Wilbur drawled, "they said Columbus was crazy, too."

As they pulled out for Chicago, they left Wilbur Wright standing at the station, surrounded by his wicker suitcases and leaning on his bicycle. Jules hardly knew what to make of him. Most of the potential aeronauts he had known had been educated at the best technical schools in the world, and were usually men of independent wealth. Here was a provincial American who had never even graduated from high school, but whose incisive mind seemed to cut through all the foolish arguments of the past without pre-judgment, in a search for new, simple truths. Jules found the simplicity of his approach very impressive.

The railway took them around the great bend of Lake Michigan and up toward Chicago, where the new skyscrapers glinted in the evening sun. All of the buildings seemed to be spanking new, bright and clean. Spratt and Huffaker departed for their offices in the Loop, but Chanute was met by a shiny black barouche which took their little group to his mansion overlooking the lake. The entrance hall was all of marble, and a staff of eight domestic employees was waiting lined up to greet them. Ariel pulled free from her governess and ran up the stairs to see if her dolls were alright. "My dear," Chanute said to his regal wife, "May I introduce Mr. Jules Kincaid?" Jules was unsure of whether to offer his hand or not. He settled for a slight bow, his right hand twitching.

"How do you do? Welcome to Chicago." Mrs.

Chanute seemed to dismiss him as another countrified disciple of her husband's. That was practically the entire extent of their conversation during his three-day stay at their house.

Jules' guest room was spacious and comfortable. The huge walnut bed would have been big enough to sleep all three of the Kincaid brothers. Adjoining the room was a tiled bathroom with a huge claw-footed tub.

A young man in a Prince Albert coat and striped trousers unpacked Jules' valise. "No dress suit?" he asked superciliously.

"I'm afraid not," Jules had to admit.

"Then I shall take this suit down to be pressed. We dine at eight. Shall I draw a bath for you, sir?"

"Yes, thank you," Jules answered without hesitation.

He luxuriated in the hot tub. It was the first time he had ever sat in a tub big enough for him to be able to stretch out his long legs. He relaxed and enjoyed the comfort until he heard the valet come and go again in the adjoining bedroom. A great six-foot towel was draped over a brass pipe next to the tub. Jules was surprised to find that it was warm to the touch when he dried himself. Touching the brass rack, he confirmed that it was steam-heated. After he had dried himself off and draped the towel around his middle, he went back into the bedroom to find that his shoes had been shined to a mirror brightness, and that his suit had been freshly pressed and laid out on the bed. According to his pocket watch, he still had a great deal of time before dinner would be served. He wandered down the carpeted corridor till he heard a squeal of girlish laughter, and peered guiltily into an open door.

"Monsieur Jules, come meet my dolls." It was Ariel, dressed in a miniature white negligee, with her blond curls freshly done up in a blue ribbon. A doll's house some six feet high took up one whole wall of the girl's bedroom. A tea-table laden with silver and porcelain dishes was set up for her dinner, and Mademoiselle was sitting there with her, trying to get her to eat, but Ariel jumped up, giggling, and pulled Jules by the hand over to her doll-house. "This is Babette and this is Octavia, and here is Thumbelina." Ariel introduced the array of porcelain dolls. Each was dressed in a fashionable gown.

"Ariel," Mademoiselle said severely, "you must come and eat your supper. Monsieur Jules, help me make her to eat." Jules took Ariel by the hand and seated her ceremoniously at the tea-table. "I'll come back tomorrow and meet your dolls again," he said. "But now you must eat your dinner like a good girl."

"Oh, pfui!" Ariel said.

When he came out into the corridor again, Jules could see guests arriving downstairs. They were all formally dressed. They had already seen him, so he had to go down. He felt very conspicuous in his ready-made lounge suit. "This is Mr. Kincaid from Harvard," Madame Chanute introduced him grudgingly. "He is one of my husband's young protegés." There were only eight other guests, but Jules was awed. One of them was the president of the Chicago Burlington and Quincy Railroad, and another was a state senator.

Jules was seated near the end of a long table and could hardly see Chanute, at the head of the table, over the flowers. A great array of heavy silver implements was set before him, and there were fine porcelain plates and ornate, crested serving dishes. As course followed course under the benign supervision of Big Sam, now more impressive than ever in white tie and tails, Jules hardly knew which forks and knives to use until the huge black butler unobtrusively picked them up for him and put them on the edge of his dish. The forbidding silk-gowned ladies, stiff with stays and lace, peered through their lorgnettes at him. Jules answered their polite questions with monosyllables. Only when Chanute drew him out about his experiences in London and Berlin and Paris was he able to make a few contributions to the conversation. Even then, he had to admit that he had seldom seen, much less talked to, the titled personages he was asked about.

The next morning Jules explored Chanute's great library. It was filled with leather-bound volumes and graced by great artistic renderings of Chanute's famous railroad bridges over the Missouri. There was also a collection of various types of wood treated with preservatives, for Chanute was an expert on the subject. In the afternoon a young man from Chanute's office took Jules on a tour of The Loop. Jules marveled at the elevated steam railway, and was later astounded at the size of the great Chicago stockyards.

His short visit to Chicago showed him a life he had never seen. Yet, duty called him to go back East, and when Big Sam delivered him to Union Station, he was not sorry to go.

In Chanute he knew he had made a life-long friend, but Jules' life was made of sterner stuff. Love, friendship, and pleasure were rare and wonderful gifts; duties and dreams were to be his lifelong companions.

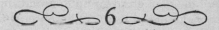

6

Jules' junior year at Harvard began with a great deal of rushing around to register himself and his two brothers. He suddenly realized what a help Aunt Prudence had been, and he missed her more than ever. Jules had to sell more of his mill stocks to pay for all the tuition fees and to outfit the boys with the clothing proper for their school. His grandfather offered no contribution, and Jules asked for none.

Then the school year began in earnest. Jules' school record was by no means brilliant, especially by comparison with that of his father before him. In his first years he had had trouble both with his written English and his comprehension of the lectures. Then, too, his reputation as a fanatic devoted to flying machines made his professors rather leery of him.

The usual campus fraternity fuss and football fever passed over Jules' head. He was earning the reputation of a grind, yet without the high grades that usually go with it.

In order to compete for a prize in physics, Jules wanted to write a paper about the invisible currents of air which he believed to exist far above the surface of the Earth. He proposed to analyze accounts by balloonists for the last hundred years, anemometer readings from mountain-top stations, and perhaps direct observation of fast-moving clouds, estimating the speed of the wind that was pushing them by making triangulations. "Perfectly absurd," his professors said. "No one insane enough to go up in a balloon could be trusted to make accurate scientific observations. Scattered anemometer readings, moving clouds; these are not scientific data. This sort of thing could make us the laughingstock of Harvard. Think of your grandfather."

Jules abandoned the project and instead dashed off a quick paper on the methods used by Sir Hiram Maxim in making the world's lightest steam engine, the one which he had mounted on his ill-fated flying machine. Jules' paper was returned without comment. The prize was won by a brilliant young man who designed an electrical circuit for the Edison Company. Jules could have designed such a circuit in perhaps ten minutes.

As Thanksgiving and then Christmas approached, their first without Aunt Prudence, the lengthening winter nights found them all at home studying hard. Henry was winning prizes at school in mathematics and Latin. With his Lyceé background, he had had no difficulties in making translations, only in writing clear English. Francis was the best football player at the Boston Latin School. Often he would come home late from school, muddied and bruised, after football practice.

"You're going to get yourself hurt, Francis," Jules expostulated. "You're going to get a broken leg or a broken arm playing with all those bigger boys. You're too slender and small-boned to be playing that game."

"Don't worry about me. It's fun. When are you going to buy me one of those padded leather helmets?" Francis asked. He went on to chatter about the horseless carriage he had seen being repaired at a local blacksmith shop. "This chauffeur fellow, he's a race driver! He just took a piece of iron, heated it up, cut it and hammered it into a new camshaft, put it into the machine and started it up and drove away in a cloud of dust!"

"Is that why you were late for supper? You should be home studying instead of hanging around blacksmith shops. Look at your grades for the first term!"

"Well, they're as good as yours, Mr. Harvard Man."

Jules' correspondence with Chanute continued through the year. Jules no longer felt comfortable writing in French, so they corresponded in English. Chanute's English was impeccable. Jules would enclose little notes in French, or cartoons, for Ariel, whom he called "the little princess," and she would answer with long run-on scribbles, switching from French to English and back again in the middle of sentences that were totally devoid of punctuation.

Chanute put Jules into contact with a Professor S. P. Langley in Washington, D.C. Langley was a promi-

nent scientist, and also the executive head of a rela-
tively new institution in Washington which was
named for a Mr. Smithson. The Smithsonian Institute
seemed to be a combination museum and scientific
laboratory. Langley was apparently another aeronautical enthusiast. He wrote requesting copies—or better
yet, the originals—of any of Penaud's plans that Jules
might have in his possession.

In the spring, Langley invited Jules to Washington to make a formal presentation of Penaud's plans to
the Smithsonian. Jules accepted warily, but with alac-
rity. He was worried about what he would do after his
graduation from college. The funds were running low,
and he felt that he could not spend any more on himself or his aeronautical experiments. What was left had
to be put aside for Henry and Francis. Of course,
Grandpa was not poor, but he had repeated again and
again that he would cut Jules off without a penny if
he continued with his "aeronautical nonsense." Jules
was irked by the idea of being dependent upon his
grandfather for anything in the future. The old man,
since the death of his second wife, was sinking deeper
into his studies of the fluctuations of the stock market.
Jules' only companions were Henry and Francis.

In Chicago, it had been embarrassing to go down
to dinner in Chantue's house and sit at that silver-
bedizened table with ladies in Paris gowns, and men
in white tie and tails, while he was in his stiff and
rather shabby woolen suit. In anticipation of his
Easter trip to Washington, he shopped around and finally found a formal suit and even a boiled shirt and
white tie at a second-hand clothing shop near Harvard. It was practically unworn. Probably some rich

student with an unlimited clothing allowance had sold it to get extra spending money. Jules had it taken in to fit him, and, when he tried it on, Francis said, "It's wonderful. You look like Edwin Forrest."

"Second-hand clothing!" Henry sneered. "Next thing we know you'll be buying Levi's riveted trousers from peddler's carts."

"Never mind, Henry. When you inherit all of Grandpa's money, you can buy me a new suit."

Jules felt very much the man of the world when he left for Washington, toting his Gladstone bag full of clothes and another filled with drawings and data for the Smithsonian Institute. He changed trains in New York, which seemed to be a dirty and bustling place, and arrived at Washington's Union Station, where a carriage and driver were waiting to pick him up. He was taken to the Cosmos Club where Professor Langley was putting him up, apparently not taking any chances at introducing an uncouth stranger into his home.

Jules read Langley's note welcoming him to Washington, and sent back a reply by way of the coachman requesting an appointment at the Smithsonian for 9:00 A.M. the next day. After unpacking his clothes and putting on a clean starched collar, he took a walk around Washington. The weather was much warmer than in Boston, and the natives, many of whom seemed to be Negroes, spoke a completely incomprehensible version of English which Jules supposed was comparable to the differences between Big Sam's Creole French and his own Parisian French.

He peered into the guest's dining room of the Cosmos Club when he returned from his walk and observed that all of the diners were formally dressed, so he walked up the four flights, changed clothes, and descended again for dinner. A white-haired British headwaiter seated him in a corner. Jules was very self-conscious until he relaxed with a delicious fruit punch and studied the complicated menu which was, blissfully, all in French.

During dinner, he watched the table manners of the other diners, and wished he had purchased one of those books on the "etiquette of the four hundred". Aunt Prudence's training seemed inadequate in this world of terrapin and champagne. Jules pulled out his wallet and signaled one of the black waiters.

"Oh, no sah. You Mister Langley's guest? You jes' sign here, sah."

Jules purchased a cigar at the counter in the lobby, went out in front of the building, and stood there, blowing smoke and trying to rock up and down on his heels the way Chanute did. Without Chanute's ample girth, though, he looked merely nervous rather than impressive.

The strange foggy city seemed to be as hot as Paris in July. Jules slept poorly. In the morning he rang for a servant, and was able to go down the hall and enjoy that wonder of wonders: a hot bath. Then, half-dressed, he repacked the papers he was giving to the Smithsonian in his smaller valise and headed downstairs.

At breakfast he was slightly revolted at the huge sideboard of fish and eggs and ham and potatoes, and an atmosphere already redolent with odor of bacon and coffee and port wine and cigars. Jules had never been able to accustom himself even to his Aunt Prud-

ence's hearty New England breakfasts. Toasted bread
and coffee was about all he could tolerate.

Jules, groomed and dressed as would suit a Harvard man, was still too early for his appointment with
Professor Langley, so instead of taking the horse-cars,
he walked briskly in the early morning sunshine to the
Smithsonian. According to his pocket watch (it was a
Waltham, ticking away at precise railroad time according to a system established by Professor Langley)
he was exactly on time for his appointment. A forbid-
dingly overstuffed female sitting in front of a writing
machine, her gray hair pulled back in a bun, greeted
him suspiciously.

"Mr. Kincaid to see Mr. Langley." Jules smiled
and handed her his card.

"I'll see if *Doctor* Langley is in," she said huffily,
emphasizing the academic title.

She disappeared into an inner office. Jules put
his valise down on the floor and began peering at the
many framed sheepskins on the wall. There were doctorates from Harvard, Yale, Oxford, Cambridge, and
even from the University of Wisconsin. They all were
inscribed "*honoris causa*". There were memberships in
leaned societies and fraternities, and citations from
such places as Manchester, in England. They were all
inscribed to Samuel Pierpont Langley.

"Have a seat, young man." The woman had returned. She returned to her work, and Jules paced
nervously, reading more of the gaudily framed diplomas.

"Please sit down, young man. Dr. Langley will be
ready for you shortly."

Jules sat down impatiently, wondering if he was

supposed to be impressed with Langley's busyness and his evident acclaim as a scientist.

"Well, well, young fellow," the great man said as he burst through the open door, exuding an air of heartiness. "Welcome to Washington! Come in, come in." He pumped Jules' hand and put his arm around his shoulder as the younger man clumsily picked up his valise and let himself be ushered into the great office. He sat in a low horsehair chair as Langley strode around his huge desk, which was littered with engineering drawings and scientific gewgaws, and, breathing huge clouds of cigar smoke, seated himself at a desk chair from which he could look down on Jules.

He seemed about sixty, and was undeniably handsome in his Prince Albert coat, with the edges of his white vest artfully showing. His carefully coiffed hair, neatly trimmed Van Dyke beard and polished fingernails—gleaming as he waved his big cigar—made him the very picture of the successful man, with an added touch of theatricality.

"I'm sorry I was unable to meet you at the station. I was entertaining Vice-President and Mrs. Hobart at dinner last night," the suave astronomer said. "I met your grandfather when I lectured at Cambridge. And your father—to all reports he was a brilliant man, and he worked so closely with Penaud. Did you know Penaud well?"

"I was very young then. I knew Ader and Lilienthal somewhat better."

"You're at Harvard. You're quite an up-and-coming young man. What are your plans for the future?"

"I'm not at all sure as yet, sir," Jules replied,

somewhat overwhelmed. "My experiments in aeronautics . . ."

"What a coincidence!" The great man bounded to his feet athletically. "That's the title of my latest treatise. Here are the galley proofs. Maybe you'd like to look at them while I'm examining the papers you have brought me. Perhaps it is immodest of me, but I do believe my work will be of historic importance." Jules half-smiled and handed his valise to the professor before bending over the long side table with its large sheets of galley proofs festooned with editorial markings. "You should be commended," Jules said, "for risking your reputation in a field which is so often ridiculed."

He could see Langley watching him out of the conners of his eyes as he riffled through the Penaud papers. Jules could hardly make sense of the nonconsecutive pages in the galley proof. "I see you used a blunt leading edge on your wings," he commented.

"We were able to extrapolate those conclusions using a faired edge in our later efforts," the older man interjected quickly. "Professor Chanute speaks exceedingly well of you," he said, changing the subject.

"His disciple, Mr. Wright, says that he could fly a barn door if it were at the right angle and had enough power. Do you know of the Wright brothers?" Jules asked.

"Bicycles. But Professor Chanute—now there's an important man."

"He has a lovely daughter, too," Jules said, and Langley looked up with a quick piercing glance. "She's ten," Jules smiled. "A little princess."

Langley shuffled Jules' papers into an orderly stack. "Perhaps we should have a press interview when you present these papers formally to the Smithsonian. But, considering poor Penaud—let's see. I'll have a special citation made for you, suitable for framing." The older man smiled genially. "I am entertaining Senator and Mrs. Maybach at luncheon today. At the Willard. My daughter will be acting as my hostess. Perhaps you would care to join us. It's always helpful for a young man to meet important personages."

"Thank you, sir. Whatever you say. And I must thank you for being so kind as to put me up at your marvelous club."

"Don't mention it, my boy."

Jules waited in the outer office, looking through Langley's new treatise, while the professor occupied himself with matters of more importance. There was still time before lunch, so Jules walked around the building looking at various cased exhibits, including cut-and-polished specimens of smithsonite, and he wondered why a bar-sinister descendant of Henry the Seventh would make such a huge bequest to the government of a foreign country he had never seen merely in order to preserve his name in aspic. The ways of fame were foreign to Jules.

A horseless carriage, glistening and chauffeured, which apparently belonged to the Smithsonian, drove them, snorting and shaking, to the Willard. Langley was greeted royally like an old habitué, and Jules like the son of an habitué. In the flower-bedecked dining room a young girl, slender and pretty, was waiting for them at their table.

"Alicia, this is Mr. Kincaid. He's here on business," Langley said with a grimace and a gesture. "My daughter Alicia." They sat down in the heavy chairs the waiters had pulled out for them. "The Institute is putting him up at my club. I'm going to show him the barn today, so you better make tea."

"How do you like Washington, Mr. Kincaid?" Alicia gave him a nervous half-smile. She appeared to be in her early twenties, and was dressed in frilly white, with her mouse-blond hair piled on top of her head in a complicated and rather disorderly hairdo. Jules wished that he had some of his brother Francis' Gallic charm as he tried to set the girl at ease. "What little I have seen of your city is very interesting," he said. "It's like a Southern town, I'm told, with men standing around on corners."

"Washington is like the little town I grew up in in Pennsylvania," she spoke less hesitantly. "Everyone knows everyone else's business."

Langley was ignoring this social chatter as he peered around the dining room nervously, occasionally breaking into a beaming smile as he nodded his head formally to great paunchy dignitaries dining at other tables, erasing the smile just as quickly as his eyes moved on. "Ah—ah," he stood up brusquely and strode forward a few steps to greet a portly gentleman and his wife who were being escorted to their table by the headwaiter. Jules, feeling ignored, stood up hesitantly.

"My dear Senator—and Senatoress," Langley was suddenly jovial. "You do us a great honor. Right over here, Mrs. Maybach. You can view the entire room from here." Langley pulled out a chair for the lady.

"This is Mr. Jules Kincaid, visiting from Harvard. His grandfather is one of their most distinguished professors." Langley's way of speaking was suddenly very Bostonian. "Marvelous, marvelous. I have ordered a nice little Amontillado before the soup course, Senator. I'm sure you will enjoy it." The senator smiled rather vacantly.

"Senator Maybach has honored us by accepting a place on our Board of Directors," Langley said to Jules. "So of course the Institute is more than happy to entertain him and his constituents from time to time." He turned back to the Maybachs. "Oh . . . Alicia you know."

"Senator, Ma'am."

"Alicia, don't toy with your gloves!" The girl put her gloves down beside her plate. Jules couldn't help noticing the strained expression on her face.

"I hope Mr. Kincaid is going to give us some guidance from his vast store of aeronautical knowledge when we show him our heavier-than-air machine this afternoon," Langley smiled.

"Oh, are you going to fly the thing?" The Senator was sipping appreciatively at his sherry. "We had a hell of a—excuse me—a most difficult time getting that appropriation through Congress."

"I hope you have found it worth your while, Senator," Langley interjected suavely.

"Are you going to fly something?" Jules spoke with the quick interest of unseemly youth.

"A model. It's steam-powered and weighs nine pounds."

Professor Langley turned back to the Senator. "Vice-President Hobart was telling me last night that . . ."

Jules, left out of the conversation, concentrated on his soup and his fish course, surreptitiously watching Alicia to see which fork she used. Their eyes met with

glances that were suddenly conspiratorial, but Alicia
would no more than give a slight ironic smile at some
of the high-flown phrases that flew over their heads,
then she would just as quickly withdraw into apparently timid acquiescence. Jules listened, sometimes
nodding, as Miss Langley spoke to Mrs. Maybach
about such weighty matters as the best bird feathers
with which to decorate hats and the newest methods
for keeping kid gloves clean. When a silence, punctuated by the clickings of heavy silver on fine china,
descended on the table like a miasma of Washington
fog, Jules was astounded to feel a tiny insistent pressure upon his foot. Yet Alicia's eyes were looking
down with maidenly modesty at her plate. Jules felt
the hairs at the back of his neck begin to rise.

"You're dreaming, young man," Professor Langley
boomed out. "You shall have a great treat this afternoon when you see the first powered heavier-than-air
machine that will have flown."

"My father was with Ader when they launched
the *Eole*, you know," Jules said carefully.

"A fiasco," Langley laughed patronizingly. "No
more than a few short hops. It barely left the ground.
But our machine—I have already reserved a spot for it
at the Institute. You will be able to show it to your
grandchildren."

"Oh, are you married, Mr. Kincaid?" Alicia asked
breathily.

"Of course not," Langley said. Alicia blushed and
looked down again at the long cream-filled Napoleon
on her plate, and poked at it with her fork.

As they stood in front of the Willard, heavy with
their eight-course luncheon, Langley gallantly offered

the horseless carriage to convey the Senator back to his offices for his afternoon nap in style, and Mrs. Maybach for her afternoon shopping, and he hailed a hansom cab to take himself, Alicia, and Jules to his home.

When they alighted on the mounting block in front of a great stone mansion, Professor Langley whipped out a golden pencil to make a note of the sum he grudgingly handed over to the hackney driver. "You go inside and get those girls started on tea, Alicia," he said. "We'll look in on Manly."

As the professor conducted him down a long, rutted drive beside the house, Jules looked back and his eyes caught Alicia's. She smiled, turned, and scurried up the front steps, lifting her skirts and reaching for the screen door.

It was a large barn to which the professor escorted him, and they mounted to the second floor by way of a wooden outdoor stairway. Langley didn't knock. He unlocked the door with a key from his watch chain. "We keep it locked. People are always snooping." He escorted Jules inside and locked the door behind him.

"Manly, this is Kincaid. Jules, this is my assistant." He introduced a slightly built, mousey little man who wore a leather workingman's apron. "I trust you will be discreet, Mr. Kincaid." He handed his hat to Manly and led Jules over to his stubby-winged model flying machine with its ingenious steam engine.

"Marvelous!" Jules' eyes sparkled with sudden interest as he squatted down to touch the shiny brass engine. "It's beautiful." Langley preened his moustache with a self-satisfied smile. The shiny little model had wings of varnished silk. It was beautifully crafted—much prettier than the muslin-covered models Jules knew. "What kind of steam pressure are you getting?" he asked.

"Er—ah, Manly, what is the steam pressure? Manly handles all the little details."

"Ninety pounds at launch," was Manly's reply.

Jules stood up saying, "You certainly are to be congratulated, gentlemen. Will it take off flat?"

"Oh ho . . ." Langley's smile had a conspiratorial twinkle. "We'll take no chances. We're going to launch it from the top of a houseboat sixty feet above the water. It has to fly."

"If the wings will sustain it," Jules said with a smile. But levity seemed to be out of place with these men.

"We're basing our estimated wing-lifting properties on Lilienthal's tables," Langley said nervously. "We are systematically and carefully exhausting all the possibilities. Manly, would you show Mr. Kincaid some of the results of our experiments? I have some very important business to take care of at the house. When you are ready, Mr. Kincaid, do come in for tea."

The older man let himself out. Manly seated Jules at a drafting table and brought him a number of bound books. "Here are the results of our tests with rubber-powered models. We have also considered using carbonic gas power and electricity."

"You certainly have done a lot of work," Jules said. "Let me study them."

He leafed through the various pages with their detailed drawings and long-winded descriptions. At first they seemed very impressive, but then as he translated the pseudo-scientific gobbledygook into plain English, he realized that all the high-flown verbiage concealed a great deal of nothing. Manly seemed to be busying himself writing out reports. From time to time he would glance over at Jules. "Are you going to be working with us, Mr. Kincaid?" he asked

"I still have another year at Harvard, Mr. Manly," Jules answered, "so I regard it as rather unlikely."

He stood up to leave, stacking the ledger books neatly on the high wooden stool he had been using. "You certainly have a well-appointed shop here," he said. "You lack for nothing."

"We are well supplied with what we need. But of course, these experiments are expensive. We must think ahead."

"Well, thank you for your hospitality, Mr. Manly, and I wish you the very best." Manly showed him to the door and let him out. Jules went up the rutted driveway, past trellises of blooming roses, to the house. He found a side door to the great Victorian mansion and knocked. A maid, in correct black and white with frilled apron and hat, bobbed and curtsied. "Dr. Langley is expecting you in the library, sir." She led the way down a corridor and knocked at one of a pair of magnificent oak sliding doors.

"Yes?"

"It's Mr. Kincaid, sir."

"Come in." The maid pulled one of the doors aside and gestured for Jules to enter.

"Well, well, my boy, did you learn much?" Langley had taken off his Prince Albert coat and unbuttoned his vest and was sitting behind a huge desk with a glass of sherry and a great cigar, papers spread out before him. "A report to the Royal Society," he explained.

"Very impressive Mr.—er, Dr. Langley."

"Have a seat, young man. Would you like some sherry? How about a cigar?" He stood up to pour some wine into a glass and handed it to Jules. "No cigars, thank you," Jules said with a smile. "I had one yesterday, and my stomach hasn't returned to normal yet."

"Well, young man, I'm not going to beat around the bush. How would you like to join my staff?" the older man began pacing up and down behind his desk, one hand behind his back, the other hand painting pictures in the air as he gestured with his cigar. "I can use someone to translate my correspondence with the various learned societies into French, and I understand you can translate from German. And then, of course, you're a presentable young man, and we are always entertaining important government figures from the War Department or the Congress, or their constituents."

"I'm really more interested in aeronautics than in entertaining," Jules said.

"According to your school transcripts, you haven't really been doing so well," Langley said.

"What?" Jules was surprised.

"Oh, I took the liberty of getting some information from one of my friends at Harvard," Langley chuckled. "I hope you don't mind."

"Up there they don't take aeronautics seriously, sir. I'm certainly glad to see such a distinguished person as yourself investing time and effort in this research."

"Not to mention money. Well, what about it,

young man? I could offer you eighteen dollars a week to start with."

"Oh, thank you, but I do want to finish up at Harvard before I consider what I'll be doing." Jules answered.

"Well, perhaps I could strain the budget and bring it up to twenty-two dollars a week. How does that strike you?"

"Don't tempt me sir. I'm sure I'll be much more valuable to you if I have a Harvard degree."

"Well, be that as it may. You think it over and write to me next year. In the meanwhile, I'll put you on our distribution list. I have the franking privilege, you know."

"Tea is ready, sir," the befrilled maid was bobbing in the open doorway.

"Thank you, Sally." Langley put his cigar out in the ashtray and buttoned his vest. "Shall we go in?" he asked as he put his coat on.

Alicia had changed into a diaphanous-topped blue tea gown and seemed very reserved as she poured the tea into delicate china cups. Langley launched into long self-serving stories of his famous spectroscope, and his expedition to the top of Mount Whitney. Jules studied Alicia Langley from the corners of his eyes. She seemed very reserved, but he sensed an inner fire there, as yet untouched. Jules couldn't help wondering what a good long kiss and a sharp slap on the bustle would do to her.

"Er—what? Lilienthal? Oh, he'll be out at Gross Lichterfelde again this summer, no doubt, gliding. I flew one of his gliders. Thirty-five yards. I was only seventeen then. It was exciting, but I admit it was frightening. I had very little control."

"That's the trouble with some of those fellows; they're not scientific. They just jump off the nearest mountaintop."

"Lilienthal's tables are considered authoritative all over the world," Jules said.

"Yes, I know. But I wonder if he faked some of them."

"Not to my knowledge. He's not that kind of man." Jules was shocked.

When the horseless carriage had returned from its afternoon rounds with Senator Maybach's wife, the Langleys bade Jules goodbye at their front door. "Please do think about my offer, young man," the professor said, shaking his hand.

"We would like to see more of you," Alicia said.

"Thank you very much," Jules said from the back of the clanking, shaking automobile. "Thank you for your hospitality. I'll keep in touch. Goodbye."

It wasn't until he was safely ensconced on the steam-cars the next day, heading North, that Jules began to sort out his various impressions. If Chanute could be considered an amateur, then Langley had to be considered the most important scientist in the United States who was giving serious thought to aeronautics. Even though Jules was rather doubtful about some of the sloppy scientific efforts he had seen that afternoon, he had to admit to himself that Langley seemed to be possessed of unlimited funds and a great desire to be the first to fly. Jules' observations on the results of Langley's experiments were curiously mixed, with quick, sudden recollections of big cigars and port wine, fancy clubs and restaurants. Alicia Langley's quick, nervous glances from the corners of her eyes kept coming to mind as he tried to concentrate. All in all it had been a most interesting weekend.

7

THE school year came to an end with graduation week at Harvard and ceremonies at Boston Latin School. Grandpa Kincaid was too busy to attend, so Jules had to go to the boys' school in order to congratulate Francis, who had been captain of his lacrosse team, and to watch Henry march up to the stage to be awarded the school mathematics prize. Henry had turned into a proper Bostonian: tall, erect, reserved, and infinitely superior to the average run of humanity. Francis retained a Gallic sparkle to his eyes and his quick smile endeared him to all.

It was Jules who organized their first weekend at Plymouth. Grandpa stayed behind to finish up his school paperwork. Jules outfitted the three of them with working clothes, cakes of Ivory soap, new brooms, and old rags, and they cleaned up the house until it was almost as spic-and-span as Aunt Prudence had kept it.

Their hard work kept them warm as they scrubbed and mopped the floors of the upper story of the barn, aired out the bedding, and cleaned up the shelves of plans. The stalls in the barn had to be mucked out, and arrangements had to be made to rent horses and a carriage for the summer. It was much too cold for swimming, but after their hard day's work they enjoyed getting dressed up and walking over the dunes and up the beach to the Plymouth Beach Club for dinner. Nothing had changed, except that Aunt Prudence was no longer with them. Jules was anxious to build a new glider and try it on the dunes at Plymouth, and everything else was forgotten.

This time it was to have a twenty-foot wingspan with wing-tips attached to a central guide-stick with guy wires, so that they could be adjusted up and down during flight to compensate for the winds. A vertical plane would also help to keep the craft stable. Having learned from Chanute and Wilbur Wright, Jules reasoned that the flyer of the craft should lie down, looking forward, since this would reduce wind resistance. "It's a step forward, Henry," he enthused. "Much better than sitting down. You can throw your weight backward and forward while controlling the wing-tips with one hand and holding on with the other."

At some expense, they shipped in some sitka spruce from upper Michigan. It was light and yet flexible, more likely to bend than break in the many crashes which were to be expected. In Boston, Jules found an old Singer sewing machine, and its treadle got much use as they sewed together the yards of cotton to fit over the spruce spars.

Sometimes, on Saturday nights, when Francis would be sleeping after having spent the whole day riding over the dunes on his old plug horse, and Henry would be off in his tennis flannels, club jacket and boater at the Plymouth Beach Club dance, and Grandpa had spent the weekend in Boston, Jules would realize how alone he was. He had spent all his life with others, some who had shared his dream, some who hadn't; first his father, then his brothers, then Leah, and then the older men in Michigan. Only on his two brief trips to Michigan and to Washington had he been really alone. Yet, he was seldom *really* alone. There were always the ghosts of the past. There were the responsibilities of taking care of his brothers, and now new worries about his grandfather.

The old man was hardly at all communicative these days. He spent more and more time in Boston, leaving the boys to their own devices. He would forget to eat, and he seemed to be getting thinner and thinner. When he was at Plymouth, he would sit in his little corner of the room making penciled calculations and muttering to himself.

"Grandpa," Jules would say, "come to the beach with us tomorrow; we'll go to the club for luncheon. You must get out. You're brooding too much."

"Well . . . maybe—never mind." Grandpa Kincaid would grimace and turn back to his littered desk.

Then one-day-old Henry did not return from one of his weekend trips into Boston. Two, three, four days went by with not even a word from him. Jules was worried. One evening, as they sat in front of the fire after dinner, toasting marshmallows, Francis excitedly describing his new-found game of beachball played on horseback, a carriage rattled into the old barnyard, and a knock came on the door just as Jules was about to unbar it.

"Who is it?" Jules asked.

"Sheriff Horsfall," the answer came. It was the local deputy from Plymouth. "You Mr. Kincaid?"

"Yes, I'm Jules Kincaid. What can I do for you, Sheriff?"

"It's a telegram, mister," the sheriff drawled. "I thought I'd better bring it out."

"Mr. Jules Kincaid, Plymouth, Massachusetts," the folded paper read. *"Please come at once if you can identify body of Professor Henry Kincaid of Harvard."* It was signed by the Sheriff of Cambridge.

"What is it, Jules?" Francis demanded. "What's so important?" Henry wanted to know. Jules held the telegram against his chest. "It's nothing, boys. I just have to go in to see Grandpa about school."

"If I can be of any help, young man . . ." the sheriff said.

Jules turned to his brothers. "Can you boys take care of yourselves for a few days? There's money where I always keep it. I'd like to catch the midnight special to Boston."

"I could look in on these young fellows if you don't have a woman to look after them," the sheriff said.

"That won't be necessary, Sheriff," Jules answered. "These boys can take care of themselves. But I would like to go into Plymouth with you, to the railway station, if I could. Just let me get my hat and coat and house keys."

Jules was silent as they rode into town in the one-horse trap.

"I'll wire ahead and have an officer meet you at the station," the sheriff said.

Jules nodded his thanks.

The late train to Boston was a fast one, only stopping at stations that had the flag up. The overhead wire whistled and hissed, throwing bright sparks to light their electric way as they hurtled through the moonlit countryside. It slowed as they came through the outskirts of Boston. The empty streets gave Jules an added feeling of unreality. He had been up since dawn.

A red-faced police sergeant was waiting at the last inter-urban stop. "Are you Mr. Kincaid?" he asked with a trace of brogue. Jules straightened his shoulders and looked down at the beefy Irishman. "I am," he said.

It was only a short walk to the nearest streetcar stop, and but a few minutes wait before a nearly-deserted streetcar picked them up. There was little to be said.

The city morgue was a cold and dreary place smelling of formaldehyde. The policeman seemed to know the way quite well. He found the right room and spoke quietly to an attendant who led them to a marble slab, one among a series of sheet-covered slabs, and pulled back the top of a sheet that covered a corpse.

"Yes, that's my grandfather." Henry Kincaid's sightless eyes stared grayly at him. His cheeks were sunken in, and his nose stood out, bony and prominent. A slight growth of beard, strangely gray and blond, made his gray face look dirty. The attendant leaned over and closed the corpse's eyes before pulling up the sheet.

The police sergeant touched Jules' arm and led him to an office. "There are a few papers to sign, sir, and you can pick up his effects."

"When did it happen?"

"It was Saturday. Down by the waterfront. He just stepped off the curb without looking and a street-car hit him. It wouldn't never have happened with a horse-car," the sergeant said. "We had a hard time finding out where you were. It was some professor over at Harvard College that told us."

"I see." He signed for Grandpa's effects, and made arrangements to send the body to a funeral parlor in Cambridge.

"I'll send you over with the paddy wagon if you wish, sir," the officer said.

"No, thank you. I'll take the trolley." Jules tucked a neatly wrapped bundle of his grandfather's things under his arm and bade them goodnight.

The Brattle Street house was silent and stolid in the cold light of dawn, looking like a sullen blind man with all its shades drawn against the summer heat. Jules fumbled with his ring of skeleton keys and let himself in to the musty front parlor. He went up to his old room, opened the windows, pulled down the blinds again, and took the dust-coverlet off the bed. There would be time enough tomorrow to make his arrangements, and go to Plymouth to pick up the boys and bring them back for the obsequies.

His brothers didn't seem very surprised the next evening when Jules told them the news. "Do you think he suffered much?" Francis asked, taking Jules' hand.

"He died instantly." Henry nodded his head without speaking and went upstairs to get into his city clothes.

Once again they stood together at a graveside, the three Kincaid boys. Their bronzed faces contrasted with their high white collars and stiff dark suits, and as they stood together, their heads bared, Jules' and Francis' blond hair blew in the breeze while Henry's dark-red shock of hair was stiff as a clothes-brush. Only some few Harvard professors and instructors who had happened to be in town were there, and the Dean of Men represented the administration. As they walked back to their black-trimmed funerary carriages, Jules introduced his brothers to the professors in whose charge they soon would be. "How did it happen?" one of them asked. "How could it have happened?"

"He's been very absent-minded lately," Jules answered. "He must have simply stepped off the curb without looking."

The meeting in a downtown Boston lawyer's office two days later was again stiffly formal. The lawyer read them the will of their grandfather. It was short and quite simple.

> "To my grandson Jules Kincaid, for reasons of which he is well aware, I leave the sum of one thousand dollars in cash, and the responsibility of being co-executor of this, my last will. To my grandsons Francis and Henry I bequeath all other properties of whatever nature of which I die possessed, as well as the responsibility for leaving yearly remembrances at the graves of their grandmother and of my beloved wife Prudence, whose

> *gentle care sustained me through so many years,
> and whose love and companionship I have sorely
> missed."*

That was it. Jules made an appointment to meet
with the lawyer and a team of appraisers who would
evaluate the estate for tax purposes. Then they went
home to a bleak shore dinner enlivened by the last of
their Aunt Prudence's gooseberry preserves. There
was nothing to be said. It had all been said before.

Yet there were many surprises in store for them.
Jules and the lawyer made the astounding discovery
that there were only a few dollars in grandfather's local
bank account. They searched the house from root cellar to lumber room, but they could find no more bank
books. It was when they came upon Grandpa's stock-
brokerage account that many things began to become
clear to them. It became obvious that the old man,
after a lifetime of penny-pinching husbandry, after a
half-century of careful investing for the future, had
suddenly become a plunger. As they checked through
the records of his stock transactions, they could see
that shortly after his wife's death and his disappoint-
ment with Jules' continuing fascination for aeronautics, the old Scotsman had abandoned his accustomed
ways, and had started betting everything on his carefully prognosticated and charted hunches. For a time
he had doubled and redoubled his holdings, but then
disaster had struck. Everything went—first his stocks,
then his government bonds, and, finally, all of his
cash.

"No wonder he was distracted," Jules said. "He

told nobody about this. There was nobody he could talk to."

"Then it would appear, Mr. Kincaid," the turnip-faced lawyer nasalized, "that there is no thousand dollar bequest for you. If your town house—excuse me—*their* town house and country place prove to be unencumbered . . ."

"Do you know what it costs these days to send those boys to preparatory school? And Harvard?" Jules paced nervously. "And I suppose it will have to be a boarding school. I can't keep house for them indefinitely. I'll have to get a job. Probably in Washington."

"Then we'll have to sell the properties, Mr. Kincaid," the lawyer said, anticipating further commissions. "Do you want me to put them on the market?"

"Yes, I suppose so."

It was July, and then August, as Jules handled the myriad details of his brothers' lives. After making inquiries, he settled upon Groton as a boarding school which would be suitable for them. The house in Cambridge would not be difficult to sell, but for the place at Plymouth—so humble, and totally useless as a working farm—they received such low offers that they decided to try holding on to it. While Henry and Francis led a lonely bachelor existence in Plymouth, Jules stayed in Boston every week from Monday through Friday to clear up the business details of his grandfather's estate, to clear the personal mementos out of the Brattle Street house, and to meet with lawyers. Only on weekends did he go out to Plymouth, to contemplate wearily the half-completed, unassembled framework of their new glider.

"There is very little money left, boys" he told his brothers. "We are putting it into two separate trusts for you, and you'll only get enough to pay your living expenses and your tuition. Then, when you're eighteen, you will come into full possession of whatever is left of the Kincaid fortune."

"Is it a lot?" Francis asked.

"Not very much. Both of you had better think about trying for scholarships. Otherwise, by the time you get out of school, you're going to be practically broke. I wish I hadn't spent so much money on that sitka spruce."

A welcome change during that trying period was a quick trip to New York to close out what little remained of his grandfather's stock-brokerage account. Jules took an overnight train from Boston and got a modest room at the Brevoort, on Fifth Avenue. The next day he took a horse-car downtown to the offices of J. P. Morgan and Company at Broad and Wall Streets. An usher in striped trousers and black coat met him, inquired of his business, and located the bank officer who would handle it.

"Mr. Kincaid?" A dapper, elderly man stood up from his desk and extended his hand. "I'm John Bellamy. Please have a seat."

"Thank you," Jules sat down beside the man's desk. It was one of those newly fashionable flat-top desks and it was devoid of clutter except for a stack of ledgers and files in front of the officer. Jules opened up the worn letter case he had appropriated from among his grandfather's things, and began taking out papers. "I have a letter of introduction here from our lawyers in Boston, and . . ."

The older man's eyes were twinkling. "Yes, I've been expecting you." He gestured toward the stack of files in front of him. "You don't recognize me, do you?"

Jules looked up quizzically. The older man smiled and broke into a torrent of voluble, if American-accented French. "Not only did I handle your grandfather's account here in New York, but I even knew your father at *Morgan et Cie* in Paris. He brought you in once. I remember it well. I've handled your family business for three generations now, and before that we handled your great-grandfather's account."

"Well, that's astounding." Jules was taken aback at the sudden rush of memories of his father and of Paris. He actually did have a vague recollection of going into a Paris bank holding on to his father's hand. "That certainly brings back ancient memories," he said, switching the conversation back into English. Mr. Bellamy's American accent bothered him. "In that case, we won't need this letter of introduction."

The older man smiled, and prepared to get down to business. "What can I do for you, Mr. Kincaid?" he asked.

"Well, first," Jules shuffled some papers, "help us clear up the residue of Grandfather's stock-brokerage account. I understand that there are a few hundred dollars, and I have a letter of authorization as my Grandfather's executor to allow you to transfer it into my personal cash account."

"Very good. I've already prepared the papers for your signature as executor. If you will just sign here."

Jules studied the paper of authorization and accepted the steel pen offered to him by the bank officer. "I can't understand why the account was kept in the New York branch. It was always handled through Boston."

"That's the way we do it. We're right on the spot here, and we take telegraphic authorizations from our Boston office. Your grandfather was quite a large speculator."

"Yes." Jules got out the next set of papers. "And here are the authorizations signed by both executors to set up custodial accounts for my two brothers. We are selling some property in Cambridge, and the proceeds should be divided evenly into these two accounts."

"Very good," Mr. Bellamy smiled tolerantly. "We wouldn't normally handle such small accounts, but considering our long-term relationship with your family, we are happy to make an exception."

"Do you remember my father very well?"

"Yes. I only met him once or twice, but he was a very nice gentleman. It was a pleasure to hear some good American English there in Paris. I remember how you held on to his hand when you came into the bank with him that time. He was very proud of you."

"We were very close," Jules muttered. "What a long time ago it was."

They concluded their business, and Jules shook the man's hand with a great deal of reminiscent pleasure as he made his farewell. It was unexpected and disconcerting to him to have run into this reminder of a time long past.

He took a stroll around New York's financial district, stared out at the busy harbor with its white-sailed ships going to and fro, and found a place to have a modest lunch. All over town there were posted advertisements for a play called *L'Aiglon* starring a

Miss Sarah Bernhardt. Jules secured a ticket for that evening's performance. He dined at the Bravoort that evening, choosing the least expensive items on the menu, before heading over to the Booth theater—a magnificent pile on Twenty-third Street. Jules was astounded to see an old woman with a wooden leg playing the lead role of Napoleon's nineteen-year-old son. He was tempted to laugh, but her performance soon captivated him. The rolling Alexandrines of Rostand's play hypnotized Jules, and the rapid, rhythmical, theatrical French brought floods of inchoate memories. Jules left the theater in a daze, and spent his last night in the expensive Fifth Avenue hostelry tossing and turning with vague dreams of the broad avenues of Paris.

Jule's last year at Harvard was a cold lonely one. He joined the Hasty Pudding Club to take advantage of living in the clubhouse and dining in their dining room. It was a so-called "waiting club", mainly for freshmen and sophomores who hoped to get into a "final club" later, so Jules was one of the few seniors to be met there.

Weekends he would often go to Groton to have dinner with his brothers, for they were seldom allowed to leave the school. Even on the rare weekends when they went together out to Plymouth, Jules could feel that the boys were growing away from him. They were becoming very American, while Jules remained always an outsider, always a loner. Francis was the kind of boy who could be perfectly at home on the playing fields of Groton, yet still be just as welcome in a blacksmith shop or in a janitor's quarters puttering with a new-fangled petrol engine. Such was his charm, in fact, that in spite of the classical orientation of his instructors at Groton, he was able to convince some of them to allow him to construct a gasoline engine as a school project.

Henry, on the other hand, had developed his innate reserve to the point where he was the very picture of the prep-school snob. Although he knew well that he was shortly destined to be a pauper, he grew adept at cultivating rich, high-society acquaintances and skilled at the art of dropping names and hints of a solidly wealthy background. In his skillful allusions, the modest Cape Cod two-room salt-box became a vast estate with a large, active stable of horses and perhaps the hint of a yacht just over the horizon. Only Francis' friends would occasionally hear laughing remarks that reduced Henry's mountain to the size of a sand-hill.

Still another difference between the two brothers would be noticeable on Sunday mornings. Henry would troop off, booted and polished to perfection, with the rest of the boys to Presbyterian services with their laughably Anglicized Latin and high-church trappings. Francis, taking advantage of minority status as a Papist, would relax in more congenial surroundings with those few Micks and Jews who had managed to slip into Groton under the rose.

Meanwhile, back at Harvard, Jules was grinding away. Sometimes he would walk past their old Brattle Street house, cherishing nostalgia for better days past. Sometimes he would indulge himself in brief and sordid affairs with comely Irish housemaids, but he found it somehow degrading, and he had heard the horror stories students told of the dread dangers of syphilis.

His correspondences with Lilienthal and Chanute

were still active, and the little notes in French with their sketches in the margins which he exchanged with Ariel Chanute were still being written, although the little girl's interests seemed to be tending more toward fancy dresses, symphony concerts, and dancing classes. Jules adjusted the contents of his notes to describe fancy balls which he had not attended and opera soireés of which he had only read.

The various publications of the Smithsonian Institute came regularly to Jules under the free-franking privilege extended by the Congress, in its wisdom, to Samuel Pierpont Langley. There were descriptions of new exhibits, and reports of high-society parties given in the august halls of the great museum after the doors had been closed to the common working man. From time to time, a note form Alicia Langley would appear tucked into one of the envelopes, saying that her father had encouraged her to write and mention such details as their dinner party for the Chief Justice, or the fact that Manly now had two assistants.

Jules looked forward to spending the entire Christmas vacation at Plymouth with the boys. It would be cold, the North Atlantic wind blowing great salt gusts straight down from Canada, but Jules looked forward to building great roaring fires with driftwood, plugging the interstices of their drafty little house with oakum, making mulled wine drinks, and indulging himself in long conversations about aeronautics. But Francis shamefacedly admitted that he had accepted an invitation to visit with the family of a schoolmate in Boston the week after Christmas, and Henry diffidently mentioned that he was going out to Pittsburgh in the private railway car of some U. S. Steel magnate's family to spend the week after Christmas with the *nouveaux riches*.

Although Jules shopped around in Plymouth, the only Christmas tree he could find was a gnarled and wind-blown old nubbin which they desultorily decorated with tired popcorn. Their roast goose was greasy and unpalatable, only made edible by copious libations of mulled wine, of which they all had too much. Jules returned to his deserted quarters in Boston with a sigh of relief, and he returned to his schoolwork with a sigh of relief. Sometimes, during this strange hiatus of solitude in his life, he thought of his years in Boston, his years in Paris, his shorter periods in Berlin and London and Michigan and Washington, and he realized that he had come to a turning point in his life. His youth—what there had been of it—had come to an end, and now a new life would open before him. Only the great free dream of flight ran like a golden thread through the lives of his mother's family, the life of his father, through his own life, and hopefully through the imaginations of his brothers, who were now growing away from him.

In February came the black news that Lilienthal was dead. At first it was only a short paragraph in the *Boston Evening Transcript* where Lilienthal was described as a retired manufacturer. Jules hurried to buy German-language newspapers from Boston, New York and finally Berlin, and the story gradually emerged. The gaunt old German, who had risked his life so many times in the pursuit of knowledge, had finally paid the ultimate price. While making a cold winter flight, his legs dangling from beneath the great gull-wings as he tested a new method of lateral control and guidance, the old man had suddenly lost control and fallen from a height of fifty feet. He spent one long day in agony, and then died. It was reported that his last words were. *"Opfer müsen gebracht werden"*—"sacrifices must be made." Jules was depressed; as depressed as he thought his father must have been those many years ago, when his life had been at a similar low point. Jules tried to shake off the memory; tried to get out and walk the snow-covered streets of Boston to clear the miasma of memories from his mind. His footsteps crunched in the crisp, frozen snow, and the cold air cleansed his mind, but he knew that this would be the end of aeronautical experimentation in Europe. The whole world respected Lilienthal. The astounding pictures of him in flight again and again had been passed all over the continent. Scientists everywhere respected Lilienthal's tables of air pressure, so painstakingly charted. And now he was gone. Who could muster the courage or the resources to follow in his path?

Even in this new world, of which Jules was also a part, he doubted there was anyone who could raise the money, brave the laughter, and risk the young blood needed to prove that man was not limited to being an earth-bound creature, but that he would one day venture above the trees, above the clouds, closer to God in his search for truth. Certainly it would not be Jules. His money was exhausted. Soon he would be penniless, perhaps eking out an existence as a guest of Henry and Francis at Plymouth. Even if he could finish another glider, it would likely crash into kindling as had so many in the past.

Who else would continue the work? Langley? He had the ability to raise the funds, God knows, and he could certainly excite the interest of scientific societies and the newspapers. But did he have the courage to risk life and reputation? Did he have the courage to pursue the quest of flight in the face of ridicule? Or would he, like Hiram Maxim, retreat from any further contact with a quest which had cost the lives and reputations of so many savants and fools?

And Chanute? What was he but a nice old man dozing atop a dune in Michigan and listening to the distant silvery laughter of a beautiful young girl, and the closer tinkling of ice in a wine bucket. These were the deadly gray night thoughts which Jules could not share with his brothers.

Letters came from Chanute commiserating with Jules for his personal losses, as well as the great loss to science which they all felt with the death knell of Otto Lilienthal. Chanute was coming East to address the American Society of Civil Engineers at their annual meeting. He invited Jules to come down from Boston for a reunion at the Plaza Hotel, a new and fabled edifice which boasted tiny wooden rooms that rose from floor to floor suspended on cables of steel. Jules counted the last of his money and decided to indulge himself in the trip. Perhaps it would cheer him up.

He packed his Gladstone bags and took the railway south to New York, marvelling yet again at the empty beauty of the countryside as it flowed by the sparkling clean train windows. It was so unlike what he remembered of Europe. In New York he cleaned himself up at the station before taking a streetcar far north past the dilapidated immigrants' shacks, which were now interspersed with great gaudy mansions peopled by the new rich with such names as Vanderbilt and Astor.

The new hotel was a great gingerbread rockpile surmounted by a shiny brass roof that glinted in the light. It stretched ten, fifteen, perhaps twenty stories into the sky. As Jules filled out the hotel registration form, giving his address as the Hasty Pudding Club in Cambridge, he asked whether Professor Chanute had arrived yet from Chicago.

"Yes, sir," the bright-faced young clerk answered obsequiously, his British accent not dissimilar to that of Harvard Square. "Suite 1-A, overlooking the park. And for you Harvard gentlemen, we have a special new introductory rate if you don't mind being on a higher floor." Jules blanched at the thought of trudging up fifteen or twenty stories, and the clerk read his mind. "It only takes a moment on our new elevating lifts, sir, and they're quite safe."

Jules' room was small, but it had a view which Jules imagined could only heretofore have been seen by a bird in flight. It was getting on toward dinnertime, and Jules changed into his old but seldom-used formal suit. The strange new contraption whisked him down to the marbled lobby and he stepped outside onto the street to buy a small twist of violets before searching for the grand staircase that would take him up to Chanute's luxurious suite. He knocked on the heavy door with some trepidation.

"*Qui. Qu'est-ce que c'est?*" It was Mademoiselle.

"*C'est moi*, Jules Kincaid!"

"*Non!*" She opened the door and turned in surprise. "*Voila, Monsieur Chanute! Voila que nous a donné le bon Dieu!*"

"*Jules! Bienvenue!*" Chanute, brilliant with shiny red face and white piqué shirt, rose from a satin *fau-*

teuil and strode toward the door. "How you have changed, *mon cher collègue!*"

Jules flushed with pleasure and his eyes lit up as he put his arms around the older man and patted him on the back with a pleasure that was simultaneously fraternal and paternal.

"*Jules—Jules! C'est toi?*" Ariel Chanute came running into the drawing room on ballet feet, a vision in white and gold. "*Ah, comme tu est beau!*" She threw her arms around him and kissed him impulsively. Jules blushed.

"*Quelle tableau! Alors, mes enfants,*" the genial old man returned to his satin throne and the younger couple sat down to join him. Mademoiselle bustled off to make tea.

"Are you coming to hear my speech tonight?" Chanute asked.

"Oh, I can't afford that sort of thing, you know that."

"Don't worry about that. We can work you in somehow. It's nice to have an ally in the audience. All this glider talk isn't doing my reputation any good."

"I hope you don't let it discourage you, or make you think of stopping your experiments."

"Oh no; the Wright boys are continuing—as well as they can afford to—and Huffaker may go down to join Langley in Washington. But what about you, young man? What are you going to do when you graduate?"

"I'm going to marry Ariel and we're going to fly off together to cloud-land."

The next few days were a rare and wonderful round of pleasure for Jules. All of his life he was to remember them. In the company of the prettiest girl in New York, he saw all of the most interesting sights that a great city could offer. They rode a two-wheeler all the way up to the Metropolitan Museum of Art, and at Mr. Hammerstein's new theater they heard an Italian opera, an entertainment which Jules didn't understand at all. Down in the theater district they dined at Lüchow's and actually saw the barbed-wire salesman Brady, diamonds flashing on his shirt front, handing Lillian Russell into a carriage. They rode the elevated steam trains, and took a boat over to Brooklyn. Ariel was as scintillating and playful as a dazzling fountain shimmering with gold and silver light. Late in the evenings, in Chanute's waxed and polished suite, Jules and Chanute would stand smoking their cigars, and discussing the future as they looked out the windows at the carriage lanterns blinking in Central Park.

"Go to Washington, young man," Chanute advised him. "Langley is a very smart man, and he obviously means well. But don't let him underpay you. Confidentially—" the older man looked Jules in the eyes to press his point. "Confidentially, he has a huge War Department grant to develop a military reconnaissance flying vehicle, and you are one of the ranking international experts in aeronautics. Sir Hiram and Lord Kelvin notwithstanding, I firmly believe in heavier-than-air flight. I just wish I were young enough to make my career in it," the old man said seriously.

"But Langley—is he a scientist or a politician?" Jules asked. "All he seems to do is to repeat the experiments of others, and then write them up in grandiloquent language. And entertain politicians."

"You're still young, Jules. I've seen you falling onto the sand, and toiling with your hands. You won't lose your ambition; a few years of meddling with the madness of bureaucracy will not do you any harm. I speak to you as a father. Do you suppose I enjoy sitting down to these fifteen-course dinners with a gaggle of old men and discussing the simplest principles of suspension bridges as though they were the *dernier cri?* I'd much rather be out in the fresh air of San Francisco Bay, or wading in the mud helping to sink a caisson into the Missouri River. But my day is past. All that is left is the glory, and it's a singularly unsatisfying dessert. So if I can help you or the Wright boys, or some unknown fellow we have never even heard of, to make progress, then I will be a contented old man."

"You will never be old, *Père Octave.*"

Jules took the Fall River Line boat back home. It was refreshing to be out on the open sea again, and it was interesting to contemplate what the last four years had brought. All in all, he was content. He no longer felt so strongly the great burden of day-to-day supervision of his two brothers, and his own progress had been systematized by exposure to the disciplines of organized academic study. Although he had very little money to fall back on, he felt that the future was bright. Chanute's confidence in him and in the future of flight itself had done him a great deal of good.

Down in the clanking boiler room of the very same steamer he had taken four years earlier was the very same bedraggled oiler and wiper. Again Jules had the pleasure of tinkering with the great steam engine, and diagnosing its multifarious ills. While upstairs in the saloon overfed financiers were clinking crystal glasses, Jules was in the boiler room glorying in the power of man's ingenuity. The way of the future, he felt, was on his side, for this was the age of invention.

Back in school for the last push before graduation, Jules felt happy and confident as seldom before. He let his brothers take him out to dinner in Boston, and described to them Chanute's continuing enthusiasm for aeronautics, and managed to infect them with his own excitement. "Once you could start building viable aeroplanes." Henry said, "you could capitalize a company for a million dollars. It would replace a whole cavalry corps as a method of military reconnaissance. The army would have to have scores of flying machines, hundreds!"

"And think of the fun of flying," Francis smiled. "The freedom of soaring, and then diving like a hawk!"

"And think of the money you could make on exhibitions," Henry said, toying with a pencil and making marks on the tablecloth.

"Thousands of people come to see the simplest balloon ascension, and they don't even know when and where it's going to come down," Francis added fervently.

"All right, boys, first things first. Control, then power. It's all the same old story. Lack of control is what killed Lilienthal. He had flown at fifty feet many times before that. We've got to get the designs of the apparatus he was testing when he died. I wonder about his tables of air pressure." Their conversation turned to pure technical discussion, just as some hundreds of miles away the two Wright brothers were sitting, one on each side of the fireplace, saying " 'Tis," and "No, 'tisn't."

Jules' correspondence with Langley began to be more copious, and he knew that Chanute was also pulling for him by letter and through the intervention of old Mr. Huffaker, who was already in Washington working on the projects. Langley made certain concessions, but he refused to make a final commitment as to salary by letter. Jules made plans to travel down to Washington as soon as he had graduated.

The families of Jules' classmates stood around them in chattering bevies as they waited for the graduation ceremonies to begin. The three Kincaid boys stood tall and handsome, although Jules had forgotten to shine his brogans. Francis, just coming into manhood, attracted the attention of a good many of Jules' classmates' sisters. While making the introductions, Jules kept his eyes open for passing professors he could introduce or re-introduce to Henry, for Henry would soon be following in his footsteps at Harvard. Henry had the knack of looking like a serious and reserved young scion of an industrial magnate, while still being ready to flash a winning smile when he met someone of importance.

Jules won no prizes, and his class standing was not especially high. His advanced standings in math, physics, and German had only forced him to study that much harder to keep up, and his professors had always resented the feeling that they could not guide him into more serious areas of endeavor. Jules was not sorry to leave Harvard Square. For his grandfather it had been a goal, but for his father and for Jules himself, it had been merely a way-station.

With the boys securely ensconced at Plymouth for

the summer, and a neighboring farmer's wife scheduled to come in to clean and cook, Jules packed up to go to Washington for his crucial interview with Langley. The half-completed glider, now dusty and strewn with hay, still rested on the floor of the haymow. With Francis galloping on the dunes every day, and Henry playing lawn tennis at the beach club, Jules felt sure that no progress would be made on it. But for young men, summers are an endless joy stretching into a rose-tinted sunset, and Jules was ready to let it rest for the moment.

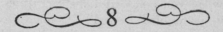

8

WASHINGTON in July was incredibly hot and humid. A maid showed Jules to a guest room in Langley's stone mansion. He discovered that the professor and his daughter were summering on a houseboat on the Potomac. After unpacking and greeting Manly and old Huffaker in their spacious horse-barn offices, Jules took a sponge bath, changed into his lightest seersucker suit, and had himself driven down to the riverside. A rowboat ferried him out to the houseboat where Langley and his daughter were roughing it with only one maid to look after them. A tall and curious superstructure of girders towering sixty feet above the water topped the commodious cabins. On the front deck, its wings shining in the sunlight, was Langley's nine-pound model flying machine. On a frilly back veranda were white-painted wicker chairs padded with little pillows, and an iron table with sparking china tea things contrasting with a gaily checked tablecloth.

"Mr. Kincaid! At last!" The professor greeted him at the side of the boat and gave him a hand up onto the deck. "We have finally inveigled you into coming down from your mansion at Newport."

"Plymouth," Jules laughed.

"Come aft," the professor said with a smile, leading him through a carpeted drawing-room that had a pianola in the corner. "You remember my daughter Alicia?"

"How do you do, Miss Langley?" Jules took off his straw boater and bowed. "It's nice to see you again."

"Mr. Kincaid, it is a pleasure to have you here at last. Huffaker is always speaking of you."

"Alicia is always hanging around those men in the barn. Lish, serve us some tea, please. And then off with you. Mr. Kincaid and I have some serious talking to do."

The two men sat down under the striped awning and squinted as they watched the desultory summer traffic on the river. Jules put his stiff straw hat down carefully on a chair, but Langley kept his floppy Panama hat pulled down over his forehead and puffed on a long cigar. With his brocade vest and his long-tailed coat, Jules thought he looked like a Mississippi river gambler.

Alicia fluttered about, serving them tea and making inconsequential remarks that seemed to irritate the professor. When she finally left, Langley got down to business.

"Here's what I have in mind, young man. You can serve as my surrogate when we have guests in from France or Germany, and there may be some Italians. Do you speak Italian?"

"A little bit. But most Italians speak French," Jules offered.

"Then there are my papers, which should be translated into French and German for the various pubications. You can do that can't you?"

"Yes, but what about substantive work?"

"Of course, of course. We are systematically going through all the possibilities—carbonic gas, steam power, following up Penaud and Ader. Of course all of these things have to be written up."

"How about the model? When are you going to fly it?"

"I'll fly it when I'm good and ready. Now look here young man, all this business that Chanute tells me about your being the heir to a great tradition. Well, we've pretty well agreed on a substantially high salary, but I don't want you to try hogging all the glory. These are *my* projects."

"Of course, sir. I don't care who gets the glory so long as we make progress. Isn't that the nature of scientific inquiry?"

"You may be a freshly-minted Harvard graduate, but you have a great deal to learn about the way research is done today. We are not running a penny-ante game, and we're not all independently wealthy." The picturesque older man snorted disdainfully.

"Some more tea, Father? Mr. Kincaid?" Alicia stood in the doorway, twisting a lace handkerchief in her hands.

"Why thank you, Miss Langley, I'd like that,"

Jules said as he smiled at her. The older man grunted.

"We've had such a hot summer," the girl said. "All the young men are out of town, and everything seems to be going at half-speed." Smiling tentatively, she sat down next to Jules, crushing his hat with an audible crunch. She jumped to her feet, brushing at the back of her muslin gown. "Oh, I've *ruined* it. I'm so sorry,"

"That's all right, Miss Langley. Accidents will happen."

Langley's laugh had an edge to it. "She's so clumsy!"

The girl looked close to tears, and Jules felt sorry for her. He laughed and stood up, throwing the shattered bits of straw over the after-rail while salvaging the Hasty Pudding hatband. "Sit down, Miss Langley, and let me pour *you* some tea. The Professor and I have pretty well concluded our talk, and I'm looking forward to moving down here." He tried to allay her embarrassment. "You certainly have a nice cool place to spend the summer."

"Rank has its privileges," Langley said. "Of course, this goes on the Smithsonian books as a research vessel, but then I've never had any trouble with the Board of Directors. They've all been entertained here often enough."

"It certainly is a fine boat," Jules said.

"Well," Langley said, "If we are so far along in agreeing then perhaps we should celebrate. Lish, why don't you go inside and have Sally bring out some champagne, and then we'd better get ready to go back to town, much as I dislike the idea."

Alicia stood up and went inside to find the maid.

"Of course you understand, Mr. Kincaid, that you will not be working directly with Manly, Huffaker and their assistants. Your first assignment will be to translate some of our papers into French. I just happen to have a stack of them here for you. Perhaps you'd like to look at them tonight." He picked up a reddish Manila envelope from the deck and put it on the tea table.

Alicia and the maid came out with a tray and a bottle of Moët-Chandon. After the champagne had been poured, Professor Langley raised his glass in a toast. "Here's to a long and profitable association."

Jules raised his glass. "To science," he said.

"Daddy," Alicia said, "it's cooler on the boat. Why don't you stay here overnight? I'm sure Sally wouldn't object. Mr. Kincaid could escort me back into town, and I could send the carriage out for you tomorrow."

"Mmm . . ." the professor pondered the idea.

"Maybe I could even take him to the dance with us." Alicia turned to Jules. "My friend Mary Lodge and I are going to the Cosmos Club dance tonight. You'd be welcome to join us, Mr. Kincaid."

"Never mind that, Lish. Mr. Kincaid has some papers he wants to look at tonight."

"Well . . ." Alicia stammered.

"I would be glad to escort your daughter into town," Jules said. "But as you say, I've got some reading to do. I'm afraid I'm not much of a one for dancing, anyway."

"Well, I'm sorry you can't join us, but I accept your offer to escort me home. I'll just go get my parasol," Alicia said, leaving the men alone again.

"Have some more champagne, Mr. Kincaid. I hate to drink alone." Professor Langley threw the stub of his cigar over the after-rail and began to go through the complicated process of piercing and clipping another, and looking around for wooden matches with which to light it.

Langley didn't get up when Alicia returned, all ready to leave for town. "Now you watch what you say to the Lodge girl, Lish. And that goes for you too, Kincaid. Her father's a senator. As for me, I'll be doing some studying for next month's schedule of events.

"All right then. Goodbye, Daddy."

"Good day, sir," Jules said. "I'll look forward to continuing our conversation tomorrow."

Jules hleped Miss Langley down into the little rowboat and rowed them to shore, where they woke up an ancient Negro who hitched up an equally ancient horse to the carriage that would take them into town. Alicia tried to make polite conversation.

"Mary Lodge is my best friend," she said. "We go to all the dances together. Her father used to teach at Harvard."

"Did he? So did my grandfather."

"Really? Maybe they knew each other. That's Rock Creek Park over there. It's a wonderful place to ride. Do you enjoy horseback riding, Mr. Kincaid?"

"Yes, but my brother Francis is the real rider in our family. He rides at our beach club. They're playing a new game called polo. It's something like rugby on horseback."

"Oh, I've heard of that."

"It comes from India. They say it's based on the Pathan tribesmen who used to use an enemy's head for their ball and bang it with lances."

"Oh, that's terrible!"

"I'm sorry, Miss Langley. I didn't mean to offend you."

When they got to the Langley house the sun was just setting. "This is when the social life in Washington begins," Alicia said. "When it cools off a little bit."

"Are you a socialite, Miss Langley?"

"Goodness, no. It's only since I started going around with Mary that Daddy will let me go anyplace alone."

"Well, I wish you a pleasant time at the dance. I'm going to go upstairs to my room and clean up before dinner."

"I'll look in on you before I leave," Alicia said.

In the privacy of his bedroom, which was darkened against the summer sun, Jules threw his suitcoat on the bed and took off his collar and his shirt, which was soaked with perspiration. After a cooling sponge bath and a drink of water from the carafe on his nighttable, he felt better and began dressing to go down to dinner. When a knock came on his door, he slipped his jacket on and went to the door. It was Alicia.

"Your dinner is all set out for you in the dining room, Mr. Kincaid. If you need anything else, just pull the bell rope." She was wearing a high necked silk gown, and Jules thought to himself that she was really very beautiful.

"Thank you, Miss Langley," he said. "Have a pleasant evening."

With hardly a glance back, Alicia went down the stairs and out the front door to where the carriage was waiting.

After a dinner of cold roast beef and fresh garden vegetables, which he ate in the solitary splendor of the deserted dining room, Jules took his folder full of pages and went into the library. He lit some candles so that he could begin a preliminary survey of all the papers he was expected to translate. There were printed treatises on geology, electromagnetism, new principles in cartography, and even one on spiritualism. All of them featured Langley's name as co-author, or chairman of some committee. Jules looked in vain on the library shelves for a dictionary of scientific terms or even a French dictionary, but all he could find were leather-bound editions of the novels of Thackeray and Scott, and picture books of the Civil War. Blowing out the candles, he went upstairs to his bedroom. Moonlight was pouring in through the French doors that overlooked the clipped and rolled grass of the lawn. Jules hung up his suit, put his shoes neatly side by side under the bed, lit some candles, and sat down in a comfortable chair by a deal-table to read some more. Even his silken union suit was uncomfortably hot in this humid climate. Although his day had been very long, a printed article on geology captured his interest. A porcelain clock on the marble mantelpiece ticked away, giving the hours and quarter hours with a silvery knell. Jules hardly noticed the time go by, so absorbed was he in his reading. Nor did he pay much attention when the rattle of a carriage came up the drive and shortly thereafter girlish laughter echoed down the hall and he heard a door slam.

Some time later, a knock came on his door. "Mr. Kincaid," he heard someone say. "Just a minute," he answered, and stepped quickly to the armoire to pull his trousers on. Barefoot, he went to the door. "Who is it?"

"It's me. Alicia." Jules opened the door a little bit and peered around the edge. The girl was standing there in a voluminous peignoir, her long blond hair streaming loose over her shoulders and back. Moonlight behind her glowed down the stairwell from a skylight. "May I come in?" she whispered.

"Er—of course." Jules stepped back a few paces and stood by the table, his hand resting on the back of the Louis Quinze chair in which he had been sitting. Silently, hesitantly, Alicia took one step into the room to stand there in the moonlight. "I know I shouldn't do this . . ." She laughed softly, a little afraid. "Maybe I had a little too much champagne."

"A beautiful girl is always welcome." Jules could hardly make out her face in the shadows, but the moonlight shone through the many translucent layers of nightgown and peignoir, silhouetting her tall, slender figure seductively.

"I just wanted to say . . ." she laughed nervously, one hand on the door. "I wanted to say again that I hope you will accept Daddy's offer. He really needs some good assistants. Mr. Huffaker—he doesn't seem to get anything done. And Mr. Manly, he's a lickspittle. They're all lick-spittles."

Jules felt a pleasurable pressure begin to rise, and stepped behind the chair to hide his embarrassment.

"You aren't a yes-man, are you, Mr. Kincaid?" Alicia gasped and raised a hand to her lips. "Your hair is like a halo in the moonlight . . ." she murmured.

Jules took a step toward her down the silver path of light that streamed through the French doors. "Alicia . . ."

"Oh—*oh my!*" She took two quick frightened steps backwards into the hall and then ran away from him, her bare feet padding silently, quickly, her flowing skirts rustling. Jules peered around the corner of the door at her until she disappeared into her bedroom and he heard the door latch. Then he stepped back into his own room, closed the door, and smiled.

At Jules' interview with Professor Langley the next day in the now familiar library, they settled the details of his employment, mostly the salary. Then there were other matters to be discussed. "Where are you going to be staying?" Langley asked.

"I really don't know," Jules shrugged.

"A rich young fellow like you should stay at the Willard," Langley suggested. "That's where all the lobbying is done." Jules did not regard himself as a lobbyist. In his family, it was his brother Henry who seemed adept at meeting the right people.

"And how about your clothes?" Langley asked. "If you're going to represent me, you'd better be a bright young man, and look like one. I'll give you the name of my tailor." Jules reflected that this would be one area in which he would try to economize. He did not fancy himself quite in the same class with President McKinley, who would order as many as twenty-five suits at a time from his tailor. But he said nothing.

Before he left town for the trip to Boston to pack his books and papers and his few clothes, and to make sure that his brothers were well organized for their first summer alone, he stopped at the Willard. The hotel manager was more than happy to rent a room to a new employee of such an important customer as Samuel Langley. After explaining that he wanted a good address, but was not nearly as wealthy as Mr. Langley seemed to think, he was able to rent a tiny maid's room on the top story. It would serve, at least for a while.

He did not see Alicia again before he left Washington.

Somehow, it was like visiting another world as Jules arranged his affairs in Boston. He walked by Kurman's Department Store and thought of his affair with Leah Dreifuss, a part of his life that seemed like such a long time ago. With his grandfather's lawyer, he arranged to have his brothers' school and living expenses doled out to them during the next year, and he envied them their monied freedom. Out at Plymouth he organized things for the boys' comfort, but they already seemed to be disappearing in the direction of the blue sea: Henry busy with the soical life at the beach club, and Francis very much occupied with horses, stables, blacksmith shops, and tinkering with the various horseless carriages that belonged to his friends. Jules, still in his city clothes, walked through the deserted rooms where Aunt Prudence had lived and died, poked at the cold and barren hearth, and climbed up to the haymow to look at his last uncompleted glider. The boys were going their own ways, and he knew that without his drive and constant obsession, no progress would be made with it. He could only hope that he could influence Langley to experiment along the same line. With Langley's unlimited resources, progress could be made, but it would be like driving an eight-horse hitch of wild mustangs, and Jules wondered whether he could do it.

The newspapers were suddenly full of Langley stories as Jules left Plymouth to move to Washington.

Apparently, he had flown not one, but two model planes for flights of several minutes on the Potomac. In some accounts, the flights were referred to as the first powered heavier-than-air flights ever made. They had lasted for the several minutes the miniature steam engines functioned. A congratulatory letter from Alexander Graham Bell, who had witnessed the flights, was quoted all over the country.

Jules arrived in Washington and took up his modest quarters at the Williard. The next day he reported to Langley at the Smithsonian. "Congratulations, sir," he said. "It seems I have joined you at a good time. I hope it's a good sign for the future."

Langley was ebullient. "A great success," he said. "Now there'll be no more trouble from that damned Admiral. The administration is going to appoint a board, and it will be packed with my friends—Graham Bell, and Roosevelt, and . . ." Langley glanced over at him sharply. "All this is confidential, of course," he said.

"Of course," Jules agreed. "Why did you make only three flights? You can't find out much from three flights."

"Yes—well, the machines *were* rather battered after landing in the water." Langley bridled at any implied criticism. "We proved that it could be done, and that's the important thing.

"Yes, sir, I suppose it is."

"Did you know that Graham Bell thought I wasn't going to publish his letter?" Langley's laugh had a derisive edge to it. "I wonder what he thought I was going to do with it, hide it in a report somewhere? I let him talk me into releasing it."

"It's being quoted all over the world," Jules said.

"Of course it is. That's why I had him there. What better testimonial could I have than an eyewitness report by Alexander Graham Bell?"

"You certainly plan ahead," Jules said as he laughed wryly.

"It's the only way to survive in Washington," Langley said with a smile. "You'd better learn, and learn fast, that they're all out to get us. They all want to push through their own appropriations and dump ours. Look at my friend Roosevelt. He may have been a great idealist, but he had to learn to work with Tammany up there in New York, and now he's learning to work with Mark Hanna. You have to be practical if you want to survive."

Jules scratched his head and tried to absorb the lessons he was learning.

"And are you all settled in?" Langley asked. "Where are you staying?"

"At the Willard, sir. They gave me a speical rate."

"Excellent. And your office? How do you like it?"

"Very cheerful. I have my first set of translations ready for you here, sir." Jules put them on the desk. "They're all ready to be machine-written, or set in type."

"Excellent, excellent." Lanley riffled through the translations. "I'm sure we will be able to work together very nicely."

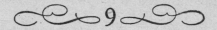

WASHINTON, *Da Capo*, in eighteen hundred ninety and seven, was like a strange new land to Jules Kincaid. Clouds of dust blew up and down the wide, deserted avenues. Herdic omnibuses clattered over worn cobblestones past deserted rowhouses and the shabby mansions of the speculators who had built them. The Willard, with its great halls, busy restaurants, and smoky pool-rooms, seemed to be a haven for the dubious types who haunted the lobbies of Congress, and then paced the halls of the great hotel spitting great gobs of tobacco in odiferous splats that stained the marble and muddied the skirts of the questionable ladies who wandered through, perfumed handkerchiefs held over their noses.

At the Smithsonian, Jules occupied a bright little

office downstairs from Langley's large office. It was a small, bare room overlooking a courtyard, furnished with old tables and chairs from the basements and storerooms of various Smithsonian buildings, and right down the hall from the electric speaking-instrument invented by Langley's friend, Dr. Graham Bell. It was one of the first to have been installed in Washington.

Jules already knew Manly and Huffaker. Langley took Jules around the Smithsonian to introduce him to the staff, beginning with his forbidding secretary. Then came the various carpenters and artificers in the workshops, and the curatorial and custodial staff, for the Smithsonian was also the American National Museum.

"And here is the office of our accountant, my good friend W. W. Karr." A spry old man of sixty, dapper in a perfectly-tailored business suit, jumped up from his desk and bowed.

"Mr. Karr, this is my new assistant, Mr. Kincaid."

"Pleased to meet you," the old accountant said, shaking Jule's hand vigorously.

"Mr. Karr keeps all of the books for us." Langley gestured at various sets of ledgers. "The Hodgkins Fund. Our War Department Fund—that's confidential. Our regular appropriation fund. If you are authorized to contract for outside work, you'll find that our procedure is to get an authorization through my office and then process it through Karr's office. He will then issue the checks." It was one of the many bureaucratic procedures that Jules had to learn. In his youth, Langley had worked in the offices of various architects and he had acquired an admiration for the generation of great reams of paper work.

After he had given his first set of translations to
Langley, Jules was given a new long-term project:
translating the master's famous book *Experiments in
Aerodynamics,* into French.

As for clothes, Jules dutifully ordered some suits,
a Prince Albert coat, a dove-grey vest, yellow gloves
and various other articles from Langley's tailor and
other purveyors, and they were soon pressed into service as Jules assisted Langley in giving a guided tour to
a group of boondogglers from the French Aeronautical Society. Jules was hard pressed to keep up with
Langley's mellifluous torrent of superlatives as he
guided the Frenchmen around the great building on
the Mall, and showed them the plans for a new national zoological park.

"Here we will have the large mammal house, and
over there the small mammal house. Directly south of
that, the antelope house. I have engaged Mr. William
H. Blackburn of Barnum and Bailey's—er—exhibiton
group to act as the first head keeper of our collection,"
Langley said, then waited impatiently for Jules to finish translating into French.

In the evenings, too, Jules found himself pressed
into service, as he sat at Langley's left through long,
rich dinners at the French Embassy or at the Willard.
Alicia Langley would often attend, twisting her white
gloves nervously or putting them into her champagne
glass to indicate that she was not drinking. Jules often
noticed her watching him from the corners of her
eyes, but they kept up a façade of polite reserve
which suited Jules well. He didn't know how to handle the particular problem she posed.

Yet, substantive work seemed to make no progress. From time to time Jules would visit Langley's

great barn to see if Manly and Huffaker and their assistants were doing anything. All they seemed to do was continually write up old experiments, or piddle with the model aeroplane which they were preparing to exhibit at the main building of the Smithsonian. In his own little office Jules would labor at making his traslations in longhand and preparing them to be machine-typed at the French Embassy, and proofreading them. Alicia would drop in from time to time, her skirts rustling in a way that drove all thoughts of aeronautics from Jules' mind, to gaze out his sparkling clean windows at the courtyard below, and to engage in nervous repartee.

"You're so serious, Mr. Kincaid. You should get out more often. We have young people's dances at the Cosmos Club every Friday. All the Strauss waltzes. You should come. I could get you a card."

"To tell the truth, Miss Langley, I hardly know how to dance."

"Mary and I could easily teach you. How about Saturday? Would you like to come for a picnic in Rock Creek Park?"

"That might be very nice, but I don't know what your father would think."

"Oh, fiddlesticks! What he doesn't know won't hurt him. I'll pick you up here at one o'clock." Alicia tucked her parasol under her arm. "And now, I suppose I must go wake up father. We have to leave cards at the Roosevelts. It's like a quadrille, all this social life." Jules showed her to the door and caught a glimpse of pretty ankles as she scampered up the stairs to her father's little hideaway office. "I'll see you on Saturday, Miss Langley. I'm looking forward to it."

It was a beautiful day for a picnic in the park that Saturday. Jules' nervousness was partly allayed by Mary Lodge's Boston accent, which made him feel at home. The park was all wild and overgrown, and Jules had to help the ladies, hobbled by their long skirts, over fallen branches and up the hill, as they sought a good spot to lay out the tablecloth and open the picnic hampers. There were wild flowers everywhere and groves of smoke-colored beeches. "You should see the dogwood blooming here in spring," Alicia said.

Jules had brought along a large bottle of champagne in a canvas bag, now soaking wet from the melting of the chipped ice with which he had filled it. Along with their cold chicken and potted meats, the three of them drank the champagne from folding silver cups, and soon began to feel frisky.

"One, two, three," Mary Lodge called out the time as Alicia taught Jules the steps of the Viennese waltzes that had been so popular of late. Mary Lodge hid her laughter behind her straw hat as she watched Jules' clumsy efforts, but she was also drawing him out in a subtle manner as she inquired about his clubs at Harvard and his other social contacts. "Father used to teach history at Harvard," she said. "I found out that he did know your grandfather."

"A small world," Jules said with a smile.

"Oh, I'm exhausted," Alicia said as she laughed. "It's your turn, Mary." Alicia subsided, laughing, on the grass beside the tablecloth while Mary got up to take Jules in hand. Jules was very conscious of Alicia's attractiveness. Her toes just peeped out from beneath her petticoats, and the gray silk gown seemed to fill out her slim figure. She was flushed with wine and panting with the effort of hopping around with Jules, and he was strongly drawn to her. He was glad that the girls had invited him to break the monotony of his work and the silence of his bachelor quarters.

As the fall turned golden, Jules would often accompany Alicia and Mary and various of the latter's swains on horseback rides in Rock Creek Park, cantering along clumsily, easily outdistanced by the girls in spite of their sidesaddles. There were dances and parties at the houses of the Cabot Lodges or their friends the Roosevelts, who seemed to be socialites from New York who held some sort of political appointment. Once they even went to the White House, where they were guests of the President's physician, a Colonel Leonard Wood. At a party across the river in Virginia at an estate called "Friendship", which belonged to the McLean family, Alicia tried to teach Jules a boring new Scottish game which involved hitting a small white ball with a stick and then strolling, hand in hand, to the next meadow to hit it again.

Jules enjoyed his different milieus, but the goads of ambition made him impatient with the apparent senselessness of his pleasant existence. Various points in his translations of Langley's old experiments began to bother him. One afternoon in December, he ascended the narrow stairs to Langley's hideaway office to ask about them yet again. He knocked on the door, waited, and knocked again before he heard stirrings of life inside, and then Langley's bear-like growl. "Yes, what is it?"

"Jules Kincaid, sir. Could I see you for a moment?" Langley unlocked the door and motioned Jules inside. The air in the little room was thick with cigar smoke.

"Well, come in. You've never been up here, have you? This is where I observe the flights of birds to try to get some new ideas." Langley gestured towards a mounted brass telescope that was pointed out one of the windows.

"I have some notes about the flights of buzzards," Jules said. "Perhaps you'd like to see them. Their wing-structure is very interesting."

"Buzzards. Charming. I hear you made a good impression on my friend Roosevelt." He changed the subject.

"Yes. He took a course with my grandfather, and we were both members of Hasty Pudding."

"He's a good man to know. Up-and-coming. Now, what is it you wanted to see me about?"

"This report about your steam-powered model, sir. Are you sure you want me to translate it? You call it a three-hundred-foot powered flight, but actually, because it was launched from sixty feet above the river, it was falling one foot in every five. A good many glider flights have done as well."

"It was a *powered* flight. One foot in five—amateurs don't know the difference. You just go ahead and translate it the way it is. You've never been in this room, have you? This is where old Fuss-and-Feathers used to hide himself away on a hot summer day when he was president. Probably met some of his lady friends here. Jackson was a randy old coot. Here are his initials scratched on the window with a diamond."

"That's very interesting, sir. Another thing in your book—these experiments with airfoils. You say you made them with a blunt edge on the wing or a faired edge? The figures seem to agree with those of Lilienthal, but I can't figure out how you arrived at them."

"Mr. Kincaid, I don't want any of my assistants double-checking my figures. Your job is to translate these things, not to ask questions. I have a large enterprise here, and I can't be bothered with details. Now, if you would be so good as to leave me alone, I have to work on a guest list for the Thursday tea. If you please." The professor, his face a little red, showed Jules to the door.

Back in his own office, Jules became increasingly irritated at the way Langley had treated him. Taking his coat and hat from the hatstand, he tucked his papers into a folder and went outside to catch a streetcar that would take him to Langley's house. The sparks flying from the third rail were like the sparks of indignation that fired Jules' rising temper. It seemed to him that Langley's attitude was one of impatience with any proper sort of correct scientific investigation, just a constant search for funds and more funds, and a continuing preoccupation with totally empty, self-serving, pseudo-scientific papers filled with impressive phrases of absolutely no import.

When Jules got to Langley's house, he stomped along the rutted lane back to the barn and climbed up the stairs two at a time to the second floor. He knocked on the door, then knocked again before it was opened by Mr. Manly. "Shh", the little man said, one hand holding the door and the other one on a roof beam above his head. "Be quiet. Come in. This is when Huffaker always takes his afternoon nap, and I hate to disturb him."

Jules stepped inside. "I wanted to ask you some questions about Langley's book," he said. "What's that?" he asked, gesturing towards Manly's hand, which was still resting on the roof beam.

"Oh, it's a little bell system I devised," Manly said with a chuckle. "We take turns watching the door. If it's Langley, we ring the little bell and everybody drops what they're doing and gets to work."

"Very ingenious," Jules said, walking into the central drafting room and hanging up his hat. "I'd like to ask you some questions about this book, if you can spare the time."

"Surely. What can I do for you?"

"On page eighty-three there is a paragraph about blunt edges and faired edges. You're simply basing your statement on an imutable law of physics aren't you?"

"Oh yes, 'Langley's Law'." The smaller man snickered.

"Did you actually make these experiments? The figures are too exact. Do you have any of the larger airfoils you used? I'd like to see them."

"Well, of course, if they work for the smaller airfoils, they work for the larger airfoils, and what difference does it make whether they're blunt edges or faired edges?"

"It could mean the difference between life and death if somebody were to follow your specifications and build a full-sized flyer."

"Well, perhaps you should take that up with Professor Langley. I don't feel free to discuss it, under the circumstances."

"Is this what you call scientific investigation, Mr. Manly? The experiments described here are either real or faked, and I'm beginning to suspect the latter."

"Professor Langley is a great scientist, Mr. Kincaid. You've taken his shilling. I'm surprised that you would raise the question of his integrity. May I ask what you've been doing all these months? True scientific experiments take place in laboratories or out in the field, not at the French Embassy or at afternoon tea dances." The justice of these remarks bothered Jules. "As for myself, Mr. Kincaid, I do not care to discuss this matter any further with you. I suggest you take it up with Professor Langley and see what he has to say."

"I have, and I got no answer at all."

"Then I suggest you leave well enough alone, sir. And now, I have some important work to do this afternoon, so if you'll excuse me—" Jules let himself be shown out, but as the locks clicked shut behind him he was getting madder and madder. He went down the stairs and stomped up the lane even faster than he had come down it, whipping at the espaliered rose bushes with his folder of papers, and cursing under his breath.

"Jules—Jules. Up here." It was Alicia Langley, peeking out from behind a lace curtain on the second floor of the house. "What are you doing here? Come in for some tea."

"I—I'd rather not." Jules was too angry to make polite conversation.

"Oh do come in, Jules. I'll make some tea for you. It's so lonely here."

Jules was tapping his folder full of papers against his leg. "Oh, all right." He thought it might calm him down to relax for a while before returning to the office, where he might do something rash.

He went to the side door of the mansion and let himself in. The house was cold and dark. Only the ticking of a grandfather clock and the rustle of Alicia's skirts disturbed the silence.

"Jules, it's so nice to see you. What are you doing here at this time of day? What's the matter? You look so angry."

"Oh, sometimes these people can be maddening."

"Come into the kitchen and tell me about it. I'll made you a nice hot cup of tea."

He followed her into the large and airy kitchen, and sat down at the table while Alicia filled the kettle, put it on the stove, and poked up the fire. "What's the trouble, Jules? Are you getting Washingtonitis?"

"I don't know. Describe it for me."

"Well, everybody gets it sooner or later. In Washington, everyone is running around talking and trying to get something for nothing, but no one seems to get anything done."

"That's just it, Alicia. I'm getting very discouraged. I've been here for four months, and I don't think we've made any progress at all. Tea parties, and meaningless reports to the French Academy, but not one solid bit of work. I'd be better off designing electrical systems and doing my own experiments."

A worried expression crossed Alicia's face. "You mustn't think of leaving, Jules. Where would I be— where would *we* be without you? Let me speak to father about putting you in with Manly. I'm sure Daddy means well. It's just that what he needs is a real scientist, not another boondoggler."

"Oh, I don't know," Jules answered morosely, sipping his tea.

"If he put you in with Manly you would be more involved in the actual experiments, wouldn't you?

That would make the whole thing more interesting for you, wouldn't it?"

"Yes," Jules agreed grudgingly.

"Let me see what I can do." Alicia reached over and touched his hand. A grandfather clock struck somewhere in the deserted house. Jules took out his watch and checked the time. "I'd better be getting back to the office," he said, standing up.

"All right," Alicia agreed, seeing him to the side door. "But don't you do anything hasty."

Jules paused outside the door, adjusted his hat, and looked back at Alicia standing beside the etched glass door. He remembered the time he had seen her silhouetted in the moonlight, and he smiled "Thank you for inviting me in," he said.

Alicia looked at him, his long blond hair glinting in the afternoon sunlight, and then she impulsively leaned forward to kiss him. Jules took her in his arms, kissed her firmly, and then smiled as she blushed and pulled away from him. "Oh. Oh my!" Alicia said, flustered, and closed the door quickly behind him.

Jules returned to his office and spent the rest of the afternoon avoiding Langley. After having his dinner alone in the back room of a little tavern on F Street, he returned to the Willard, picked up his mail at the desk, and trudged up the four stories to his diminutive room. Then he lit the candle at his little desk and opened up a letter from Henry and Francis. Henry had declined his invitation to join Jules for Christmas, explaining that he had already accepted an invitation and would be in New York for the holidays, but he said that Francis was looking forward to the trip to Washington, and would be arriving on the fifteenth. Henry, efficient as usual, said that he would put Francis on the train personally in New York and gave Jules the exact time of his arrival in Washington. Both of the boys seemed to be doing rather well. Jules was getting lonely for them.

The other letter was from Octave Chanute. It told of new experiments by the Wright brothers at some obscure place in North Carolina. They had apparently gone there because the weather bureau reported steady winds and unobstructed sand flats, perfect for gliding experiments. Jules knew that they closed up their bicycle shop during the cold months of each year and devoted themselves to experimentation. He wished he had their freedom.

Jules got out his atlas and tried to locate Kitty Hawk. He wondered if the Wright brothers would welcome him as an uninvited guest to their experimental camp. It would be a pleasant break for him to be able to get away from the stifling atmosphere of the office, and it would give him a chance to sort out in his own mind what he should do.

A knock came at the door. "Yes?" Jules asked as he stood up, glancing at his watch on the mantelpiece in surprise. It was already nine o'clock and he didn't expect the chambermaid to be coming around at this hour. "Who is it?"

"It's Alicia," a muffled voice said. Jules opened the door and Alicia came in, dressed in a long cloak with a hood that covered her hair and shadowed her face. "I hope you don't mind me coming here," she said. "I just had to talk to you."

"You shouldn't be here, Alicia. What would your father think?"

"I don't know and I don't care. That man . . ."

She turned away from Jules, unfastened her cloak, and tossed it on a chair. "I told him I was going to the Ladies Aid meeting, but then I slipped across the street."

"What's the trouble, Alicia?"

"I spoke to Father. He says you've been snooping. And when I said you might leave, he said that would suit him fine. He said he didn't need any second-guessers at the Smithsonian." She turned around and looked Jules in the eye. Her soft wavy hair framed her face and fell to one side of her neck, which seemed somehow so vulnerable in the soft candlelight. Jules thought to himself, *She's absolutely the most beautiful girl I've ever seen.*

Alicia noticed his gaze, and a hand went to her mouth. "I shouldn't be here . . ."

"Your father would be very angry if he found out."

"Yes. And do you know why? Because I might hurt his reputation. Not mine. All he ever thinks of is himself. My mother wasted away to nothing, and he didn't even notice."

"I suppose he gets involved in his work. My father was that way. An interesting experiment, and he'd forget to eat, forget to go home . . ."

"Not Daddy. He doesn't care about experimenting—it's just a means to an end. And the end is more glory. More money. More fancy medals and honorary doctorates. He . . ."

"You shouldn't speak of your father that way."

"I don't care! I *do* care. I hate him. I hate him, the pompous old windbag. 'When I led the expedition to Mount Whitney',"—she imitated his intonation. "'When I led the expedition to Mount Whitney—' If

I've heard that once I've heard that story a hundred times."

"Well, he can be . . ."

"You have no idea. He's completely false—a great pompous façade concealing a nobody. He came from nothing and he'll go back to nothing. Ashes to ashes and dust to dust." She laughed bitterly. "I'm glad I don't have any brothers. His name will die and be forgotten. That's why he hates *you* so much. You're everything he pretends to be, you're from a brilliant scientific family on both sides, with a diploma on the wall and friends in high places."

"He has a lot of diplomas."

"All honorary. He never attended *any* college. Harvard, Yale, the Univertity os Wisconsin. Wisconsin? A cow-town college. But he chases them and he butters them up—gets them invited to the White House. 'You pat my back, I'll pat your back.' And what for? You listen to me, Jules. He'll steal your ideas just like he steals Manly's, just like he steals everybody else's, and then he'll shove you out of the way and go down to the footlights and take his bows."

"If you feel that way, why don't you do something?"

"What can I do? Simply smile and follow some man around? Run away from home and be a suffragette? Work in a sweatshop? I can't even sew! 'We'll find you a good husband. Just be patient, we'll find you someone who's presentable.' And of course, no-one is good enough for the daughter of the great Samuel Pierpont Langley. He wants me to sit on his footstool and look up at him in awe, the way Mother did." She burst into tears.

Jules automatically put his arms around her to

comfort her, but a hot urgency was rising in him as he felt her arms go around his neck, her hands go under his night shirt, and her fingernails bite into his shoulders. Alicia's knees seemed to give out and Jules took a step, almost a dance step, holding her, and lowered her onto his bed. Her face, cheeks wet with tears, kept turning away from him but her hands pulled down his robe and clawed his back as she let out little animal cries. Jules kissed her neck, and pulled down the bodice of her dress, and buried his head in her breasts. She made no resistance as he feverishly undressed her, but lay there panting, her head tossing from side to side, her eyes wet with tears as he towered over her, tearing off his own clothes.

"Oh God—*oh God!*" She gasped as he tried to force his way inside her, but her hands were running up and down his back, pulling him to her, her nails leaving long red scratches.

"Oh God, it hurts," she moaned. "Oh God, it's so good."

"Alicia—Alicia!" Jules felt like an appendage to the piston of a great steam engine as he burst inside her again and again with a power he had never before felt so strongly. Alicia locked her arms and legs around him and gave little sharp gasps and cries that seemed only to urge him on. As his thrusting began to subside, she pulled him still closer, running her hands through his hair and burying his face in her breasts until he had trouble breathing. He turned his head away and seemed to drift off, hardly conscious of her languid caresses.

Then they both became conscious of a disturbing hot wetness. "Oh my God. . . " Alicia pulled away from him and reached to the floor to find a white undergarment and press it to her groin. It came away covered with blood. Jules got up to find a towel. He ached with a dull throb.

"Alicia—you're a virgin?"

"Well, I was." She laughed self-consciously. "Oh, look at the mess I made." She took the coverlet from his bed and put it on the floor, and then got into the bed and burrowed in the blankets, pulling a sheet up to her neck.

"Did I hurt you?" Jules leaned over her, concerned.

"Yes, but . . ." The tears on her cheeks were now dry, and she smiled and reached up to put her arm around Jules, pulling him down for a long kiss. She held him to her until he realized how cold he was and burrowed under the covers with her. Alicia hid her face on his shoulder and said, "Oh, Jules. Do it again."

"Are you sure? I don't want to hurt you."

"Again, Jules. Please do it again."

10

THE next day Jules searched Langley out, and, after an annoying wait, was finally admitted into the august presence. Langley offered him a chair, and Jules got right to the point.

"The Wright brothers are testing down in North Carolina. I thought I'd go down and see what they're doing."

"Well, I suppose I could spare you for a short time, and it would give both of us a chance to think things over. But I want you back on the sixteenth. There's a delegation from the French Academy coming in."

"Then it's all right?"

"Yes, yes. Let's find out what those penurious bumpkins are up to. I'll write it off as a field trip. You

153

can give me a written report when you get back. All in the interest of scientific advancement, of course."

"Of course."

"Not that we can expect much, but it's a good idea to keep abreast of new developments. And now, if you'll excuse me, I'm expecting the Chief Justice shortly."

"Certainly." Jules rose from his seat and made his way to the door, not quite turning his back on the older man. The professor's expression was inscrutable, already falling into the façade of jovial benignity with which he habitually greeted the world. Jules closed the door behind him softly.

Before he left Washington for his sabbatical, Jules filled up a wicker suitcase with English biscuits and tins of potted meats, for he had heard that the camp which the Wright brothers had established at Kitty Hawk was far away from civilization, and he thought he might be able to contribute to their larder. On the way to the railroad station he stopped at a florist's shop and had a dozen long-stemmed roses sent to Alicia Langley.

On the train down to North Carolina, he tried to sort out his feelings about Langley and his job, about Alicia, and about himself. He was astounded at the incredibly passionate nature hidden behind Alicia's innocent exterior. He had seen his back in the mirror that morning, and had been surprised to see it tiger-striped with scratch marks. Behind her sweet, virginal manner, there had apparently long smouldered a burning resentment of her father, and it had taken only a touch to convert that hatred into passion.

And Jules was surprised at himself. He had always thought of himself as cool and objective, yet her sudden flare-up had changed him in an instant into a thrusting, panting animal. And she had savored him inside her.

When he arrived in Elizabeth City, North Carolina, Jules discovered that the only way to get across to the little village of Kitty Hawk was to hire a boat. It wasn't easy to find a boatman who was willing to take him across Albermarle Sound to the narrow bar of sand that separated the Sound from the ocean. At Kitty Hawk, all of the natives seemed to know the Wrights, but no-one wanted to take him to their camp, which was several miles away. "You can't miss it," they said. "Down to Kill Devil Hill. Just keep walking south. You'll see it. There ain't nothing else there." So Jules pulled his cap more firmly down on his head, picked up his two suitcases, and started walking. There were neither hills nor trees, and the wind blew steadily, chilled with the salt of the ocean.

After a time he came to two deserted shacks. An anemometer spinning merrily on top of one of them let him know that he was at the right place. "Hello! Anybody home?" He shouted into the wind, but then realized that no-one could hear him, so he picked up his suitcases again and trudged to the door of the nearest shack and knocked. When it opened, he was surprised. "Dr. Spratt! It's me, Jules Kincaid!"

"I'll be darned. Hey Will, look what the wind blew in!" Wilbur Wright, bundled up in sweaters and scarves, his bald pate shining, got up from the table where he had been sitting with another man and came to the door. "Jules! What the hell are you doing here?"

"Chanute told me you were down here, so I thought I'd bring you some supplies."

"Well, I'll be damned! What do you think of that!

Come on over here, Jules. I want to introduce you to my brother." Jules put his suitcase down as Spratt closed the door, and stepped over to the table.

"Orv, this is the young feller who was up in Michigan with us, the one who's working with Langley. He knew Lilienthal." Orville Wright stood up and slowly put out his hand, looking at Jules suspiciously. This younger Wright brother looked to Jules like a smaller, more advanced model. "Welcome to Kitty Hawk," he said. "Have a seat. We were just making some coffee."

"Dr. Spratt, if you open up that wicker suitcase I think you'll find some sweets for your sweet tooth." Wilbur and George Spratt were still beaming as they asked Jules about his progress with Langley.

"Hey, look here," Spratt said, "a real Christmas fruitcake."

"That has liquor in it, doesn't it?" Orville Wright asked disapprovingly.

"It's made with rum—as a preservative, of course," Jules said, smiling.

"When is Langley going to build his big aeroplane?" Wilbur Wright asked. "Aerodrome, he calls it, don't he?"

"That's what he calls it," Jules said. "It's from the Greek. We seem to spend a lot of time thinking up fancy names, but not much actually building the machines."

"Is he using Lilienthal's figures?"

"Yes, and I don't want to be the one to crash like Lilienthal did."

"We're using them too," Wilbur said, "but I'm sure we've got better controls. I figure it was controls that failed, rather than a fault of the machine. We've got—"

"Well," Orville Wright interrupted. "We like to

think we made some improvements, but we don't want to tell the world about them until we've had them patented."

"This sure is the place to practice though, Jules," Wilbur went on. "Steady winds, no sudden gusts. We load the flyer down with thirty or forty pounds of chain, and it still lifts."

"When can I see it?"

"Well, we had an accident. We won't be able to fly today or tomorrow. Not 'til it's fixed. But you're sure welcome to share our bed and board."

They talked far into the night on the subject of aeronautical design.

Jules discovered that Chanute had sent Dr. Spratt down to North Carolina when he had heard that there were no doctors within a hundred miles. "Durn nice of the old feller," Wilbur said.

"He's a wonderful man," Jules said. "And that daughter of his! Did he tell you that I was with them in New York? Ariel and I saw everything from the ballet to the Bowery."

Before their accident, the Wright brothers had erected a derrick. They hoisted their machine into the air, and suspended it in the thirty-mile-an-hour wind by attaching ropes to the control surfaces they were using, but every time the subject came up, Orville steered the conversation in a new direction. He was very secretive, as opposed to his brother, who had that open and breezy air that Jules was learning to associate with Westerners.

It rained intermittently the next day. While Orville and Spratt went to the other shed to work on their mysterious machine, Jules and Wilbur walked several miles south down the island until they came to a patch of trees.

"The whole island used to be a farm," Wilbur said, "but the ocean just dumped millions and millions of pounds of sand on it. See them bushes over there? They're treetops. And there used to be a farmhouse, too. The sand covered everything up. Great place for hunting, though. Birds everywhere and they say there are even a few b'ars in the woods down there."

Albermarle Sound seemed to be teeming with fish. Jules could see eight or nine of them every time he looked into the water.

"Look at that buzzard," Wilbur said, pointing up. "See how much trouble he has keeping his balance, in spite of the dihedral on his wings?"

"A hawk would just soar in that wind."

They shot three pheasants on their way back to camp and then sat outside the shack and plucked them. Wilbur continued to talk about the buzzards as they worked.

"When those buzzards are soaring down to leeward at maybe a thousand feet, maybe about a hundred feet high, the cross-section of their wings is only a line," Wilbur said. "And when they're soaring toward you, the wings appear broad. This would indicate that the wings are always inclined upward, which don't seem sensible." He looked hard at Jules. "I think we got a machine that is bigger and stronger and lighter than any ever built yet. Once we learn how to handle it, then putting a motor on it will be no problem at all. And if the motor quits, we can just glide down instead of crashing."

It started raining again, and they had to move inside to finish preparing the birds before dinner. Served with potatoes and turnips, followed by fruit-cake and fresh-brewed tea, they made a regal repast compared with what the brothers had been eating.

After dinner they sat and talked. The brothers asked Jules about his experiences in Washington and the people he had met.

"Do you know anybody over at the War Department?" Orville asked, and Jules had to admit that he didn't.

"Dr. Langley usually handles those people," he said.

Later, they got out the photographs of Lilienthal's last apparatus, and tried to figure out where he had gone wrong.

"He should have worn a helmet and some football padding. It might have saved his life. A lot of men have fallen from fifty feet and survived," Spratt said.

"He did wear a helmet. You can see it in the pictures. The controls were attached to it."

"That's where he went wrong. He lost his head!"

"That's not funny, Dr. Spratt," Jules said.

All the fresh air and hours of exciting talk made Jules sleep like a log, in spite of the fact that his bedding was but a few blankets, and that he had to sleep directly on the hard sand. The next day was just as rainy as the one before, and Jules suspected that even if the Wrights could get the machine repaired and into the air, they might not want him to see it. He was beginning to get a bit bored.

"Will, I've had a nice time, but if it's going to rain like this, maybe I'd better get back to Washington. I'm expecting my little brother for Christmas."

"Well that's a durn shame, Jules. Sure you don't want to stay and do some fishing with me?"

"No, not this time. I'm not much of a fisherman anyway."

Wilbur accompanied him back into the village of Kitty Hawk after he had said his goodbyes to Orville and Spratt. As they walked along, each carrying a suitcase, the wet sand blown by the strong wind stung their exposed hands.

"Too bad you didn't get in any soaring," Wilbur said. "But you see how Orville is. He don't want no broken legs. Why, the wind picked up that machine, with me holding to the wing-tip, and threw us both twenty feet."

"It must be some big machine," Jules said.

"Biggest damn lifting area I ever built," Wilbur boasted. "And the next one will be even bigger. Has to be, to hold a man and a motor too."

"Well, good luck to you. I hope you'll keep us informed of your progress," Jules said as Wilbur helped him into the boat that would take him back to the mainland.

"Same here, young feller." Wilbur said. "Let us know when Langley gets ready to fly, and we'll be there with bells on!"

Jules enjoyed the solitude of his trip back to Washington. Instead of going into the office the first day, he spent the time making notes on what he had learned of the Wright brothers' experiments. It wasn't much, but it gave him some food for thought. That evening he went downstairs for his solitary dinner, returning to his room afterwards to gaze out the window at the carriages clip-clopping past. He was still not quite sure how to deal with Langley. He had been trying to save his money, but there wasn't enough yet to launch out on his own, and not a better job in sight. He thought it would probably be best to stay on, save more money, and look around.

Then there was Alicia. He didn't know what he felt for her, if anything. She was perhaps the most ladylike of any of the girls he had known—vertically ladylike; horizontally, she was a tiger. Jules didn't know whether he should feel guilty, or pleased; victorious, or conquered.

A knock came at the door. "No—*C'est pas possible!*" Jules stepped to the door and opened it. Alicia was standing there. A gray veil which fell from her hat partially obscured her features. They stared at each other silently for a moment. Then Jules smiled.

"Come in, Alicia, come in."

She stepped inside and threw her veil back across her hat. They were both very sober.

"Thank you for the roses," Alicia said.

"How did you know I was back?"

"Fourth window from the left." She stood looking at him.

"Oh, Jules—" With two running steps she had her arms around him, her fingers running through his hair. Jules took his hands out of his pockets and put his arms around her.

"Hot house roses," he murmured.

As they lay together that evening, Alicia told Jules of her life. It poured out in a torrent of words, as if she had never had another person she could talk to. She told him of her days at Annapolis, where her father had been the official astronomer. She told how he would spend his whole pay on tailored clothing and entertaining at the Officer's Club, while her mother scrubbed and sewed and cooked in their modest military quarters without any help. Alicia told of her life in Pennsylvania, where her father had taught so long at a minor college. " . . . and then he got his historic brainstorm and invented a spectroscope to measure light rays. I don't know where he got the idea. Probably from one of his graduate students, but he made the most of it. He made sure the world knew all about it. Every scientific publication, every obscure newspaper reporter was invited to the house, and mother was running back and forth from the kitchen, pouring tea like an Irish housemaid. She worked her fingers to the bone. And then, just when it started to pay off, she simply expired. From overwork, I think.

"That's how he got to Washington. He pulled every string he could, and then he got this Smithsonian thing. Quasi-official, a huge budget, and he doesn't have to account to anyone except his Board of Directors, and he certainly knows how to keep *them* happy."

"You really hate him, don't you?" Jules asked.

"Yes—I mean no, not really. He's a very strong man, and you have to admire him for that. It's just what he did to mother, and what he tried to do to me. He doesn't want a daughter. He wants someone to sit at the foot of his throne. He wants someone to grace his tea table and fetch his slippers. He's making an old maid out of me."

"You certainly don't behave like an old maid," Jules said, grinning. Alicia raised her head and looked at him fiercely, and then she burrowed her face into the curly blond hair on his chest and bit him.

The Smithsonian had survived nicely without him. He ran into Langley as he was entering the building the next day. "Well, here's our world traveler, back early." The professor had apparently forgotten their differences, and he was as jovial as ever as he slapped Jules on the back and escorted him personally to his office. "Tell me about our bicycle boys. How are they coming along?"

"They're working on a very large glider which they're flying like a kite. No engine."

"No engine? They're years behind us."

"But they're . . ."

"Never mind, Jules. I don't think we have to worry about the bicycle makers. You must come over to dinner tonight. I'm having Manly in, a rare treat. We'll discuss our next series of tests. Perhaps you should work more closely with him."

Jules wondered if Alicia had been working on him.

When Jules finished his work day, he went home to clean up and change clothes, then walked to Langley's house. A maid met him at the door and conducted him to Langley's study. She knocked and opened the door. "Mr. Kincaid, sir." Manly was already there. Apparently, the two men had already been discussing the situation. They all shook hands as if they hadn't seen each other for some time. "A glass of port? How about one of these new-fangled cigarettes?" Langley offered them some machine-made cigarettes from a miniature humidor, and poured some wine from a decanter. Jules puffed on his cigarette and sipped at the wine. It seemed to be somewhat inferior to that which Langley usually served.

"Well, gentlemen, it would seem that some reorganization of our aeronautical work is desirable. Jules, we have decided that as far as titles are concerned, Mr. Manly will remain in charge of all of the aeronautical experiments—under my supervision of course—and as such, his name will also appear on all of the papers. Of course, that doesn't mean that your position will be in any way diminished. Quite the contrary. You will appear on the Smithsonian staff, and will be an advisor to me and to Mr. Manly on aeronautical work even more than before. I cannot spare you from some of your representational duties and your translations, but we will find time for you to participate more and more in our planning and experimentation in aeronautics."

"That's fine, Professor. I don't care about the credit, I'm just interested in making progress."

"That's the right spirit," Professor Langley smiled. "This is confidential, of course, but the results of our three little flights with models five and six are more far-reaching than you might think." Langley and Manly seemed to share a flecting secret smile. "Doctor Graham Bell's enthusiastic letter about our flights—the letter that's been in all the papers—has created a very favorable atmosphere. A commission has been formed and we shall be able to get some government financing—so we don't have to depend so heavily on the Smithsonian funds. Of course, I have some very good friends on the commission, including Assistant Secretary Roosevelt and Alexander Graham Bell. We're going to quietly expand our aeronautics research department. I think we'll probably be taking over most of the Smithsonian workshops, and you two gentlemen will be in charge."

A knock came on the door and Alicia opened it. Her father looked up, irritated at being interrupted. "Dinner is served," she said smiling, ignoring her father.

Langley stood up. "Well, gentlemen, shall we?"

They seated themselves in the dining room with Langley at one end of the table and his daughter at the other. The dinner seemed to be a rather more simple repast than that which Langley usually served—a salad, a roast, boiled vegetables, and bread pudding. No wine was served, which seemed most peculiar to Jules.

Alicia seemed somehow more sure of herself than she had ever been before. She drew Manly out and asked Jules about his experiences in England. She even led her father to tell his anecdote about the famous expedition to the top of Mount Whitney. The old man's self-esteem seemed to expand to encompass the entire dining room as he recited his adventure in well-polished phrases. He was so expansive that after dinner, when they adjourned into the library for further discussions, he even offered his younger colleagues some of his imported cigars. Alicia excused herself, giving Jules a secret wink.

"Mr. Kincaid, as you know, has been visiting the enemy camp," Langley said when they were finally seated, puffing on their cigars. "He has actually flown. Gliders." Langley snickered.

"But don't you think that is a perfectly legitimate approach to ultimate flight mastery?" Jules asked earnestly.

"Perhaps so," Manly said. "But it is quite different from the approach that Dr. Langley and I have been taking."

"You don't seem to understand the implications of my *Experiments in Aerodynamics*," Langley said. "The most important thing is the engine, and that is within our grasp. Our experiments prove that the greater the speed, the less force will be required to sustain the aeroplane in the air. I wouldn't say it in public, but I believe that once our aeroplane attains speeds that approach those of which automobiles are now capable, hardly any force will be necessary. The elasticity of the air will hold the aeroplane up. We'll probably be able to turn the motors off and use them strictly for maneuvering."

"That's the essence of Langley's Law," Manly said smugly.

"Then it's a matter of engines and propellers," Jules said.

"Precisely," Langley agreed. "That's your department. You and Manly. I'm an astronomer. You're engineers. Build me an engine."

"All right," Jules agreed. "But in addition to building propellers and engines, we must be able to build wings strong enough to withstand the initial impetus we'll need to get us up to a high speed. We also need to work on the apparatus that will allow us to land safely. With the designs we have now, the aeronaut is going to get dumped in the water every time he comes down from the air, and the machines may break up if we're traveling at the high speeds you envision."

"First things first," Langley said. "The main thing is to demonstrate, with a full-sized aeroplane, and a manned flight, that we can fly. Then we can get the funds we need to iron out the bugs."

"All right, sir, but what about control in flight?"

"That's not your department. For all we know, the wind currents of the upper airs gust so strongly, and change direction so quickly, that an aviator will not be able to react in time to control his machine. It must be made completely automatic. All we need to do at this point is to attain a straight level flight. You can adjust the Penaud Tail in such a way that it will automatically correct the level and altitude of the aeroplane, can you not?"

"That leads us to the question of what angle the wing should be at," Jules insisted. "In spite of your own experiments, which indicated that a five-degree angle is optimal, you're still using a zero-degree angle in your flights."

"Well, it worked, didn't it?"

"According to the professor," Manly interjected, "it is immaterial what angle is used. If you have enough speed, the air will support the machine."

"You gentlemen seem very confident of this. I suppose that confidence is based on your experiments with the turntable and the whirling table," Jules said warily. "But perhaps we should try confirming your theory with some wind-tunnel tests."

"Wind-tunnel?" Manly raised his eyebrows.

"You remember those patents I pointed out to you," Jules said. "And now they have that huge new wind-tunnel at Catholic University. I hear they're getting wind-speeds of up to twenty-five miles an hour."

"Yes, but we can't use it. I've tried. That fellow Zahm has it all tied up for his own experiments. We don't need it anyway. Didn't your friend Wright say that he could fly a barndoor if he had enough power on it?"

"That's right, he said that."

They went on to discuss particulars of their next experiments. Jules suggested a number of lines of inquiry, and was pleased to have them accepted. He felt that he would be able to work with Manly much better, now that he would be able to take a more active role in the experiments. He was still worried about various aspects of their work, but he accepted Langley's decisions. He still felt that learning to fly through gliding should be pursued, but he thought that perhaps he would be able to pursue more gliding during his summer vacations, or eventually make his opinions carry more weight at the Smithsonian.

Alicia was reading in the front parlor when Langley showed them out. She bade them goodnight with a cool self-assurance that Jules had never seen in her before. She gave Jules' hand a meaningful squeeze as they said goodnight, and Jules wondered if the others noticed that extra sparkle in her eye as she waved goodbye to him. All in all, it had been an interesting evening, and Jules felt much better about his ability to cope with the problems of working in aeronautics at the Smithsonian.

During the next two weeks, Alicia came to Jules' tiny room at the Willard several times. They were strange sessions of raw passion; Jules and Alicia went at each other like two tigers—clawing and panting, pausing, and then attacking again. Jules never used the word love, and the only time it passed Alicia's bruised lips was in a moment of extreme passion.

They talked. Jules found himself speaking to Alicia as he had spoken to no one else in his life. He spoke of the loneliness of his life in a way that he had never spoken to his grandmother or to his brothers. He spoke of the lack of understanding which he had been faced with when it came to aeronautics. He spoke to her of his grandfather's death, and the chilling discovery that he had come to the end of his resources. He spoke of Chanute and Lilienthal with their private funds and the freedom to experiment. Alicia would listen silently, holding his hand against her thigh and occasionally stroking the delicate line of blond hair on the back of his hand.

The change that Jules had noted in Alicia at her father's dinner party became even more marked, and he thought he saw even a physical change. Her youthful nervousness had given way to a mature and self confident womanliness; even her way of walking and moving became smoother, more graceful. If she had once been a nervous and insecure girl, she now exuded the devil-may-care personality of a radiant woman. Jules was astounded. All *he* felt was tired.

Jules had to warn her that Francis was arriving on the following Saturday, otherwise she would have been in his room all afternoon, as she had been the previous Saturday.

When he went to pick Francis up at the half-completed Union Station that Saturday, he was astounded at how the boy had grown. All the horseback riding, beach ball, tennis, and even polo of the previous summer, as well as the lacrosse, soccer, and football in the fall at school, seemed to have filled him out, and had even added inches to his height. His face was rosy-cheeked and glowing, and his hair, usually sun-bleached by the summer sun to a golden whiteness, had darkened to a honey-blond. But his voice still cracked and strangled between a childish piping and a pleasant tenor, and his flashing smile was as warm as ever. Jules thought he saw something of his father in him, but a "Carl Kincaid" whose personality was all dappled sunshine rather than shadowed with the cares and worries his father had known.

"Francis, how are you? *Mon Dieu*, how big you are!" Looking incredibly fit in his tweed jacket and school tie, Francis was all sinew and bone, with not an ounce of excess flesh on him, and he seemed almost as tall as Jules.

"Come on, let me take your bag. We'll catch a herdic." After they had made their way around the scaffolding and out to the sidewalk, Jules found two nickels in his pocket and slipped them into the fare box at the front of the horse-drawn conveyance. They took their seats among several other passengers, Francis' bag on Jules' knees. Jules pointed to a passing streetcar.

"A third rail!" Francis said. "Gee, you're getting very modern."

"You're just a country boy who's never been to the big city before," Jules laughed. "How was your trip?"

"It was like Massachusetts, miles and miles of Massachusetts. Acres and acres of land with nobody there." Francis' Boston accent grated peculiarly on Jules' unaccustomed ear.

"That's right, you've never travelled very much, have you?"

"Look at all the black people! You didn't tell me about the black people."

"Wait 'till you hear their *patois*. You'll never understand them in a million years."

When they got to the Willard, Francis was impressed. He screwed up his nose at the odor of chewing tobacco and cheap cigars, but he gawked at the elegantly dressed ladies who swept by them so regally. "So this is where you live!"

"I've got you Milburn's room, with a private bath. He's a Congressman from Ohio, and he went home for the holidays."

Jules went up with him and lolled on the spacious bed while his brother hung his suits up in an armoire.

"I hope you brought your school uniform," Jules said. "We're going to visit the White House on Monday."

"Wonderful. What's the occasion?"

"Oh, I have to usher a bunch of Frenchmen around, and I thought you might like it. You haven't forgotten your French?"

"*Je parle Français* like a native—a native Bostonian," Francis said with a laugh.

"Do you know how to dance?"

"Of course. Henry took me to the club dances last summer. You should see me do the schottische." Francis did a hopping little dance step, and Jules laughed aloud.

"Come on, let's go downstairs and split a bottle of champagne. But no cigar for you."

"Aw, come on."

"Not on your tintype."

Monday afternoon found Jules looking smart in a cutaway (except the buttons had long since fallen off

one sleeve) waiting in the main lobby of the Smithsonian to escort a variegated group of French provin-
cials from the Grenoble *Académie des Artes et
Sciènces* on a quick tour through the exhibits. Then it
would be on to the White House, before he finally
abandoned them to their fate at the French Embassy.
Francis accompanied him, trim and handsome in his
school uniform, his blond hair barbered to perfection.
When Langley emerged from his office to make his
standard speech, this time mercifully short, since the
Frenchmen wouldn't understand him anyway, he was
accompanied by Alicia.

"Dr. Langley," (Jules now invariably used the
spurious Doctor title with just a touch of malicious
glee) "may I introduce my brother, Francis?" Francis
stepped forward and extended his hand to Langley.
"And this is Alicia Langley, Francis."

"How do you do?"

Jules raised his voice to the tone his grandfather
had used in addressing Harvard undergraduates and,
in French, introduced Professor Langley to the
Frenchmen. While the professor spoke, Jules stood by
with a smug and hypocritical smile on his face.

"You're going to the White House? May I come
along with you?" Alicia smiled with something of the
self-assurance one might have expected of the boss's
daughter.

"Of course," Jules answered. Alicia attached herself to Francis, and vice-versa, and that was the end of
Francis' help in dealing with the vociferous Frenchmen. Through their brief tour of the Smithsonian, and
in the carriages to the White House, and then as they
traipsed through the Oval Room, the East Room, and

the rest, Francis and Alicia hung back at the end of
the line, arm in arm, whispering to each other and
laughing gaily.

President McKinley, being a man of some sense,
was not visible, nor were members of his family, but
through the hall came an unsuspecting functionary;
the President's physician, Colonel Leonard Wood.
Jules trapped him, introduced him, and promoted him
to general on the spot, retailing wildly exaggerated
stories of the Field Marshal's incredible battles with
the *peaux-rouges*. When Francis was introduced, he
shook the Colonel's hand with a twinkle in his sparkling blue eyes. The grizzled old veteran responded
with all the warmth which everyone always showed to
Francis' charm.

After they had left the sore-footed Frenchmen to
their gourmandizing fate in front of the French Embassy, Jules joined Francis and Alicia in the one carriage they had retained, almost jealous of their instant
intimacy.

"Francis is taking me riding in Rock Creek tomorrow, Jules. Isn't that nice of him?" Alicia smiled contentedly.

"Be careful of him, Lish." Jules answered. "He
rides like a regular *peau-rouge*—a red Indian. But
what can he wear? I don't have any boots and
britches."

"That doesn't make any difference," his brother
laughed. "I could ride bareback and still ride rings
around Buffalo Bill."

"Don't get smart, young man. Alicia will be riding
sidesaddle, and I don't want any accidents."

"Don't worry about that, brother. I'll treat her

like the goddess Diana, Queen of the Hunt, and I
won't disgrace you. I'll raid your wardrobe, and find
something spiffy."

"You won't spiff yourself there," Jules laughed.

"Am I still here?" Alicia asked. "I feel like a pawn
in a chess game."

Jules' wardrobe was indeed raided. In the armoire Francis found a pair of purple-mauve Beau
Brummell trousers that Jules had unaccountably purchased from a tailor who was glad to get rid of them.
They were the kind that fit over the instep of the shoes.
The fact that they were too big in the waist was hidden by his jacket. Otherwise, they fit him to perfection, showing off his muscular thighs and calves.
Worn over Jules' elastic-sided Congress gaiters, they
made Francis look the very picture of the English fop,
except that the shoes were a bit too long for him. He
had to stuff the toes with paper. Jules saw them when
they rode up beneath his office window to greet Professor Langley. Jules had never seen Alicia looking so
handsome. A few strands of blond hair had escaped
from her broad black hat, but with her black gloves,
her gold-topped leather crop, and her shiny black
boots, set off by a ruffle of petticoat from beneath her
long skirts, she looked marvelous. He almost wished he
were free to ride some Pegasus other than the one he
had long since chosen.

Wednesday and Thursday found Jules hard at
work with Manly in the Langley barn, helping a photographer make photographs of all the many Penaud-
type models they had made. On Wednesday he joined
Alicia and Francis for tea at the big house, but on
Thursday, somehow they forgot to invite him, and he
looked out of the barn window to see Francis emerg-

ing from the house with Alicia and the Cabot Lodge
girl, apparently accompanying them on a shopping
foray to the stores on Constitution Avenue.

Friday night was the young people's dance at the
Cosmos Club. When Francis picked him up in his
room, just as he was tying the white tie of his ancient
but honorable dress suit and tucking his white gloves
under his arm, Jules asked him, "Why don't you get
yourself a soup-and-fish? You can afford it. You're
rich."

"My school uniform is all right," Francis smiled.
"I never liked those suits, anyway. Maybe next year or
the year after for the Assembly dances."

"Assembly dances? You're moving in high society."

"Not me. That's Henry's forte. I just go along for
the fun of it." Francis slapped his gray mocha gloves
against the seam of his trousers. Smiling good-
naturedly, he looked like a cavalry ensign from the
French Embassy.

Jules had reserved a table for them by the dance
floor at the club. "That girl is always late," he said to
his brother, referring to Alicia.

"She's worth waiting for, Jules. You don't know
how lucky you are." Considering that the eight-year
difference in their ages was on his side, Jules found it
strange and wonderful, and perhaps apropos, to get
big-brotherly advice from Francis.

"Ah, here they are." The two Kincaid brothers
stood up.

"Hi, boys," Alicia smiled reassuringly. "Mary you
know, and this is her friend, Alice Roosevelt." A thin
and hoydenish girl of thirteen or fourteen, gawky, although correctly dressed in a white decolleté gown,

(the ruffles of which failed to conceal the fact that she was rather flat-chested), thrust out her hand and said, "How-de-do". Jules bowed over her hand and gestured. "My brother, Francis Kincaid. He's down from Groton for the holidays."

"A snotty Grottie, huh? My brother's a Grottie. Maybe you know him. Teddy Roosevelt?"

"That wizened little thing is your brother? Who would have guessed it?"

"Half-brother, actually."

The rest of them looked at each other and shrugged their shoulders as they sat down. Jules tried to signal a waiter. "I had to bring her along," Mary Lodge whispered to Jules. "Her father's my daddy's best friend. I never would have heard the end of it if I hadn't."

"Well, she certainly found a soul-mate," Jules said. The younger couple kept up a continual chatter until they suddenly jumped up and joined in a Virginia Reel, galloping up and down the floor with reckless abandon, and faking the steps amid shrieks of laughter when they didn't know them. Jules and Alicia waited for the more sedate Strauss waltzes, at which he felt he did not cut such a ridiculous figure. Mary Lodge, aside from her other charms, was the daughter of a Senator, and very popular with the stag line.

After the dance was over, Alice and Francis insisted upon taking a midnight carriage ride through Rock Creek Park.

"What will your father say?" Mary Lodge asked. "What will *my* father say?"

"What kind of a sissy-cat question is that, Mary?" the Roosevelt girl demanded. "Blame it on me if you want to. I blame everything on my wicked step-mother." Alice gave a raucous laugh and clambered into the carriage.

Nothing would do but what they had to stop in the park and have a snowball fight. Mary Lodge joined in their fun while Jules and Alicia, holding hands, sat in the carriage with tolerant, superior smiles. Their top-hatted Negro coachman looked on with sober disapproval.

On Sunday, the Kincaid boys lolled around in Francis' luxurious room, eating a big breakfast from silver trays. Tuesday was Christmas, and it was rather sad, as had been all the Kincaid Christmases for a number of years. Alicia prevailed upon her father to invite the Kincaid boys to his cold stone mansion. She cooked dinner for them herself, since the cook and the maids were off for the holidays. But the full dress suits, the heavy table silver, Langley's preoccupied air, and the oppressive atmosphere of the formal dining room itself put a damper on Francis' naturally high spirits. It was all Alicia could do to keep up the role of the charming, bubbly hostess. Even her delight at watching the boys open up the matching sets of initialed gold cuff-studs she had given them was dampened by her father's frown of disapproval.

When the time came for Jules to put his brother on the train North, he was not overly sorry to see him go. Much as he loved him, the boy's high spirits were a little hard to take. It was not only the difference in ages, it was also a difference in temperament. Jules was phlegmatic, sober, and methodical. Francis was a smiling blur of constant motion. If he had ever stepped in front of one of Mr. Brady's glass plates, he would have appeared in the photograph as a laughing shadow.

* * *

After the holidays, Jules' renewed interest in his work was balanced only by his astoundingly frequent nocturnal, and even afternoon, activities. Alicia was insatiable; gentle, wild, demanding, yielding, and so often there. And there, and there, and the other place too. Jules hardly knew whether to feel guilty or absurd when he slipped away from the barn during the boys' afternoon naps, tip-toed through the side door of the house, and made love to Alicia on the huge table in her father's august dining room. Once, he was sure, Manly spotted him from the upper window of the barn as he walked across the grass to the house, keeping out of sight of the kitchen windows, and he was sure that Manly reported it to the professor. But if so, Langley said nothing. Perhaps he couldn't believe that one of his menials could dare approach the throne unsummoned.

One day in February, Jules and Manly were hard at work in the basement of the main Smithsonian building, trying to get a large turntable to revolve at a steady speed by using the motive power of a discarded steam engine Jules had hooked up to it. They had a biplane model aeroplane all rigged up on the turntable with guy wires and pulleys to measure the amount of lift, but they could not get the turntable to revolve at a steady speed. They were cursing and tinkering and burning their fingers on the boiler, and the air was thick with steam and alcohol fumes when Alicia Langley walked in, befurred and behatted. "Oh, excuse me." Manly straightened up, putting his hand to his mouth and biting his nails.

"I wonder if I could see you for a moment alone, Jules."

"Of course, Miss Langley," Manly muttered out of turn. "I'll just go out and get some fresh air."

"Jules. Jules!" He didn't seem to hear her. The wheezing steam engine made an ear-splitting racket in the enclosed basement. Alicia stepped over, eyed it, and then, with her gloved finger, pressed down a lever that let all the steam out with a sibilant rush.

"Now what did you do that for?" Jules asked, emerging from beneath the turntable, his fingers covered with grease. "Oh, hello Lish. Where's Manly?"

"Jules, I have to speak to you."

"Of course, what is it? Your father back from Quantico?" The tiny steam boiler, its alcohol fire still burning with a hiss, made strange bubbling noises.

"Jules, I'm pregnant. Isn't that wonderful?" Alicia eyed him with a cheerful smile that did not conceal her anxiety as to his response.

"Oh my God." Jules put his fingers to his chin, leaving long grease-marks like black-face, and sank into a sitting position on a dusty sawhorse. "Oh my God," he said. "What are we going to do?"

"Why, get married, of course. And raise a family."

"Jesus, I can't get married. I'm only twenty-two. And I'm as poor as a titmouse!" The steam engine bubbled merrily.

"What difference does that make?" Alicia fiddled nervously with the buttons of her gloves and eyed him out of the corners of her eyes. "You have a good job. We could buy a little house in Georgetown. Daddy would help us."

"Daddy, daddy. I don't want anything from that old . . . fellow." Jules stood up, wiping his hands on his denim apron. "There are operations for that sort of thing, you know."

"Jules! Would you kill your own flesh and blood? Don't you love me at all?"

An increasingly high-pitched squeal from the steam engine didn't improve their conversation as they raised their voices higher and higher. "Of course I love you, Lish, it's just that—"

"Jules you're a miserable, unfeeling, selfish, cold-blooded dog." Alicia stormed out, buttoning her gloves on the way.

"Lish, I . . ." The boiler exploded with an ear-splitting bang, scattering brass fittings all over the basement, but Alicia didn't even turn her head as she stalked out.

Jules wiped steam out of his eyes. All the grease on his face made him look like the end-man in a minstrel show. When the last of the nuts and bolts had fallen to the floor, a silence descended on the basement, only broken by the quick clatter of Alicia's boots as she ran up the steps. Manly's little head, his slicked-down hair now standing up in strands like a rabbit's whiskers, peered around the corner of the wall by the stairwell. "What happened?" he piped meekly.

It promised to be a thoroughly scarifying scene in Langley's library when Jules met him by appointment upon his return from Quantico. Alicia had nerved him up to it, but he felt like a mouse caught between two great cats. Alicia stood firmly behind him as he took his seat in the great leather chair in front of Langley's huge desk. At this crucial moment of her life, Alicia felt a strength she didn't know she had. Fighting for the life of her unborn child, she felt able to stand up to her father, to Jules, to all of Washington society, to the entire sidereal hemisphere if necessary.

"Er, Mr. Langley—Dr. Langley, I mean . . ." Alicia poked him in the shoulder. "Go ahead," she muttered.

"What is it, my boy?" the smug Cheshire asked, stroking his whiskers. "How are my aerodromes progressing? Are you getting along with Manly?"

"Uh—" Jules looked over his shoulder at Alicia, and she nodded sternly. "It's not that, Professor. I'd . . ."

"Well?"

"I'd like to ask for your daughter's hand in marriage, sir."

"What?" The professor stood up and ran his hands through his smoothly barbered hair. "Is this what you two have been up to, Alicia?" the old man asked, pacing nervously. "Manly said you two were up to something. I should have known better than to leave you in the house alone, Alicia. This is what comes of not having a mother to look after you. Well, young feller, what do you have to say for yourself? Do you know what it costs to keep a fashionable young lady like this dressed in the latest Paris gowns? Do you have any idea?"

"No, I . . ."

"I don't care if I have to live in a shack, Father, I . . ."

"What is your income, Mr. Kincaid? Aside from the over-inflated salary you extorted from me? You can afford to live in the best hotel in town, but what kind of house can you give her? And how many maids am I going to lose?"

"To tell the truth, Professor, I don't have a *sou.*

Everything we had for two generations has gone into paying for our educations, and for our experiments."

"What? What kind of a . . ."

"Daddy, I don't care. Actually—" Alicia raised her hand in an arresting gesture that was unlike her. "Actually, we don't have a choice."

"What do you mean by that?" Langley stopped in his tracks.

"We're going to have a baby!" Alicia smiled proudly. "You're going to be a grandfather. Isn't that wonderful?"

"A child? A bastard child? Is that what I raised my daughter for?" Turning to Jules, Langley towered over him. "Is this how you repay my generosity? By getting my daughter pregnant?" Jules sank deeper into the big leather chair. "And my housemaids? How many of them have you been diddling?"

"Father, it isn't like that at all. Jules and I are very much in love. Jules even wants a nice church wedding, don't you Jules?"

"Er—I guess so," Jules mumbled.

"It's Daddy who pays. But I'll tell you one thing. You'll have a nice quiet wedding and then it will be Daddy who *stops* paying for all the dresses and all the maids and all the carriage rides. Your fancy Mr. Kincaid can start paying for these things. You won't get another penny out of me, you can be sure of that." The old man stormed out of the room and the sliding doors crashed together behind him.

"You stood up to that very well, Jules," Alicia said with a laugh, almost gleeful at her first open defiance of her father.

"How are we going to survive, Alicia?" Jules

asked. "That's not much of a salary to support a wife and child."

"I don't care, Jules. I'll be so happy to get out of this big mausoleum that I'll even learn to cook and sew. You'll see, I'm going to be a wonderful wife." Alicia leaned over Jules to give him a kiss and then sat down on the arm of his chair.

"How did I get into this?" Jules muttered. Alicia slipped down into his lap and put her arms around him. "Kiss me," she smiled.

"Here?"

"It wouldn't be the first time."

If Jules had been bathed in sweat during that crucial interview, the next few months seemed like a Turkish bath. The boys had to be invited down from Boston for the wedding, and discreet little notices were prepared to be sent out at the last minute for the Washington papers. A date had to be reserved at the old Presbyterian meeting house across the river in Alexandria, and the bride, of course, had to be fitted out with a white gown with expandable waistline. Jules hadn't given a thought to where they would live. Professor Langley, in varying states of high and low dudgeon, kept disappearing down to Quantico.

Jules tried to immerse himself in his work, as he often had in the past, but he couldn't. Alicia kept interrupting him with a million little details. She seemed to be growing bigger and taller and more mature every day; she glowed with that radiant beauty that a woman can only have when she is carrying within her the future of the world. She kept fluttering in and out of the workshops with her friend Mary, asking Jules absurd questions about the boutonnieres for the ushers, and such-like. When she wasn't there, Manly would make snickering little remarks, and Haffaker would make gross jokes.

Right up to the quick-time of their wedding, Jules didn't know where they were going to live. Finally, Alicia had to make the decision for him. "While we're looking for a house, we'll stay right here in Daddy's place, as much as I hate it. Let him go down to the houseboat. It'll keep him out of our hair."

"Whatever you say," Jules said.

The wedding itself was a small affair that filled but a few pews of the austere old meeting-house. The younger Kincaid boys, resplendent in cutaways, gray gloves and ascots, stood up for their brother. Professor Langley, albeit unwillingly, lent his always impressive presence to the ceremony. The only bridesmaids were Mary Lodge and Alice Roosevelt. There were only a few guests—Manly and some of the shop assistants, an attaché from the French Embassy, and Langley's forbidding secretary. After a picture-taking session in the snow, the boys' silk top hats gleaming in the winter sun, it was but a small party that rode back to Langley's mansion in their rented carriages. The wedding dinner was a somber affair, punctuated by Langley's and Henry's formal toasts, until it took off on wings of champagne.

Later, all alone in the great mansion except for two giggling Irish maids, all alone in the great wide bed of the front guest room—although it was certainly not for the first time—the bride and groom lay together in their bed, holding hands.

"Poor Jules. Are you mad at me for trapping you?" Alicia stared up at the canopy above their heads. Jules rolled over and buried his head in the curve of her shoulder.

"Oh, I feel something," Alicia gasped. She took his hand and ran it up under the heavy skirts of her nightgown to massage her stomach. "Do you feel it?"

"Mmm . . ." Jules commented judiciously. He was thinking about the pitch and thrust of the new brass-bushed propellers they were making. Then he began to think of other things.

They found a little row house in Georgetown. The down payment was almost as much as Jules' accumulated savings. "*Georgetown*," Professor Langley snorted. "Slave quarters." Jules asked nothing of Langley, and Langley offered even less, but Alicia was as merry as a grig, searching out old Federal pieces in furniture emporiums, and cleaning and cooking with a will. She packed Jules' lunch in a black working-man's lunch pail, and he took the new tram line to work every day; she cherished her privacy and peace throughout the day just as much as she loved the intimate comforts of having her own home with her own husband and no forbidding father or snickering maids to interfere. No-one they knew lived in Georgetown, and except for Mary Lodge, no visitors ventured over into the *terra incognita* of the once fashionable site of ante-bellum mansions, tiny slave quarters, and the newly-conceived row houses. While the dogwood was blooming, Alicia grew with new life.

11

JULES was vaguely aware that an American battleship had been blown up in Havana Harbor the month before. Francis had been chattering about it at the wedding, and Jules had even seen Huffaker and some of the boys during their lunch breaks reading Hearst newspapers with huge war-scare headlines. He paid little attention. When, toward the end of April, Spain suddenly declared war on the United States, and the United States on Spain, Jules was astounded. But the war really came home to him when Langley stormed up the stairs of the barn one morning and almost broke the locks getting in.

"The Spanish are coming, the Spanish are coming!" the red-faced old man puffed. "They've sent the whole fleet to bombard our East Coast. They'll burn

Washington just like the British did in my father's day."

"Gracious me," Jules said, putting down his screwdriver.

"We've got to hide the boat," the professor panted. "We've got to hide the boat! Manly, get out the survey maps. Where can we hide the boat?"

"How about Mallow's Creek?" Manly pointed on the map to an inlet on the Maryland shore.

"Manly, you're in charge," the professor said. "Take the whole crew. Get some more men from the main building and go down there right now and get that boat out of sight. Jules, you'd better stay here. You have a family. Maybe we should go over to the War Department and borrow some Gatling guns. Do you know how to fire a Gatling gun?"

"Hmm . . ." Jules scratched his head. "We've got an army for that sort of thing, don't we?"

"They're going to take the entire army out someplace in the Midwest and train them all together. There'll be nobody left here to protect us, just like it was in 1863. We'll be digging rifle pits on the White House lawn."

"Oh now, Father," Jules said, hoping that a little needling would put the quietus on the older man's fear. "How quickly can they get here? The ships Queen Isabella sent took four months."

"Jules, your mind is flying around in the clouds, as usual. Come down to earth." The old man stomped down the stairs, leaving Jules the master of all he surveyed. He liked it that way.

Surprisingly enough, the F-Street line was running that night. When he heard the artillery booming from Fort Myer, Jules began to think that perhaps his father-in-law was right. He got off the streetcar and bought some newspapers to read on the way home.

"Alicia—Alicia!" he called when he got there.

"In the kitchen, darling," came her reply. Jules hung up his bowler hat, put his furled umbrella into the closet, and went into the diminutive kitchen. Alicia was cleaning the ashes out of the bottom of the stove, and, as always, she had a smile for him.

"We've sunk the whole damned Spanish fleet," he said. "Somewhere in the Philippines, wherever that is," he said, pointing to a headline in the Washington Post.

"Isn't that nice," she said, leaning over his shoulder and giving him a kiss. "I have a letter from Henry here. He wants to know if you're coming up for his graduation."

"Yes, I suppose I'll have to, and I'll have to get him a graduation present, too," Jules said, reaching under the sink for a bottle of wine.

"You go up and change, dear," Alicia said, taking the bottle from him. "I'll have a glass with you on the back stoop. Your son has been kicking me all day."

Thus did war come to Georgetown. After Langley's initial scare, Jules heard very little more about it, not being a man who listened to gossip, of which there was a great deal. He did hear stories of Alice Roosevelt's father quitting his job to form a volunteer cavalry unit, and other stories about the entire standing army attacking Cuba as one unit as soon as they were properly trained. He paid little attention. Outside of his work and his happy home life, he had only the impending week off to go to Boston for his brother's graduation to occupy his mind. Even for that, it was Alicia who went to the trouble of going out to buy him a new Gladstone bag. She also ordered the new initialed cuff-links that matched his own to give to Henry for graduation. Alicia had decided not to go with him.

"Daddy is so lonely," she said. "And besides, I have some beautiful old Irish lace that belonged to my grandmother that will make a wonderful christening dress for . . ." Alicia chattered on, but Jules' mind had wandered off on a new tack.

All the way north on the train to Boston, Jules studied his various notebooks. According to Langley's Law, any engine powerful enough to drive a plane surface through the air at forty miles an hour or more could depend upon the elasticity of the air through which it traveled to support the structure. Apparently, the shape of the wing and the angle at which it flew had little to do with Langley's calculations. Jules was beginning to have doubts on the subject, so he was glad that they were doing simultaneous research on the various propellers. They had already made great progress over the steam engine designed by Sir Hiram Maxim for his flying machine. They had experimented with boiler coils of various sizes and shapes made with different alloys, and in that respect, Professor Langley's knowledge of metallurgy came in very handy. Their nine-pound model aeroplane had flown very nicely, but whether the same principles, when applied to a larger machine, would still work, was very questionable indeed.

When Jules got to Boston, he put up at the Hasty Pudding Society. Having heard that he was in Washington, the students bombarded him with questions about Teddy Roosevelt's volunteer cavalry, the state of preparedness in the regular army, and the whereabouts of the fleet squadron that the Spanish king had sent to bombard Washington and New York. Jules couldn't even begin to answer their questions. He paid courtesy calls on several of his old professors, and then went out to Groton. Henry and Francis were glad to see him. He took them out to dinner, and broke the news that he and Alicia were expecting a baby in October. Francis was overjoyed at the idea, but Jules could see Henry mentally counting the months. Yet, Henry's innate reserve cracked open a little bit when Jules gave him his graduation present, with love from Alicia. He was very pleased with his new gold cuff-studs. Francis smiled broadly and said, "I'm sure glad you got them for him. He's always borrowing mine."

Jules' conversations with people who had any sort of scientific background could not long stray from his obsessive interest in aeronautics. Yet, when he tried to tell the boys of his newest experiments, Francis kept talking about the war; the great victory in Manila and the vengeance our troops would wreak on the dastardly Spanish in Cuba; while Henry's mind was occupied with his graduation ceremonies the next day and his impending trip to Newport for a month's cruise on somebody's yacht. "Who's going to take care of Francis?" Jules asked. "You can't leave him all alone at Plymouth all summer."

"I'll be all right, Jules," Francis said enthusiastically. "When I'm tired of my own cooking I can go to the club. And besides, we're going to play some real polo this year, if the army hasn't requisitioned all our polo ponies."

"I'll go out with him to make sure he's settled in all right," Henry said. "I have to go out there to store my things for the summer, anyway." Jules had been doodling on the tablecloth. "See the brass fitting at the end of the propeller blades we're making? That's how we get our variable pitch. We just turn it . . ."

Henry's graduation was a triumph. He took two prizes in physics, the top prize in mathematics, and, surprisingly enough, one of the lesser school prizes in English composition. Francis accepted several awards on behalf of the soccer team, of which he had been the captain, and one for the football team, for which he had made a crucial seventy-yard touch-down that had excited considerable attention. All in all, it was a good day for the Kincaids. Jules decided to return to Washington immediately after the ceremonies. What he said was that he didn't want to leave Alicia alone too long, but actually, he was anxious to get back to his experiments.

12

"HELLO, Lish. I'm back." Jules put his suitcases down and hung up his hat. "Anybody home?"

"Back here, Jules. Come on out."

Alicia was on the back stoop shelling peas for dinner. "You're back early. How nice." She turned her face up to be kissed.

"I couldn't stay away any longer. Lordy, you've grown a foot!"

"I think I have. Get yourself a glass of wine, and tell me about Francis."

"All right, I will." Jules hung his coat over the bannister and took off his tie and collar. "Shall I get you some?"

"I'd better not. Hurry up. I'm dying to hear about your trip, and then I've got some things to tell you."

She raised her voice as Jules went inside and groped under their ice-box for the wine bottle. "You won't believe this, Jules, but Daddy was over here last night."

Jules pulled out the pan beneath the ice-box and set the wine bottle to one side. The pan was full of melted ice-water, so he took it to the sink and dumped it out before replacing it, and poured his glass of wine. "Not Our Lord and Master?"

He went outside and sat down on the steps, taking out his cuff-studs and putting them carefully in his pocket before rolling up his sleeves. Alicia smiled to see the red sleeve-suspenders she had made for him from an old pair of garters.

"You're as big as a house, Alicia! I think you're going to have twins."

"That's not a bit funny," Alicia said as she made a wry face. "But tell me about Francis and Henry."

Jules picked up some pertinacious pea-pods and began helping her shell them. He described his quick trip, and told her that Henry had been very pleased with his graduation present. The smell of mint pervaded the air. Alicia had crushed fresh mint leaves on the doorstep to prevent ants from coming in. "And what has been happening here? I feel like I've been gone for a year."

"Well," Alicia said, drawing in an anticipatory gulp of air and putting on a Cheshire cat smile that indicated that she had been incubating something more than the pride of the Kincaids. "Well, you know how mad Daddy was that he couldn't go to Europe this summer because of the war. That makes two summers he's missed."

"Oh, him and his trips to Europe. All he does is collect sheepskins."

"Yes, but he has been rather lonely since we got married. I've been spending some time with him, and he was not at all happy about being stuck here at the hottest time of the year. It's even hot on the houseboat this year. Well, now that's all changed. I don't know what happened, but all of a sudden he's full of new plans. He wants to build a new houseboat, two or three times as large as the old one. He's also going to let you and Manly hire as many assistants as you want."

"Well, well. What's this all about?"

"I had to pry it out of him. It's a deep dark secret and I'm not supposed to tell you, but I will. You'll find out tomorrow, anyway. He's got a big War Department grant, and he's going to have you and Manly construct a full-sized aeroplane, just like your test models."

"What? Those things flew only three times! And that may have only been a fluke of wind. We need a lot more testing."

"There's no more time, he says. This is war. He keeps talking about 'Manifest Destiny' and the 'New American Century.' Daddy says we're going to take Cuba, the Philippines, Puerto Rico, and Hawaii, and then maybe Mexico and Guatemala and the de Lesseps Canal. He says it's inevitable."

"He's been in Washington too long. It's midsummer madness."

"He says we'll need a big army and a lot of aeroplanes to scout for the army and navy. He says that our enemies will never be able to surprise us again if we can observe them from the air."

"Now who's got his head in the clouds?"

Jules was bemused with the potential of these

new developments as they had dinner, and later as they relaxed in their backyard, sipping iced tea and listening to the birds singing in the cool of the evening. Later, as they lay together in their comfortable bed and drowsily watched the moonlight streaming through the window, Alicia said, "Do you know that you're the best tummy-rubber in all the district? Ooh, did you feel him kick?"

"Yes." Jules was suddenly awake. "I think he's going to be a rugby player, like his uncle."

"Or a hootchy-kootchy dancer."

She eyed him contentedly and touched his shaggy blond hair. "There was one more thing, Jules. Daddy's giving Manly a raise in salary, but he wants to keep all of the glory for himself."

"Doesn't he always?"

"Yes. I told him that was all right, but I made him promise to put you on the Board of Directors of the Institute. That carries a stipend. He didn't want to do it," she giggled maliciously, "but I told him you had an offer from some company up north, and he wants to keep you here."

"Alicia, you're a terrible liar."

"Yes, I am. Isn't it awful?" Alicia laughed again and rolled over to kiss him on his closed eyelids. "Shall we do some experimenting?" she murmured, running her hand up under his nightclothes.

As soon as he arrived at his office the next day, Jules was summoned to a conference with Manly and Langley. The old man was ebullient, showing his teeth and banging on his desk like his friend Teddy Roosevelt. "Unlimited funds! A new War Department grant! Those spoil-sports in Congress won't even know about it until it's all over. We're going to attack with all out armies simultaneously. Jules, you can let out contracts for the construction of an internal combustion engine immediately. The specifications will be for an engine of twelve-horsepower, weighing one hundred to one hundred-and-fifty kilograms, with provisions for a duplicate engine to operate the other propeller. Manly, you can start building the airframe now. Just enlarge everything in our test models five and six, and make an allowance for engine and pilot. We'll have to let out contracts to build a new houseboat three times as large as the one we've got."

"Surely you're not going to stick with that houseboat idea?" Jules said. "A simple railroad track laid out into the direction of the prevailing wind would be much more practical—and cheaper."

"Never mind the cost. Our penny-pinching days are over. This time we'll have a full pantry, and more servants quarters."

As they laid out their plans for the coming year, Jules began to get more and more exicited about the possibilities, but he still had his doubts. "I'm forced to play the devil's advocate, Father," he said, and Manly winced at the evidence that he might be overshadowed by his employer's son-in-law. "We must have more tests on models five and six before we spend a lot of money on a machine that may not fly at all. After all, we've only had three successful flights, and they were very short."

"They were the first powered flights in the history of man," Langley beamed. "I have twenty years of experience at this, and proven designs. We're standing at a crossroads of history, and the outriders of fame are galloping down upon us," Langley said enthusiastically. "You're going to have the honor of being the first man to fly in a heavier-than-air machine, Jules. We'll call it the *Langley Flyer*."

The ensuing weeks were filled with conferences, with the hiring of draftsmen and workmen, and with the letting of contracts. Jules hardly paid attention to the huge headlines in the Washington Star which announced that the United States Marines had landed at Guantanamo Bay in Cuba. He had to make hurried trips to New York to find an established engine-maker who would accept a contract for a light-weight engine that could produce such high horsepower; and upon taking their old model flyers down to Quantico for further tests, he discovered that the steam propulsion units had desiccated to the point where they were no longer operable. It involved a lot of time, and painstaking effort, to find out what was wrong with the engines and set them right again.

The copious war news went right over his head, but Langley would bounce into his office daily, enthusing about the battle of Santiago and his friend Colonel Roosevelt, who was rapidly becoming a national hero. Colonel Roosevelt's Rough Riders had charged up a San Juan hill, taking incredible casualties, and then, firing automatic weapons at the fleeing Spaniards, had bravely conquered a sugar-cane distillery. Little was said about the two regiments of black troops and the division of regulars that shared in the losses. The McLeans of "Friendship" preferred to glorify their home-grown heroes, rather than the dull sluggards of the regular services, who were mostly Civil War holdovers. After all, it was *their* war, a war they had created out of newsprint and adjectives.

On July 3rd, the United States Navy destroyed

the Spanish fleet at Santiago in Cuba, thus avenging the *Maine*. On July 7th, the Hawaiian Islands were annexed by the United States. On July 9th, Jules returned from a quick trip to New York to find a nervous Alicia, great with child, anxious to see him.

"Jules, did you get my wire? I telegraphed the Plaza."

"No. What is it?" Jules put his bags down in the tiny entryway of their house and eyed Alicia's spotted apron as she went to get a telegram from the kitchen. "Francis has disappeared," she said. "Henry sent a wire from Plymouth. No one has seen him since the beginning of June." Jules eyed the terse telegram Henry had sent him the week before, and wished that he could telephone up to Plymouth, but there were probably no telephones in that town. He had a quick and terrible vision of his trip to the Boston City Morgue to pick up his grandfather's body.

"I suppose I should get up there and see what I can do," Jules said. "And we have a meeting of the Board of Directors tomorrow. Vice-President Hobart is presiding. Your father won't take it kindly if I absent myself on private business at this time."

"That's something you will have to decide for yourself," Alicia said, drying her hands nervously on her apron.

Jules took a hurried bath and changed clothes before going down to the kitchen to join Alicia for a quick repast of home-baked bread with a glass of wine. "I'll go over to the office and call Boston," he said. "I'll sleep in your father's office upstairs if I can find the key, and then I'll leave right after the meeting tomorrow. That Francis! He may be lying dead in the gutter."

"Oh, don't make it worse than it is. You know him. He may just have decided to take a boat ride somewhere without telling you."

"Will you be all right here, all alone?" Jules asked.

"I'll be fine, and if I start feeling uncomfortable, I'll just move back with Daddy. He has kept my room just the way I left it."

It was the first time that Jules had had to attend a meeting in the luxurious boardroom of the Smithsonian. Presided over by the Vice-President, it was an impressive group of senators, representatives, and several of the outside directors, including Dr. Graham Bell. Jules had to address them, and, perspiring and nervous, he described his frustrating search for a sub-contractor who would build their gasoline engine for them. "They are all involved with automobile manufacture," he said, "and they are keeping their trade secrets to themselves." When Jules had finished, he sat down, shifting nervously as Manly, and Karr, the accountant, made their reports. Jules was breaking out in prickly-heat in his hot cutaway and high collar, but his father-in-law beamed at him, cool and confident at this, one of the high points of his life.

It was a festive occasion as they all stood together in front of the Smithsonian, and a smiling Langley saw the various dignitaries to their carriages. Jules skipped out on the handshaking and went to wait for Langley in his office. "Well, me boy," Langley said as he bounded in. "Wasn't that wonderful? Forget about the Hodgkins Fund. We're going to put a bill through Congress so fast that their heads will spin. Your speech was very impressive. Congratulations."

"Dr. Langley, my little brother has disappeared. I must go up to Plymouth and see if I can locate him."

"You can't leave right now, Jules. I want you to go over the plans for the launching apparatus. I'm taking your advice, and switching from the overhead launching rail to one mounted on the floor of the turntable."

"Surely you can understand, Father. You're a family man. There's no one else to look out after Francis. Henry's just a boy. I must go. As a matter of fact, I'm leaving directly from here. Surely you understand . . ."

"Well, if you must go, you must. Who'll look out after Alicia?"

"I hope she'll be all right. That's another very good reason why I'll be returning as soon as possible. Please keep your eye on her."

By the time Jules got all the way up to Plymouth, he had begun to feel that he had spent his life on jostling, noisy steam-cars. He left his bags at the station, and walked out to the house. It was unlocked, and there were certainly signs of habitation, but no one was there. Cursing with frustration, Jules left a note and retraced his steps, walking all the way to the Plymouth Beach Club. There he found Henry, immaculate in tennis whites, batting a ball about with a Harvard undergraduate whom he vaguely knew, while two straw-hatted girls hopped about in their long skirts.

"Jules! What are you doing here? Didn't you get my telegram?"

"What telegram? Where's Francis? He must be all right if you're . . ."

"I sent you a wire two days ago. At Georgetown. Didn't you get it?"

"I've been on the cars, getting here. *Where is Francis?*"

"He's in Cuba. He's a corporal in the army. He joined the Rough Riders. He's a hero!" Henry took off his straw hat and extracted a perspiration-soaked telegram from the hatband and handed it to his brother. Jules unfolded it and began to read. It was addressed to Henry.

I AM FINE STOP HAVING WONDERFUL TIME STOP JOINED ROUGH RIDERS BUT TRANSFERRED TO GENERAL SHAFTER'S STAFF AFTER REQUISITIONED MOTORCYCLE AND AUTOMOBILE STOP NOW CORPORALING AS COURIER AND DRIVER STOP PLEASE TELL JULES STOP HOPE I HAVEN'T CAUSED ANY TROUBLE STOP HOME SOON STOP LOVE FRANCIS

As the news slowly penetrated his fatigue-befuddled mind, Jules got so angry that his face turned beet-red. "That little snipe!" he cursed. *Quelle cochonnerie! Je m'en fous!* I'll tan his fifteen-year-old hide."

"He's a hero, Jules," Henry said. "There will be medals galore!" Jules threw up his hands and walked away.

When Jules returned to Georgetown after another brief stop in New York, where he finally managed to locate a subcontractor who would attempt to build an engine for them, he found the little house in Georgetown spic-and-span, and Alicia knitting white booties, much relieved at having received his wire about Francis. One of her father's Irish maids had moved in with them, planning to sleep on a trundle-bed in the living room. Three people in that tiny house were too many, and Jules secretly resolved to spend more of his nights at the office or on the houseboat.

As soon as he had reported to Langley and put his affairs in some order, he paid a visit to a friend at the War Department, telling him that his brother must have lied about his age and should not be in Cuba at all. His friend sent a confidential message to Havana. An answer from General Shafter's Chief of Staff came two days later, and was sent over from the War Department via an armed messenger, an army corporal wearing the new summer-tan uniform. It said that General Shafter regarded Francis as indispensable to the smooth operation of his headquarters, and stated that in the absence of any documentary evidence that Francis had falsified his enlistment papers, he would be unable to release him from his assigned duties. He also stated that any further communications on the subject should be channeled through Colonel Roosevelt's Rough Riders, since Francis was on temporary duty assignment from that unit. Jules, by now familiar with governmental red tape to some extent, had the suspicion that the war would be long over before he could get any action from the War Department.

He was more than a little surprised when acquaintances at the Smithsonian came up to congratulate him, and showed him news stories in the Washington Star which had been picked up from the Boston and New York papers. It seemed that the English journalist who had sent Francis' first wire out of Cuba had written a story about the young man, characterizing him as a youthful hero and an automotive genius who set up a fast courier service between the various units of the Cuban command. He was called a young Mercury, dashing from headquarters to headquarters on his snorting, gasoline-gulping steed with messages of historic import. He was described as wearing Army blues, a cowboy hat, and riding boots. Jules could well imagine his brother in a wool uniform buttoned up to the neck, perspiring in malarial jungles. Deciding again to go through unofficial channels, he called upon Mrs. Roosevelt and asked her to see if she could have her husband return Francis to his own regiment and get him out of Cuba as quickly as possible. Alice Roosevelt, standing by, winked at him conspiratorially.

"It's a pest-hole down there," Mrs. Roosevelt said. "My husband is trying to get the entire command sent back as soon as possible, before they all die of yellow fever. I'll ask him to see what he can do."

Jules spent most of August at Quantico, preparing the old number five and six models for their new tests. It seemed that every time he got them ready for launching, the weather would turn bad. He discovered that the best time to do the testing was either at dawn or dusk, when the river was almost always as smooth as glass, unruffled by passing ships or vagrant winds; but to ready the planes, and develop a hundred-and-ten pounds of steam pressure within two minutes of lighting the fire, created continual problems. The fine copper tubing of the boiler coils had been imported from France, and there was none available in the United States at any price. No sooner would they get them repaired and try them out on the test bench, then the steam pressure would blow out the coils again, necessitating further tedious repairs.

While that work was going on, Jules convinced Langley to let him build a quarter-size model of the ultimate aeroplane design. "We can run both propellers on one engine," he told Langley, "if we could ever get the protoype engine completed. Without a pilot, the weight will not be excessive. We should do a great deal more testing before we risk the life of any aviator in a machine with the power of fifty horses."

"No. We have too much else going on. All this testing you're talking about would interfere with your other work," Langley said.

Jules decided to acquiesce, and he changed the subject. "Oh, incidentally, Dr. Langley, I heard from Chanute. He says the Wright brothers are performing all kinds of tests this summer in Dayton, and they'll be back for more gliding at Kitty Hawk again this winter. They are being very conservative. They haven't even tried an engine yet." Jules laughed deprecatingly.

Langley peered at him with a sudden sharp gaze, and Jules was reminded that the old tiger might be distracted, but he was always dangerous. "You understand, my boy, that this is all highly confidential. I'm even getting armed guards from the War Department to keep our work secret. There are countless thousands of dollars at stake. Scores of thousands. I have made contractual provisions so that I can apply for patents on the Langley flying machine, but I'm not going to apply and neither are the Wrights. The minute anything goes into that Patent Office, anyone can read it. Look at the Mouillard patents! But once I can start producing my own machines and selling them to the government, there will be a fortune to be made. It will all go to Alicia. Bear that in mind."

Jules assembled his rough sketches of the quarter-sized model and got up to leave. "Yes, yes indeed," he said thoughtfully. He had never regarded scientific research as a way to get rich.

While supervising the draftsmen who were employed in making engineering drawings for the new launching structure, Jules also consulted with Manly about the ingenious new airframe which they had devised. Instead of a metal centerpole to which the wings would be clamped, Manly had planned a tubular steel structure which would leave room inside for mounting the engine, and for a place for the pilot to stand in order to make instant adjustments on the Penaud tail to control the upward and downward movement of the aircraft. He had invented a pulley-and-wheel arrangement to tilt the rudder up and down. Special fittings were already being manufactured in all of the Smithsonian workshops. Jules was impressed with the little man's ingenuity.

At the beginning of August, the island of Puerto Rico was invaded and occupied by the United States Army, and on the 12th Spain sued for peace, but Jules was hardly aware of politics. What worried him was a letter from Colonel Roosevelt, which was reprinted in the Yellow Press. It said that nearly five thousand of the troops in Cuba were ill with yellow fever, malaria, or dysentary, and if they were not evacuated soon, thousands would die. The weeks went by with no further word from Francis.

Jules shuttled back and forth between Washington and New York, trying to keep his eyes on the contractor who was developing their gasoline engine. The man had rented a huge loft, and engaged almost a dozen new employees to work on the project, but progress was dismayingly slow.

A needless complication was the paperwork involved. Jules had to get authorizations through Langley's office and process them, in order to make payments to the New York manufacturers. They never seemed to go through on time, and the contractor had trouble meeting his large payroll. Telegrams would arrive frequently from New York, requesting an immediate dispatch of funds. Finally, Jules went to Karr's office to complain.

"Mr. Karr, when are we going to get this check for New York? I sent in the request two weeks ago, and I'm sure its been authorized and processed through your office, but here's a telegram saying they haven't received the check yet."

"You young people are so impatient. They must be holding it at Morgan's in New York. These things happen. You'll get used to it. That's the way these things go."

Jules was very irritated at having to act as the buffer between the manufacturer and the Smithsonian. Unexpectedly, he had to make a trip that same night to New York to deliver the design of a new machine part. Rather than face, unprepared, the ire of the contractor, he stopped over at Broad and Wall Street to make inquiry at Morgan's. He was pleased to see old Mr. Bellamy still at his desk.

"*Bonjour, M. Bellamy. Je suis Jules Kincaid.*" The older man was overjoyed to have an opportunity to show off his French.

"*Bienvenue, M. Kincaid. Qu'est-ce-que on peut faire pour vous?*"

Jules switched back into English. "It's not my personal account. I'm at the Smithsonian in Washington now, and our accountant, Mr. Karr, says that you're holding a check for one of our suppliers here in New York. I wonder if I could pick it up and hand-deliver it."

"Oh, yes. Mr. Karr. He's a very active customer.

All of the Smithsonian accounts are very active. Let me find out." Bellamy sent a clerk to get the files on the Smithsonian accounts, and meanwhile, he reminisced about Paris with Jules. When the files came, the banker rapidly checked through them. "There's a big transfer from this special account to the stock-brokerage account, but I cannot see any check that we are holding."

"Stock-brokerage account? Could I take a look?"

"Oh no, I'm afraid not. You would have to have a letter of authorization."

"You're sure there's no check being held?"

"None that I can see here," Bellamy said. "I'm sorry, Mr. Kincaid."

"Then I suppose I will have to go over there without it." Jules stood up and thanked the elderly banker. On his way over to the contractor's loft, he puzzled over why there should be a stock-brokerage account for the Smithsonian, and, if there was one, why it should be as active as Mr. Bellamy had described it. It seemed to him that speculation with Smithsonian funds would probably be prohibited by law.

When Jules delivered the engineering drawings to the contractor, he found a telegram from Alicia waiting for him. She passed the news that Francis was back from Cuba. He and the entire Rough Rider unit were at Camp Wyckoff on Montauk Point in New York, but they had all been quarantined. They were not allowed to leave the compound.

Jules took care of his business as quickly as possible, and went out to Montauk Point on the first available train. At the camp, an armed guard stopped him at the gate. "Nobody's allowed in or out, mister. Absolutely nobody."

"I came all the way from Washington. My brother's in there."

"*Nobody* in or out. Them's the Colonel's orders. What's your brother's name?"

"Corporal Francis Kincaid. Courier service or something."

"Yup? You his brother? He's in charge of the lion. I'll send for him. He'll be up by the fence and you can yell at him there. He's quite a young-un." While the guard sent someone to fetch Francis, Jules passed the time by talking to the young, white-uniformed officer of the guard. "I see you all have your summer uniforms, now that fall is here," he said.

"Yes, as soon as we got back from the tropics, they caught up with us. Those army blues were so moldy with jungle rot that we had to burn them."

"How could I make an appointment with Colonel Roosevelt?" Jules asked the officer of the day.

"The Colonel is at his country estate. It's not far from here. Ask any reporter; they'll tell you how to get to Sagamore Hill."

"Jules—*Jules!*" It was Francis, up the hill behind a wire fence. Jules waved at the officer of the day and ran as far as he could up the hill toward his brother.

"How are you? You look wonderful. What's that thing?"

"That's Josephine, our mascot." Francis was holding the leash of a young mountain lion. Jules thought his brother looked tanned and healthy, but very thin.

"Have you been sick? How are you feeling?"

"I'm much better now. Get me out of this place, will you? It's like a prison."

They shouted up and down the hill eagerly, Francis asking about Alicia and how Henry was doing, and Jules anxious to hear about his brother's adventures. Soon they were interrupted by the loud clanging of a triangular piece of metal suspended in front of a mess tent. "I've got to go to chow now, Jules. I'm dying of hunger. Get me out of this place."

"All right. You'll be hearing from me," Jules shouted. "It's wonderful to have you back." He kept waving as Francis disappeared into the crowd of khaki-clad men.

It was no trouble finding out where Colonel Roosevelt lived. His name, and the name of Sagamore Hill, were being featured in every newspaper in the United States. In the village near there, Jules rented a one-horse rig to drive him out to the estate. Jules sent in his card, and the Colonel received him immediately in a messy library room decorated with books, framed Holbein prints, more books, and the stuffed, mounted heads of various wild animals. The Colonel had a broken arm.

"Fell down a mountainside yesterday while I was out taking a tramp with the family. Bully! It's grand to be home. Have a seat, young man."

Jules smiled nervously in the face of so much unbounded energy, and explained why he was there. "Kincaid? Oh—Alice's little friend. He lied!" The Colonel's eyes were flashing with indignation.

"Yes, he did," Jules had to admit. "He's just a boy, and he wanted to be with you."

"I cannot abide a liar. Take him. You're welcome to him." Picking up a little glass bell from a side-table, Roosevelt summoned a uniformed aide, who immediately wrote out an order to the camp commandant. The colonel signed it laboriously with his left hand. "There's just one problem," he said to Jules. "When he left me to go with Shafter, he signed up for another year's enlistment in the regular army. That's your problem. I wash my hands of it."

Jules was quietly overjoyed at having received what he came for, but he tried to mollify his host by asking after Alice and Mrs. Roosevelt, and some of their mutual acquaintances in Hasty Pudding.

It was only a short trip back to the camp to present the colonel's order, and then an hour's wait while Francis was given a quick medical examination and released. He came out of the camp gate with a bundle of souvenirs. They embraced like Frenchmen, pounding each other on the back. Francis was overjoyed and chattering away as they rode in the carriage to the nearest railroad station. While retailing the stories of his many adventures, he insisted upon stopping at the first tavern they saw to have a hearty civilian meal. All the way into town, and then on the tram car up to the Plaza, Francis smiled and jabbered unceasingly. They sat on the edges of their beds at the great new hostelry, and talked through half the night.

"I had a wonderful time," Francis smiled. "I had some money put aside, and as soon as Henry left Plymouth, I took a train down to Texas and just walked into the Rough Riders' camp. Colonel Wood remembered me, and he sent me right in to Colonel Roosevelt. Of course, I had to fib a little, but one of the orderlies had just got sick, and they signed me up. I hope you weren't too worried," he said as he smiled winningly.

"I thought Alicia was going to have a conniption fit," Jules said grimly. "It's not good for a pregnant woman to get these shocks."

"Well, nobody got hurt. You should see those cowboys breaking mustangs. All the horses we got in Texas had to be broken. And getting them on the train to Tampa! They kicked out the sides of the cars until we hobbled them. I think the colonel was happy to have somebody around who spoke Boston.

"Then, when we got to Cuba, they put me on as a courier, riding from Shafter to Roosevelt's camp to Lieutenant Parker's command. You should have seen them going up that hill with those Gatling guns!"

"You mean they were shooting at you?" Jules asked.

"Not for very long. No sooner would I get to one place then they sent me off to another. I was in the saddle from dawn to sunset. One of the officers taught me an old cavalry trick. I'd rub my whole backside with Pear's soap, then by ten o'clock I'd be riding along on soap suds. The cowboys all said that I was so scared that I peed in my pants, but I didn't care."

"Did you get in on any of the big battles?"

"Oh, I was there at San Juan Hill. Christ," Francis was suddenly serious, running a hand through his sun-bleached hair. "They charged right up the hill. The Spanish mowed them down. Almost every officer I knew. Fifteen hundred wounded. The cowboys were cursing and spitting tobacco and sweating and stumbling. It was only the new carbines that saved us. Ninety casualties in our regiment alone."

"What's this business about a motorcycle?" Jules asked. Francis gobbled up another sandwich from the plate they had ordered from room service, and laughed. "Oh, that was funny. We took this village of El Canny, and I was up early the next day, trying out a new filly. The one I had before got shot out from under me. I saw this fancy hacienda, and I rode into the courtyard. The whole place was deserted, and there was this beautiful Panhard automobile sitting in an open barn. So I dismounted and tied my horse to the luggage-rack, got the engine going, and started driving out, when some old fellow in white pajamas came running up. It turned out that this car had belonged to some Spanish general, as near as I could understand. So I just confiscated it, wrote him out a receipt, and signed it William McKinley."

"You are a terrible fellow," Jules said with a laugh.

"That was just the beginning. I drove it back to camp, and the first thing you know I had to drive it to General Shafter's headquarters, and he confiscated it from me. But I was the only one who could drive it and keep it going, so he put me on *his* staff. Colonel Roosevelt was furious."

"But what about this motorcycle? How did that get started?"

"The same way. I was always hungry. I would always be driving around after sunset, trying to find a good meal. I told the captain that I had to fix the engine and then test it. Once I ran into Spanish cavalry patrol, but I just stepped on the gas and drove right through them. Got a bullet in the radiator for that one, but I fixed it up at the next blacksmith shop."

"And the motorcycle?"

"Oh, I found it outside of a little *bodega* back of

the San Juan Hill complex. There was nobody around, so I just loaded it into the back of the car and drove off. That thing was more fun than a thoroughbred stallion. I used to bounce down those little mountain trails at forty—maybe fifty—miles an hour. It was a lot more fun than shovelling manure. Thirty-horsepower engine. I was always scrounging for gas or cleaning the sparking plugs or changing the tires. I hope I see it again. General Shafter said he would have it sent up to Washington and I could start a whole courier service for the army."

"Well, you're not going to. We'll get you out of that. It's time for you to think about going back to school, young man."

"Back to being a Grottie snotty? No, sirree. I'm not going back to being a schoolboy. I'll be down in Washington where you can keep your eye on me. You can even get me permission to live off-post. After all, your baby needs an uncle. You're going to name him Francis, aren't you?"

They were both wall-eyed with fatigue by the time the sun began to creep in through the heavy damask curtains of the suite to which they had been assigned. Only then did Jules recognize it as the suite which Chanute had occupied. The hotel management, upon seeing a Rough Rider uniform, had given them the best rooms in the house.

The next day they sent telegrams to Henry, to Langley, and to Alicia before going down to the factory loft where the new internal combustion engine was being built. The workmen were utterly thrilled to be in the presence of a newly-minted war hero, but Francis was not at all interested in retailing his war experiences. He found the designs for the new engine fascinating.

"A radial five. Is that the piston-firing order? It's perfect. There shouldn't be any vibration at all. What about cooling? You can't have water jackets if you're going to come in under that weight limit. My motorcycle has cooling grids molded into the cyclinder walls to cool it."

"That's solid cast-iron," Jules said. "But we're going to have machined steel with a cast-iron sleeve if we can find a way to weld them together."

"It could be done . . ." Francis' eyes flashed with lively interest. Jules' heart was warmed as he felt some of the cares begin to slip from his shoulders.

They went to Washington together the next day and stopped at the Smithsonian before going over to Georgetown. Langley swelled with pride at having one of the first returning Rough Rider veterans at his beck and call. "You can't go over to Georgetown, my boy," he said to Francis. "They don't have any room at all for you there. Come stay with me. You say you have another week before you have to report to the War Department, and Heaven knows, they don't have any motorcycles for you to ride. We'll see what we can do for you. I have friends over there. My, my!" The old man rubbed his hands together. "Let's send a carriage over for Alicia, and have a family party this evening."

They gathered again that evening around Langley's polished table, and were all regaled by Francis' anecdotes, if not by the rough soldier-language into which he occasionally lapsed. Jules had heard it all before, and at the first opportunity he began making an informant report to Langley on the state of development of the internal combustion engine being made in New York. They were both pleased to find Francis chiming in with certain suggestions. His experience at requisitioning, driving, and maintaining internal combustion engines made him an expert in their eyes.

"How would it be if I got you detailed to the Smithsonian for the rest of your army enlistment?" Langley smiled grimly. "General Shafter won't like it, but he'll find out who wields the whip-hand, war hero or no war hero. And suppose I send you over to my tailor tomorrow for a new dress uniform. I suppose corporals have dress uniforms?" Jules and Alicia exchanged quick glances of amusement at this unusual display of generosity on the part of the Lord of the Manor. Apparently, he was looking forward to having a new bauble to show off at his dinner parties.

"While we're on the subject of business, Dr. Langley . . . I hate to bother you with details, sir, but I'm having an awful lot of trouble getting checks through Karr's office to our New York contractor. I checked up at the Morgan bank and got some rather peculiar ideas of the way our accounting office is being run."

Langley's eyes suddenly blazed. "I'll thank you to keep your nose out of the accounting office, Mr. Kincaid. That's Mr. Karr's business, and my business. You just attend to your Ps and Qs." Jules was surprised at the feline speed and fury of Langley's reaction. From time to time he tried to bring the subject up again in the following weeks, but Langley always shut him off.

13

FOR some short time Francis was one of the most popular dinner guests in Washington. Under the sponsorship of Professor Langley, he found the legs of his tailored trousers crossed under the tables of the capitol's wealthiest hostesses. His novelty value as one of the first Rough Rider veterans to be seen, and a genuine corporal in the United States Army, (albeit one who was not likely to spit gobs of tobacco on the oriental carpet), and his sheer decorative value as a handsome and healthy young fifteen-year-old, was enhanced by the quickly-learned knack of telling clever anecdotes about General Shafter, Colonel Wood, and Colonel Roosevelt.

Jules found his brother a rooming house near the Smithsonian in which to stay. Professor Langley, with his connections at the War Department, arranged for his temporary transfer to duty at the Smithsonian, and for permission to live off-post. Francis soon became a general assistant and liaison man for Jules and Manly, especially in the area of engine development. As his social life began to slack off a bit, he spent more and more time tinkering with the motorcycle that had finally been shipped up from Cuba in advance of General Shafter. His anomalous position as an army corporal without permanent assignment was cleared up when Shafter returned. The general, in fact, found him an embarrassment. To the great satisfaction of all involved, he got him an immediate discharge from the Army. Francis spent his discharge pay on the purchase of a small motorcycle of his own, with which he proceeded to make his fingernails dirty and his nights hideous with noise.

Jules found himself more and more involved in the design and construction of the new houseboat. The boat would have a turn-table weighing about thirteen tons, supported on a double circular track which had to be held up by the side walls in order to avoid having columns in the middle of the floor. By utilizing a turn-table, the new aeroplane could be launched into the wind, whichever direction the wind might be coming from. The springs which would provide the impetus for the aeroplane launch had to be estimated carefully, and built and installed. Many were the nights that Jules, tired after a long day's work, could not face the train trip back into Washington and then the trolley ride to Georgetown. He would sleep on the smaller houseboat, now moored off Quantico, trying to avoid being there when Langley was in residence.

A new and previously unconsidered area of interest for Jules was that which he later dubbed "instrumentation." He designed various simple machines, which would automatically record the number of revolutions of the engine, the velocity and direction of the wind relative to the flying machine, the height of the aeroplane as shown by a specially sensitive aneroid barometer, and the angle of the machine with the horizontal plane of the earth. Once an agreed-upon design had been achieved, Jules let out contracts for the construction for these new, delicate instruments.

Delays in payments to the subcontracting companies proved to be a continuing irritation. Sometimes the cash advances would process through Langley's and Karr's office immediately. Then again, at other times, there would be inexplicable, irritating delays. Jules would complain to Karr, but the old man smugly referred him to Professor Langley, and Jules didn't want to beard the lion in his den any more then necessary.

Alicia seemed more and more closed in to herself as the end of the term of her pregnancy approached. She seemed to draw an inner strength and serenity from the biological creation; from the chemical changes in her body, which made the outside world ever more superfluous. Except for periodic visits to the Washington lying-in hospital, and occasional forays into the stores for some forgotten item, she spent her days in the cool of their tiny Georgetown house. From time to time she would develop strange cravings for obscure viands such as hot corn bread or black-eyed peas, but usually she spent her days humming a tuneless melody of inner contemplation.

Her last weeks of pregnancy were spent in the

great stone mansion where she had passed so many years of her young life. Her increasingly nervous husband, usually preoccupied with aeronautics, would find himself sitting in his little office at the Smithsonian, or at the great drafting board in Langley's barn, staring off into space, his mind drifting aimlessly. When the fateful day in late October came, it found him poring over engineering drawings at his Smithsonian office. By design, he was the last to know. Alicia, the calmest of them all, with the help of old Mr. Huffaker and one of the maids, hied herself to the hospital. She had already been prepared for the birthing and was experiencing periodic labor pains when Jules was summoned, and arrived, panting.

"Are you all right, Alicia?" He put his hat down on the bed and took her hand. "How do you feel?" She was dressed in a peculiar tent-like garment that gaped open at the sides, and her expression, so serene of late, was now an inscrutable compound of calmness, expectation, and a touch of fear, which crinkled the corners of her eyes with new, deep lines. "I'm all right, Jules. Sit down."

He looked around nervously and, without letting go of her hand, drew a wooden chair up beside her high hospital bed. Her strong right hand seemed damp and limp in his own hot, dry palms. Alicia suddenly squeezed his hand, closing her eyes in pain as a contraction shook her. The pain went away as quickly as it had come.

"And how are we doing, Mrs. Kincaid?" A tall and businesslike nurse, dressed in stiffly-starched white from head to foot, stood in the doorway, a stopwatch in her hand. "How often are the contractions coming?"

"Oh, hello." Alicia opened her eyes and seemed to have a little trouble focusing them. "This is my husband."

"How do you do? Do you have a watch, Mr. Kincaid?" Jules took his watch from his vest pocket. "If you would just time them—the contractions—let me know when they start coming every three minutes." The nurse strode out with a smile, her starched petticoats rustling.

"It'll give you something to do, Jules, and keep you out of trouble." Alicia smiled at him reassuringly. "When I come home tomorrow, you will have a fire all built and the baby's clothes laid out in our bedroom, won't you?"

"You're not coming home tomorrow, are you?" Jules asked, dismayed. "Won't you need . . ."

"Why shouldn't I? I want to be in my own home, with just my husband and my baby. Oh,—here they come again." Jules reached for her hand, simultaneously fumbling for his watch.

"Ah, that's better." Alicia relaxed, and Jules used his handkerchief to blot the perspiration from her forehead. "I think you're right," she whispered. "I think he's a football player." Jules leaned over and kissed her hand. In the cold, white light that shone on the hospital bed, she seemed suddenly old.

"Have you given any thought to what we should name the baby?" Alicia asked. "Yes," Jules admitted. Alicia raised her eyebrows and waited. "If its a boy, I thought we might call him Samuel Langley Kincaid." Alicia closed her eyes, and murmured a soft "All right." From down the hall came the muffled screams of a woman in pain.

When the time came to deliver, Alicia seemed to know it, and called out to Jules to get the nurse.

He ran down the hall and found the nurse. "I think she's ready," he shouted to her.

"Very good, Mr. Kincaid." She followed him back to the room, where Alicia lay expectantly, and checked on her progress. She turned to Jules. "We're going to take Mrs. Kincaid into the delivery room now, sir. Would you please wait downstairs?" Jules retrieved his hat and waited by the door as attendants moved the wheeled bed out into the corridor. Just before they took her away, he leaned over to kiss her white, dry forehead. "I love you," he whispered.

The waiting-room downstairs had a cold white floor made of great square blocks of some stone Jules could not identify. He paced back and forth. The cold stone floor, the echoing sounds, and the faint antiseptic odors and echoing cries that occasionally wafted from the upper floors, recalled to Jules the Boston morgue of chilling memory. In spite of the comfortable horsehair sofas and leather chairs, and the daily newspapers neatly stacked on a side-table, he could not relax. He would glance at a newspaper, read perhaps a paragraph, and would then put it down and peer outside into the corridor without knowing what he was looking for. Then he would pace again. Langley was in New York for some meeting or other, which was just as well. Jules was in no shape to put up with the captious moods of his unpredictable father-in-law. Where Francis was, he didn't know; supposedly in one of the Smithsonian workshops. Another nervous man came into the room, but Jules had nothing to share with him. They hardly nodded. Finally the doctor came. His cravat and the points of his high-collared shirt peeked out from above a clean white apron. "Mr. Kincaid?"

"Yes?" Jules stood up, holding his hat in both hands.

"Congratulations. You are the father of an eight-pound, six-ounce son." Jules' face lit up with a smile. "And Alicia—my wife? How is she?"

"She's just fine; very happy. If you'll wait just—" He pulled his watch from his trousers pocket. "If you'll wait just five minutes, it will be all right for you to go up and see her."

"Thank you, Doctor." As the doctor went away, Jules looked around for his hat, and then discovered it in his hands. Clasping his arms behind him, his felt hat banging against his legs, he walked up and down the corridor. A smile came to his face as his thoughts jumped from one thing to another. *Samuel Langley Kincaid*, he thought. *Sam Kincaid.*

When he got upstairs, he found Alicia in her narrow bed, covered up to the chin and firmly tucked in. Beside the bed was an ordinary wicker basket scrubbed to bleached perfection, and in it, likewise bundled up, was his son. Jules kissed Alicia and took her hand, but he couldn't take his eyes off the baby. Its little face seemed all pushed together, and a thin cap of black hair covered its head. Jules put his finger in the tiny hand, and felt it gripped tenaciously. Alicia looked on with a tolerant smile. When the child opened its eyes, Jules gasped. "His eyes are blue—just like mine!"

"All babies' eyes are blue, silly!" Alicia said, and she pulled Jules' other hand to her lips to kiss it.

* * *

Thanksgiving, in that year of Manifest Destiny of 1898, was the happiest holiday that Jules, for all of his twenty-two years, could remember. The night before, on the way home from the office, he had purchased a fine fat turkey and carried it, cold in its cheesecloth covering, home with him. When Thanksgiving day dawned, clear and cold, he helped Alicia to prepare the savory stuffing for the great bird. Soon the house was alive with the spicy smell of roasting turkey.

Jules sipped at the mulled wine he was heating on the stove, and awaited his guests: Francis and Professor Langley. His father-in-law had insisted again and again that Jules and Alicia should move back into the city, but Alicia had adamantly refused, for she enjoyed the peace and quiet, the independence, and the dearth of visitors those few extra miles from the Capital afforded her. Langley was to be dropped off by his driver and picked up again at four.

Francis arrived with a great thundering roar, his motorcycle spitting and popping and slipping on the icy street, and his long blond hair streaming out from beneath the cap he had pulled down over his forehead. A crowd of small boys quickly gathered to inspect this new mechanical marvel as he manhandled it, leaning it against the house underneath Alicia's gayly-painted flower boxes, now dormant with peat moss. "Hey, you kids," he laughed. "Don't touch it. The motor's red-hot."

Jules came out onto his front stoop, a cigar in one hand, a mug of hot, spiced wine in the other. "Happy Thanksgiving, Jules!" The two brothers embraced, Jules laughing and holding his arms out wide as Francis exuberantly put his arms around him and banged him on the back, spilling his wine.

"You're burning a lot of oil with that monster," Jules laughed, drying the back of his hand on his shirt-sleeve.

"A new engine!" His brother smiled. "I put it in at the shop last week. Don't tell the old man."

"I won't," Jules said with a smile. "We'd better get inside before you freeze to death." They went inside and Francis hung up his cap and leather jacket.

"Mmm—that smells wonderful!" he said enthusiastically.

"You woke up the baby!" Alicia smiled from the top of the narrow stairway. "Happy Thanksgiving!"

Francis bounded up the stairs and kissed her on the cheek. "Let's see him," he said. As he bent over the crib, he smiled delightedly, and the sleepy infant grabbed his finger. "Look at those brown eyes," the proud uncle said. "He looks just like Henry!"

"Oh, he does not. He looks just like me," Jules insisted. "His hair is going to be blond, and his eyes are blue."

"No, they're not. They're brown."

Jules appealed to Alicia, but she merely shrugged. "Too bad Henry couldn't come down," she said. "It would have been a real family party."

"He has a lot of studying to do. I remember what it was like when I was a freshman," Jules said. "Wait until next summer. I want to get the whole lot of us together at Plymouth. It'll be a real reunion."

"How are all of us going to fit into that little house?" Francis laughed.

"If you could live in a tent in Cuba, then you can

live in a barn at Plymouth," his brother said as he
smiled, and poured him a mug of wine.

Their Lord and Master arrived directly from
church in a shiny silk top-hat and Chesterfield coat.
With a basketful of baby, and the four of them all together gathered around the overloaded table in the
tiny living room, there was hardly room to breathe.
The Kincaid brothers were full of good spirits, which
could not help but affect the older man, even though
he grimaced noticeably at the vinegary taste of the
inexpensive red wine which his son-in-law had poured
for him. Alicia presided with motherly good cheer
over her big brood of boisterous boys. From the nervous and flighty young girl she had been the year before, she had turned, in the space of one year, into a
contented wife and mother, not at all harried by having to look out for her infant, her two overgrown boys,
and her overbearing father. At the moment, Langley
was at his ease, as he leaned back in his wooden chair
after a heavy meal, one hand on the baby's crib, the
other one holding a long Havana cigar. When she took
the baby upstairs for his nap, her father lay down in
her bed beside the baby and fell asleep. The two boys
took a walk, leaving her alone with a great table full
of dishes and pots of water boiling on the stove. She
looked out the tiny window at the two brothers wan-
dering off together, gesturing and waving their cigars.
She had never been so happy.

That winter brought the greatest snowfall since
the terrible storms of 1888, which had wiped out the
fortunes of so many Dakota ranchers, including that
of the Roosevelt family. Jules had laid in a great
smoked ham, which hung with the frozen carcasses of
game birds and almost a whole side of jerky beef on

the crowded back porch of his little house. When, just before Christmas, a great blizzard dropped twenty more inches of snow on the city, all business was suspended, the Smithsonian was closed, and all railroad traffic in and out of the city was suspended. Jules would get up each morning, bundle up and trudge through the great snowdrifts to a neighbor's barn for a bucket of fresh milk. By the time he had made his way back home, the milk would be partially frozen in the pail, and the cream was a round, yellowish cake which rose two inches above the top of the pail. While Alicia prepared breakfast, he would gather in the diapers—frozen stiff as boards—that dangled only a foot above the top of the snow from the backyard clothesline. Jules would then go in to have his breakfast, stoke the fires, and look out the window at the vast expanse of whiteness, meditating on the peaceful, but unearthly silence that seemed to envelop their world. He thought that this was what it must be like above the clouds—an endless, silent ocean of white.

When Alicia joined him, they would both gaze out the window, and talk about their life together.

"I never dreamed things could be like this for me," Jules said, "A steady job, a wife and child, a home of my own."

Alicia, standing behind him, put her arms around him and nestled up to his cheek. "You are a very fine man, Jules Kincaid," she murmured.

Jules turned, put his arms around her, and held her close. "I love you," he said, wondering to himself what the words really meant.

The year 1899 was the final year of a Century of Progress; dubious progress perhaps, but certainly a century of great change. The century had begun with Montgolfier balloons rising on hot air and drifting they knew not whither, sometimes dumping their occupants out to be dashed to death on the earth below. It had begun with men traveling and fighting wars in much the way they always had. It had been a century of relative peace, devoted to progress in manufacturing and transportation, but it had also refined the art of mass slaughter of man and beast, and developed the hypocritical religiosity that nurtured Victorianism, pan-Germanism, the exploitation of distant conquests, and the Manifest Destiny that was to become the white man's burden.

Progress in all the various aspects of the Smithsonian research went forward by fits and starts, in spite of the new influx of funds and additional employees. When they tried to obtain turnbuckles, to which the wires were attached that would guy their wings, they found that none of the manufactured articles available were light enough for their purposes, and they had to design and manufacture their own. They conducted stress tests on the silken wings, turning them over and loading them with layers of sand until their weight-supporting qualities and elasticity were determined. Propellers of various sizes and shapes, mostly perfect helices, were constructed and tested until they had a veritable library of propellers. Karr's accounting office continued to be a stumbling-block to progress.

By June, when Professor Langley left for Europe to visit several congresses and, ostensibly, to canvass the various European motor manufacturers to try to locate a more promising lightweight engine, the two model aeroplanes, together with a number of extra sets of wings, all of which were capable of being set at various angles, were ready for testing on the Potomac. For a period of two months, Jules had the small houseboat towed out into the lee of an island, and, in spite of continuing delays, would get the machines into the air with the help of his brother Francis. On one day the boilers would develop leaks because of defects in the copper tubing; on another an air tank would burst from excessive pressure. On another day, the winds would be too high for any sort of safe flight. The complicated miniature steam engines had to develop a steam pressure of 110 pounds within ninety seconds after the fires had been lit. It was nearly the end of June before the conditions were all finally right.

The first test flight was flown, with Francis jumping up and down on the deck in excitement. The miniature aeroplane flew straight ahead for about seventy-five feet, wisps of smoke coming from its smokestack, when suddenly it turned its bow up into the air at an angle of about fifteen degrees. Jules thought that it would slip down into the water, but the machine was caught in the wind and blown backwards toward the houseboat. At that point, the Penaud tail functioned as it was supposed to, and the machine resumed its forward flight until its tiny supply of fuel was exhausted, and it came down to a smooth landing in the shallow water. They picked it up with the power launch and brought it back to the houseboat, where it was dried and prepared for another flight.

"The wing setting of five degrees seemed to be about perfect for horizontal flight," Jules said.

"With a slightly higher setting," Francis hazarded

a guess, "maybe it would climb higher before the fuel is exhausted. We'd get a longer flight that way."

"We can only tell by trying it."

On the next flight they clamped on a different set of wings, a bi-plane arrangement with which they had been experimenting. The wind created by the propellers, however, seemed to have an adverse affect as it blew back on the back-wing, and the flight was unsatisfactory.

The next day the wind, which had been blowing at half a gale strength all day, gradually quieted down toward sunset, and at five o'clock was very light, blowing at only two miles an hour. One of the rear super-posed wings had been damaged the previous day, when Jules and Francis had hoisted the aeroplane back onto the houseboat after its failed flight, and it was decided to use the monoplane wings this time. When everything was ready, the burners were lighted, and the boys waited for seventy seconds until the steam pressure had risen to 120 pounds. The aeroplane was launched. It flew perfectly straight for about 800 feet before suddenly turning to the left in a short half-circle. When it was about 200 feet from the shore, a sudden gust of wind caught under the Penaud Tail, raising it and forcing the aeroplane down into the water. It was not damaged.

"This is as bad as the balloons, Jules," Francis said. "You never know where it's going to come down."

"On the bigger model," Jules answered, scratching his head, "a Penaud Tail will control its ascent and descent, we hope, but the lateral guidance will still be dependent only on the shifting of the weight of the pilot—and we still don't know how well that will work against the pressure of the side winds."

In August, they closed all the workshops against the muggy heat to allow themselves and all the employees a full month's vacation. Langley was still in Europe. Jules and Francis looked forward to their reunion with Henry in Plymouth. For Alicia, it was an exciting prospect. She had never traveled very much, and never before without the oppressive company of her father. Francis went ahead by himself, bouncing and roaring along the rutted summer roads, parking his motorized steed in the livery barns of the little hotels he stayed in. Jules and Alicia loaded up their trunks and carried their baby with them, stopping for a few days in New York, where Alicia shopped. While she was at the stores, Jules took care of young Sam, and when she returned he went to inspect the dubious progress being made on their internal combustion engine. When they finally arrived at the little station in Plymouth, it seemed to have been from a journey as long as that from Cherbourg. Jules picked up the rented horse and buggy he had reserved in advance, loaded up their trunks, and drove them out to the house. The boys came running out, laughing with pleasure.

"Henry, you've grown a foot!"

"Welcome to the old homestead." Francis smiled, helping Alicia, burdened as she was with the baby, down from the carriage.

"The house is so small!" Alicia marveled. "How are we all going to fit in it?"

"We'll build the Samuel Kincaid annex," Francis said with a laugh, unhitching the horse.

"That's not such a bad idea," Jules said as he unloaded the trunks.

Summer was long, cool, and golden under the sun. After the terrible blizzard of the winter before, it was a pleasure to sit on the warm sand underneath Aunt Prue's beach umbrella and play with the baby. "It's so cool," Alicia said, "in comparison with Washington. It's like another country."

While Jules helped the baby with his first steps, and listened to his squeals of delight and fear when the cold water gushed up over his toes, Alicia, gaining strength with every day of freedom, ran up and down the beach with Francis, laughing like a schoolgirl and collecting driftwood for the fires they had to build every night in the fireplace. She adored the great shore dinners at the club, and loved the fresh clams Francis would steam for her in layers of seaweed, yet she lost weight, as the extra pounds she had put on during her pregnancy melted away from all the running, swimming, and riding on the beach with Francis. Her honey-blond hair streamed out through a hole cut in the top of her wide-brimmed straw hat, and became bleached out in the sun to the beautiful streaked color of wheat. She was turning into a Kincaid, and the change gave her a beauty, a serenity, and a self-confidence she had never known. She was turning into a Kincaid, just as her husband had been changing under her very eyes into the same sort of cynical opportunist that her father was. She was glad to see Jules separated, if only for such a short time, from the endless round of dinners and luncheons and translations of other men's work, and the time-consuming concentration on the details of other men's experiments. He played with the baby and taught him little nursery rhymes in French. He laid out plans for an addition to the house. He listened tolerantly to the babble of the girls at the beach club as they surrounded Francis, giggling and begging him to tell once again his exciting anecdotes of San Juan Hill and Havana. As a welcome change from playing second- and third-leads in the Samuel Langley stock company, Jules enjoyed playing the role of the tolerant older brother, the family father, and doting doyen of the Kincaid clan.

Henry had moved out into the barn after Jules had helped him to clean up the haymow. Together, they sealed the cracks between the worn siding boards that let in the sea air. It was unlike the impeccable Henry to live in a haymow, but he managed to emerge always immaculate, seemingly untouched by this earthy lifestyle. Lying every night cheek-by-jowl with the unfinished components of the last Kincaid glider, he began to speak again of the engineering problems that had prompted its design.

"Those variable wing-tips, Jules. We used to call them ailerons. If, instead of setting them before each flight according to the wind, we could run control wires out from a central stick and adjust them in flight, we would have great control, just as you do with the Penaud Tail. And you wouldn't have to dihedral the wings. What you lose in lift on the wing during a turn would be gained by the wing-tip acting as a wing."

"It's a totally different approach, Henry, than the one we're using in Washington right now, although I think the Wright brothers are trying it. We're proceeding directly from powered flight because we've had successful experience with it—if only in small models.

What you're thinking of is glider flights, and I would
regard gliding as a step backwards at this point."

"My God, Jules! You're getting Langleyized!"

In his own reserved way, Henry was becoming
very fond of little Sam. Perhaps he saw something of
himself in Sam's brown eyes and husky figure. Henry
was a poor baby-sitter, letting Sam squall and complain in the sand while he studied his physics textbook. Alicia would come dashing out of the surf frequently to upbraid him for his callousness. They
would take silent strolls on the beach, with little Sam
holding on to Henry's finger as if for dear life, and
looking up wide-eyed at his uncle, who looked down
at the boy with a shared, silent sobriety. Their bond
was not demonstrative, but it was there: a bond of
blood.

Henry's first year at Harvard had cast him in an
ambiguous role until he found a compromise suitable
to his complicated and multi-faceted personality. He
wanted to do well in his studies, and as the grandson
and replica of old Henry Kincaid, the son of the brilliant Carl Kincaid, and the brother of the "eccentric"
Jules, he was expected to do well. On the other hand,
all of his friends seemed to wish for no more than an
average grade. They looked down on anyone who had
the reputation of a grind, and made sneering allusions
to the possibility of a touch of the Hebrew in the family tree of such unfashionably hard-working students.
Henry went along with their prejudices, and hid his
intellectual superiority behind a facade of easy-going,
empty-headed undergraduate tomfoolery—just as he
passed off his secret hours of hard study as confiden-

tial forays into the fabled fastnesses of Irish washer-women's bloomers.

When he won school prizes or was praised by his professors, Henry shrugged it off as an accident. He led his friends to believe that he could gain superior marks with no effort at all, and changed the conversation to discussion of the Harvard football team, or of the relative merits of various yachts owned by his classmates' fathers. Henry was respected and liked, but few of his classmates understood him.

Their cool and sunny Plymouth family vacation soon came to a peaceful ending. The three Kincaid brothers—all so different, yet joined by a common strength and intelligence that would unite them for-ever in the history of flight—had been joined by a woman of intelligence, maturity, charm and beauty; and by a running, shouting baby boy who would one day become the hope of the future for those Kincaids who managed to survive.

Alicia—more than any of them—had changed. In the two short years of her marriage, she had matured and developed an individual sort of beauty that would turn men's heads for the rest of her life. She was learn-ing a cool objectivity that would one day help her to shape her destiny, as well as that of others. As much as she despised her father's consummate political skills, she had learned them, too, by osmosis. As she grew older, she would find men coming to her for advice—important advice. And she would know how to guide them, for she had been a Langley long before she had become a Kincaid.

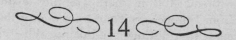 14

THAT fall, Professor Langley came home from Europe with a brand-new honorary doctorate from the University of Grenoble, as well as high-society tales of meeting a cousin of a niece of the Italian royal family while taking the waters at a North Italian spa.

"But what about a new lightweight engine?" Jules insisted. "Did you find a new manufacturer for us? They're not doing well in New York. They keep promising, but they keep failing."

"That's your department; you and Francis take care of it. All they want to do in Europe is make automobiles."

"What about that aluminum engine block? It would certainly save a lot of weight."

"Much too brittle. Anyway, we have more impor-

tant things to think about. I heard a rumor that there's
going to be a great victory dinner for Admiral Dewey
at the White House. It's going to be *the* social event of
the season. I'm going to entrust the responsibility to
you, my boy, to see that we get as many tickets as
possible."

"*Merde!*"

"The Navy has given us a great deal of money out
of their limited budget," Langley said, ignoring Jules'
expletive, "and they want to see something for their
money. We no longer have our friend Roosevelt over
there. See if Chanute would like to come. That would
impress them. And if there are any distinguished
guests from Europe—someone from one of the Acade-
mies—but with a distinguished name. What about the
houseboat? Will it be ready for occupancy—that is—for
advanced testing before Christmas?"

Jules found himself caught up again in all the
multifarious, and yet meaningless, details of Langley's
gilded world. In between bouts of designing a superstructure for the new houseboat and worrying about
engine development, he would find himself skulking
about the corridors of the White House, trying to find
out who was in charge of issuing invitations for the
great dinner for the Hero of Manila. When he did try
to discuss their experiments and new designs, he
found Manly preoccupied with writing up old experiments and making the new airframe for the fullsize
flyer. Francis would apparently be hard at work at
the drawing-board designing components to be built
in New York, but upon closer examination, Jules
found that Francis was actually applying the few advances made in lightweight engines in New York to

use on motorcycle engines. More than once, he found that he had to cover up for his brother so that Langley would not scream about the waste of Smithsonian funds.

Now that Francis had outlived his temporary popularity as the favorite dinner guest of Washington society, Langley no longer found him so charming. He would criticize Jules' brother in scathing terms for coming late to work and leaving early, and for tinkering with his noisy motorcycle in the Smithsonian shops. The blame for the lack of progress in achieving a lightweight motor with high horsepower was laid increasingly on Francis, and Jules had to suffer the criticisms in silence. They were all too just. Yet, complaints about the delays in the accounting department were not tolerated. Jules couldn't understand why Langley seemed to treat Karr as sacrosanct. He would brook no discussion of the old accountant's deficiencies.

With finite guile, Jules managed to obtain ten tickets for the great Admiral Dewey dinner, much as they were in demand by McKinley's party hacks and all the Washington hostesses. Langley was overjoyed. "I shall wear my medals," he beamed. "Jules, you are becoming a master at the old Pennsylvania shell game. You'll be the next head of the Smithsonian." Jules could not imagine a lifetime of celebrating smithsonite boulders and writing grandiloquent reports, but he was glad to have made his father-in-law happy. Alicia, too, was looking forward to the party.

"What can I wear? What would go with my new hairdo?" Alicia had taken to wearing her sun-bleached hair in a long curl down her back. Her Saturday forays into the fancy stores in search of gala dresses were perfectly agreeable to Jules, as long as Francis was available to baby-sit.

Octave Chanute sent a cordial reply to Jules' letter, saying that he and Ariel would be very pleased to attend the dinner for Admiral Dewey, but that his wife had already made plans to spend the season in Baden-Baden. He proposed to combine the trip with a visit to New York, where he had to make a speech, and he said that he hoped to visit the Wright brothers' camp in Kitty Hawk if they were planning to be there. It was the first Jules had heard of the Wright brothers in some time, for Wilbur was a poor correspondent, and Orville had never been friendly. Jules was interested to find out what they had accomplished lately, although he wasn't very sanguine about their prospects.

Jules set aside several of the tickets to the Dewey dinner for the use of the representatives and senators who were on the Board of Directors of the Smithsonian, but that still left a few. One day, in the great flood of mail that inundated the secretary's office, he found a request for a guided tour of the Smithsonian from the French Center for Arts and Crafts—the *École Centrale des Arts et Mètiéres*. When he showed it to Langley, the old man agreed that the addition of a prominent French engineer or two to the White House party would be pleasant for Chanute and would look good, so Jules wrote back saying that while hotel reservations for the whole group were impossible to obtain in December, he was putting aside two tickets for the dinner at the White House for them. As the fateful day approached, however, with both Langley and Alicia fluttering about the details of their toilettes, Jules received several cancellations from the congressmen.

They deemed it more important to be home mending their political fences in this last Christmas before a national election, than to have their names appear with hundreds of others on a White House guest list. Langley was astounded. "Their wives will never forgive them!" he exclaimed. "What are we going to do with the tickets?"

"Well," Jules smiled, "there's Francis, and my brother Henry. He's never been to the White House." Langley grunted. "And there's the Roosevelt girl. She's a friend of Francis'. Her father has tucked her away in New York City to keep her out of trouble, but she would be thrilled to get an invitation."

"I don't know what Theodore would say," Langley commented.

"Let Francis find out," Jules said.

Admiral Dewey was the hero of the hour, but it had been Assistant Secretary of the Navy Theodore Roosevelt who had issued the orders to him which had resulted in the destruction of the Spanish fleet in Manila. Now, Roosevelt had been elected Governor of New York, and he was already being talked about as a possible candidate for senator, or even secretary of state, in the coming McKinley administration. Langley nodded his assent.

Francis was very pleased to get his invitation to the big party. He resuscitated his army dress uniform with the golden corporal stripes and the gold fourragère that marked him as a general's aide, and polished up the one medal which had been awarded to all of the Rough Rider veterans. Henry's invitation was the envy of Harvard Square. He was more than pleased to accept it, and promised faithfully to pick up the French party in New York and escort them down to Washington, as well as the Roosevelt girl, who had received her father's permission to attend the party, providing that she was properly chaperoned.

While he was looking forward to seeing Chanute and Ariel again, all the fussing and feathering bothered Jules a great deal. For all its asininity, it was the occasion for a not inconsiderable spat with his wife.

"You're going to get a new dress suit, aren't you, Jules?" she asked.

"Why? The old one is perfectly all right."

"You've had it for years, and it never did fit very well. You'll look like a waiter from the Cosmos Club— and a shabby waiter at that."

"I am *not* going to waste money on a fancy suit that I'll only wear once or twice a year. I'm a scientist, not a cigar-store Indian."

He never heard the end of it.

The day of the big party found Jules bustling about from one end of the city to the other in a rented carriage, all day and all night. While Langley pontificated in his office, it fell upon Jules and Francis to meet Henry and their guests in the spanking-new and grandiose halls of Union Station. Francis spirited Alice Roosevelt off to the house on "N" Street where she would be staying overnight; Jules, Henry, and their two French guests took the carriage to the Willard.

The stocky and voluble Monsieur Blériot from the *École Centrale* was quite young, and apparently a successful engineer. His provincial French was hardly comprehensible to Jules, and a total loss to Henry. The shy and handsome dark-haired young lady with him turned out to be not his wife, but his niece Marie, which created no end of trouble since they would have to have two hotel rooms instead of one. Only after Jules threatened to raise the roof did the manager of the Willard agree to put Miss Blériot in Henry's room and give Henry one of the tiny maid's rooms on the top floor.

Jules left them to their own devices for a few hours as he made a quick foray into a notions store to pick up some white ribbons for his wife. He delivered them to Georgetown, where his cold lunch was counterpointed by a barrage of hot remarks from Alicia as she bustled about worrying through last-minute changes in her attire. Then it was back to the Willard, and a guided tour of the Smithsonian for the Blériots, culminating in a visit to Langley's office. Then, after dropping off the Blériots at their hotel, he had to pay a visit to Chanute and Ariel at *their* hotel. Ariel was a delight, as always, and she invited him to stay for tea. It was a pleasant interval in a hectic day. Chanute amused him with anecdotes of Chicago's Gold Coast, and Ariel's chatter was like the tinkle of a silver bell. She was seventeen now, and more beautiful than ever.

By seven o'clock, Jules was famished. His wife could not spare the time to set out a sandwich for him, so he had to sit in his cold Georgetown kitchen with yesterday's bread and butter and a glass of wine, while the coachman stomped and cursed outside and his wife fussed and primped upstairs with the help of the maid who had come over to baby-sit for Sam.

"Jules, aren't you ever going to come up and change? We don't have much time."

"What's the hurry? They're not serving until nine."

"Come on, Jules. I want to get there early so I can look at the gowns." Jules grumpily went upstairs to change into his dress suit. He found it uncomfortably tight around the middle, and had to have Alicia let out the two little belts in the back of his vest. "It's a good thing you don't have to button it," she said. "You're getting fat."

The White House was ablaze with electric light as their carriage finally got them to the head of the line at the north portico. Jules discovered that he had forgotten his invitation. He had to go inside to find an usher he knew who could get them in, and in the meanwhile, Alicia stood out in the cold in her ball gown, and their carriage blocked the way until the marines made them move it.

The reception was in the East Room. Jules soon found the Blériots and Henry and introduced them to the Chanutes. Francis, at this moment when a French translator was sorely needed, was—needless to say—nowhere to be seen. Alicia, tall and majestic, had never looked so handsome. She eyed Ariel and Marie with suspicion. "You never told me Ariel was so beautiful," she whispered to Jules.

"Oh, she's just a kid," Jules said with a shrug.

Old acquaintances kept coming over to greet Alicia, for she had not been out in public since long before Sam's birth. "You look wonderful, Alicia," they would say. "We were worried about you. Those premature births are so dangerous." Alicia would grit her teeth and smile, and introduce the rest of the party.

Professor Langley's entrance was a royal procession. His chest gleamed with medals, and his gray-white hair gleamed with pomade. Aside from the young embassy attachés in their beautifully bemedalled uniforms, he was easily the handsomest man in the house, for McKinley and Dewey and most of their cohorts were well-padded examples of Victorian *embonpoint.*

"Well, are we all here?" He greeted the party jovially. This was Langley at his best, and Alicia's blue eyes sparkled with pride.

Francis and the Roosevelt girl skittered in at the last moment, and Francis proceeded to charm the two French girls with voluble if ungrammatical French, while Alice Roosevelt made snide remarks about the other guests. It was Langley who shepherded them with pride through the reception line, and it was Langley who presided over their table in the dining-room with charm and dignity. Jules was not enjoying himself at all. After their long and heavy dinner, after the speeches and the presentation of medals by the President to the Admiral and his staff, there was dancing. Jules, self-conscious about his poor figure on the dance floor, sat back and watched Henry dance with the two French girls and with Alicia. Francis and the Roosevelt girl disappeared for a while, and returned giggling and whispering about sneaking up a back staircase to the private living quarters of the White House. Apparently they'd had a grand tour, until they had been indignantly ejected by a secret service man.

By the time they got home, Jules was exhausted. Although Alicia wanted to indulge in a delighted post-mortem of the party, Jules fell asleep in his chair. She let him spend the night there.

15

THE luxurious gourmandizing at the White House, the visit of the Chanutes and the Blériots, and his unimportant but irritating spats with his wife made Jules very discontented during the rest of December. He would go down to the offices or the shops and find no progress being made. The entire staff seemed to be thinking of Christmas and the New Year's celebrations, or writing up old experiments, or making photographs or plans of equipment which had already proved to be of no value. Jules took to walking alone in Rock Creek Park, his high-topped shoes crunching in the snow, staring at the trees so gaunt and black against the leaden sky.

The week after Christmas he made an appointment through Langley's formidable secretary to see

The Master. Langley had hardly been in the office at all during December, and even though Jules had gone to the unusual step of making an appointment, Langley kept him waiting.

"Ah, yes, Mr. Kincaid. Come in." Langley kept up his facade even in front of his secretary.

"What's this all about? Here, put those page proofs aside and sit down. What's the trouble? Everything's been going very well. Do you want a raise? Is that it?" The old man turned his back on Jules and went to gaze out the windows behind his desk, rocking back and forth on his heels, his arms clasped behind him. He was still an undeniably handsome man in his well-tailored cutaway, but the windows cast a cruel light on the deep lines around his eyes. Jules suddenly realized again how hard that face was in repose, a face so often masked with good-fellowship.

"No, it's not money." Jules was discontented by this unexpected mention of a subject he hadn't even thought of. "It's just that we're not making any progress. A few piddling little flights measured in seconds with our toy aeroplanes, and a huge investment in building the full-size model, the houseboat, the launching apparatus and the gasoline engine."

"That's your brother's affair, and I must say he's not pulling his weight."

"It's the manufacturer, and we're well protected from default by our contracts. But even if we do finish up the full-size aeroplane, and do succeed in designing and having manufactured a light enough motor, it will be 1901 or 1902 before we're ready to test. Even then, we will have to do all sorts of dangerous and extremely expensive testing without a pilot—probably breaking up the machine with almost every attempt. We wouldn't dare risk the life of a pilot, and an unmanned, 350-pound machine pulled with the full power of fifty horses will smash to pieces with the slightest gust of wind. We're spending too much money with too little promise of any results whatsoever."

"Now you listen to me, young man." Langley spun around and jabbed his finger repeatedly at Jules. "We flew those smaller machines, we're going to recreate the same conditions on a larger scale, and we're going to fly a piloted flight!" Langley quickly suppressed his temper and smiled a fox's smile. "For all your success on Embassy Row, you still don't really understand how things are done here. Those salaries will keep rolling in. The War Department wouldn't dare abandon us after the expenditure of so much money."

"At least let's get rid of that houseboat, the turntable, the tug we have to hire and the whole complicated apparatus. All we need is a spring-loaded launching apparatus and a line of rail. You could set it up any place where there's flat land. North Carolina for instance. Why start from sixty or a hundred feet up in the air when we can start from the ground? If it crashes, less harm will be done."

Langley's face flushed red, and he banged his fist on his desk. "Now you listen here, young man. I'm running these experiments. This will be the Langley Flyer, not a Kincaid toy. I designed and built and flew the first heavier-than-air machines ever flown. And we're going to do it again exactly the same way." He was pounding the desk now. "We are going to do it exactly the same way on a larger scale. Make no mistake about that. You go back to your drawing board and your piddling tin manufactory, and leave the planning and administration to someone who knows how to do it!"

Now Jules was beginning to get angry. "We simply cannot gamble everything on one flight that may reduce the whole machine to smithereens, not to speak of risking the life of a man. We have to have more flight experience." Jules stood up and leaned forward, putting both hands on the desk and staring Langley in the face. "What we have to do is build a quarter-size model of the Flyer, like I suggested before. Without the simulated weight of a pilot, we can easily put in a gas engine of two- or three-horsepower. Even if we smash it up, repairs will cost nothing in comparison with a smash-up of the full-size machine. We can build it exactly to scale, and the aeronautical properties should be identical. You *must* agree. If we don't have the money, then we can suspend work on the houseboat."

"Sit down, Jules." The old man was silent for a moment, staring out the window. "That's not such a bad idea. The money is no problem. Do you think we could get something in the air before the campaign?"

Jules didn't know what he meant. "We can have it flying by August if we drop numbers five and six and really go to work on it."

"That's not such a bad idea, Jules. You *do* come up with some good ideas, even if for all the wrong reasons. If we can show photographs of some impressive tests, it would be a feather in McKinley's cap. It would make things much easier with Congress." Langley turned back toward Jules with sudden decision. "Do it," he said. "Forget about those steamers. Get started on the engine right now. Let out a contract.

But don't take any men off the houseboat. That's my affair."

Jules got up to leave before Langley had time to make any more restrictions, but he paused at the door and turned to look back. "You know what little Sam said yesterday? He was playing with some spools, and all of a sudden, he said 'Grandpa'."

"My, my," Langley said as he walked toward the door and opened it up for Jules. "My, my." He shook Jules' hand. "You just keep giving me reports on your progress—and Sam's progress too."

Jules often got his best work done at home in his tiny living-room after dinner. Sam would be upstairs sleeping, and Alicia would be in the kitchen washing the dishes. In the peace and quiet of his own home, Jules could concentrate. Yet, from time to time, he would gossip with Alicia as he worked.

"You know, darling, I don't really understand where your father gets all the money for his trips to Europe every year," Jules said one evening.

"Neither do I, dear." Alicia looked through the doorway, dish-towel and plate in her hand. "As far as I know, he only has his salary, and that's never been all that large, I should think," she said seriously.

"Perhaps he gets a percentage of the fees for instituting that system for correct railroad time with the Pennsylvania Railroad."

"No, he always boasted that every penny of that money went directly to the Allegheny Conservatory when he was president there."

"It's certainly very mysterious. There must be a Langley fortune there someplace."

"Well, if there is, I don't think we're going to get any of it."

Jules pinned up a new piece of paper on the improvised drafting-board he had set up in their tiny living room. "Alicia, would you mind very much if I didn't go to the New Year's Eve dance? You'll be with your father and Francis and probably the Lodge girl anyway, and I do have a lot to do."

"Darling, it's the end of the century. What's the matter? Are you mad at me?" She came in from the kitchen, drying her hands on her apron, and leaned over to kiss his cheek as she ruffled up his hair. "The Twentieth Century. Don't you want to see it in with me?"

"Somebody has to baby-sit. We can save a little money. Besides, you should be there with someone like Francis, not with an old stick-in-the-mud like your husband."

"Oh, don't say that. Think it over." She kissed him again and nuzzled her cheek against the blond stubble of his beard.

The house was very quiet after Alicia left on New Year's Eve to go to the Cosmos Club gala. Only the occasional chink of the fire in the kitchen stove disturbed the snowy silence. Jules found himself working quickly and efficiently, and it was very gratifying. The design of a tiny two- or three-horsepower engine presented intriguing difficulties. To keep the weight down, there were no provisions for cooling the engine. It only had to run for two or three minutes to provide sufficient motive power for a flight adequate for testing the stability of the flying machine. Yet, such an engine had never been built before, and each tiny component had to be designed and machined and assembled and tested.

Jules was so engrossed in his work that he didn't hear the ticking of his pocket watch on the mantelpiece beside him, and he didn't feel the cold that gradually crept in from the doors and windows as the fire in the kitchen stove died down. Only when his feet began to go numb did he realize how late it was. Standing up stiffly, he stamped his feet and went into the kitchen to add more kindling to the fire. He fancied he could hear muffled explosions in the distance. He checked his watch and then stomped upstairs where Sam was sleeping peacefully. Jules looked out of the window and then picked Sam up, blankets and all. Draping a comforter over the boy's head, he took him to the window. President McKinley was having a fireworks show on the snowy White House lawn, and the explosions and the displays were visible even in Georgetown. They lit up Sam's sleepy face with their intermittent flares.

"Mama," Sam said sleepily, and pulled on Jules' long blond hair.

"It's the new century, Sam. See the lights? Our century. Your century."

Francis and Jules worked together on the final designs for the new miniature engine. On a bench test, they thought it would probably overheat within three minutes at least, causing gasoline to explode prematurely, thereby losing power, but they hoped that during the brief flight the air would cool the motor sufficiently to sustain it at tip power for a while. From his experimenting with motorcycle engines,

Francis was able to contribute a great deal to the design. He showed Jules how the cylinders could be machined down so that they would have radiating ribs. "That way they have more surface area," Francis said enthusiastically. "The cool air blows over a larger area. The walls are very thin, but the radiating ribs give them strength."

While the manufacturer in New York was ready to take on new contracts to produce the new engine, Jules and Francis could only continue to entertain doubts of the man's ability to deliver on his promises. It had been a constant and frustrating series of setbacks, as they had to design and then reject, and then design new parts, constantly keeping in mind the totally new problem of keeping the weight down. It was a different concept from that which all manufacturers were accustomed to. In automotive engine designing, weight, size, and even shape were of much less importance. It could be argued that the heavier the engine the smoother the automobile would ride. Even the tiniest components of their engine had to be adapted or totally redone—the shielding on the ignition wires, the carburetor, the piston rods. Everything had to be done in miniature.

Francis went to work to try to devise a better sparking method for both engines. Jules took as many of the shop assistants as he could pry away from Manly and began to construct the frame of the quarter-size model of the Langley Flyer. The problems of fore-and-aft stability on the new model Flyer were different from those of the previous experiments. The design had to place the center of gravity above the center of air pressure in order to maintain level flight, and the problems of balancing the aeroplane were different. The Penaud Tail had to be designed to be self-adjusting, so that air pressure on the top of the tail would push it down if the machine descended, and air pressure on the bottom of the tail would push it up if the machine was climbing at too great a rate. Due to the dihedral slant of the wings, lateral stability was not expected to be a problem.

Even before the designs were completed, Jules could see that the propellers would have to be much larger than planned. Although they had wanted to make the quarter-size model an exact duplicate of the large one, they found that the frame would have to be expanded. It was spring by the time new wings were constructed and the frame completed, but the engine was still far from ready. After going to New York and inspecting the progress that had been made, Jules cancelled the contract for the smaller engine and took all the available parts back with him to Washington. Working feverishly with Francis, they redesigned it yet again. By the first of June they were ready to give it a bench test in the shops. The usual power-test apparatus proved to be impractical, and they had to construct an absorption dynamometer for the tests. On one of his rare inspections, Langley, who didn't really seem to understand what they were doing, insisted that a method must be devised to measure the thrust of the propellers while the machine was in free flight. "Our records have to be exhaustive and complete," he said. "A mere description will not suffice. You have to show them figures." This, too, involved a delay, while Jules devised a method to attach a pencil which would record on a drum brazed to the drive shaft. When they were finally able to make adequate tests of the new engine, they found it worked at its best while it was developing one-and-a-half to two-horsepower. However, it was impossible to maintain this power steadily for more than thirty seconds.

After many more setbacks, it was finally possible to crate up the quarter-size machine and ship it to Quantico for air trials. Langley had already closed up his house, and was living on the houseboat. He was very pleased that he would be able to supervise the tests personally before he left for Europe on his annual jaunt.

They had to wait several days before they got exactly the right conditions for the launch. "Unless there's a gale blowing tomorrow night, we're going to launch it. I've invited photographers, and official witnesses from the War Department, and Dr. Graham Bell. We must fly it."

"What if it crashes?" Jules asked. "There will be thousands and thousands of dollars and man-hours lost. Don't you want to wait until we have tested it adequately before exposing us to ridicule? Lilienthal made hundreds of flights before he let a photographer snap him."

"What's the matter, Jules? Losing your nerve?"

During Langley's summertime sojourns on his comfortably equipped "research vessel", far away from the inquisitive and impressionable eyes of vagrant congressmen and sore-footed tourists, Langley always took on the appearance of a Mississippi riverboat gambler. It was picturesque, but it was not one of his more attractive poses.

"We're going to fly it tomorrow. I've already got the cameramen equipped with telescope lenses on shore, and I'm going to rent a tugboat for the day for the Washington Star cameraman, and station it directly down-wind. Then, when everything is ready, we will signal the boat so that they'll be ready to photograph the machine."

The next day dragged on interminably. Jules checked and rechecked the flying machine. Francis seemed to get underfoot all the time. Langley kept bustling to and from the shore, meeting people and stationing them where he wanted them, and showering them with verbiage.

Early in the evening, the Potomac was as smooth as glass. A light wind was blowing at something less than two miles an hour, according to the dynamometer. Jules lined up the turntable to launch directly into the wind, and signaled the tugboat down-wind to make ready. The model, which was the largest they had built, being almost twelve feet long and having a wingspan of twelve feet, was poised and ready. Jules gave the signal. Francis quickly adjusted the motor and turned the tandem-mounted propellers. The engine erupted with a series of ear-splitting bangs, and at Francis' sign that all was well, Jules released the catapult springs and the machine sprang off the turntable. It dropped for a few feet, and Jules' heart dropped with it, but then it leveled off and flew on an absolutely even keel into the wind. After it had gone only about a hundred feet, however, it began to descend slowly and evenly, finally touching the water about a hundred-and-fifty feet from the houseboat. It had been in the air for only four and six-tenths seconds, according to Jules' stopwatch. Langley stood up from his wicker chair on the lower veranda deck, champagne glass in hand, and said, "Fly it again. Send out the launch. We'll still have time for another flight before it gets dark."

A crew of assistants was already waiting in the large launch, and they rowed quickly to the model, pulled it on board, and returned it to the houseboat. It was only necessary to dry off the parts and pour in a little more gasoline before it was ready to launch again. This time the aeroplane flew straight ahead for three hundred feet before it began to descend, finally touching down about three-hundred-and-fifty feet from the houseboat, having been in the air ten seconds. "Well," Jules said to his brother, "let's hope for better results tomorrow." Langley was laboriously climbing the stairs to join them. "Excellent, boys, excellent. Now we can show them something for their money."

"What do you mean by excellent?" Jules exclaimed. "A total of less than fifteen seconds in the air. Two little flights. It must have been pulling about one-and-a-half horsepower."

"One-and-a-half horsepower? Then tear it down and rebuild it."

"Tear it down? We should do another twenty or thirty tests."

"What? And crash it? You've got to learn to leave well enough alone. We'll have the photographs, and they will carry a lot more weight than the descriptions of the eyewitnesses. Tear it down. Take it back to Washington tonight." Langley walked away.

At the top of the steps he paused with an afterthought, and turned back toward them, his hand resting on the banister. "Would you care to join the victory party on the afterdeck? We're having champagne and fresh shad roe. Mr. Karr and Dr. Bell will be with us." Francis looked over at Jules, and then replied for him. "No, thanks," he said.

While the bewhiskered elders were holding their candle-lit seminar on the afterdeck, Jules and Francis dejectedly supervised the dismantling of the machine. Together, they caught a late train back to Washington. "A ten-second flight, Francis. Why? It should have stayed airborne for another twenty or thirty seconds at least."

"Loss of power? It must have overheated. Those cylinders are too small. Let's make some new ones."

"That father-in-law of mine! All he wants is the fame and the money. He leaves it to the wage-slaves like us to figure out why it flies and why it doesn't fly. God forbid he should get his hands dirty. But I could put up with all that if he'd just quit interfering. I've had two years of his interfering. Two years of afternoon teas and polysyllabic circumlocution. I tell you, Francis . . ."

Except for occasional diatribes to his wife in the privacy of their bedroom, to which she only half listened, Jules had never unburdened himself of his frustrations in dealing with Langley and his satraps. For forty miles, all the way into the city, he harangued Francis about it. It didn't occur to him that Francis was still only sixteen, and very impressionable.

The photographs of the test flight were very impressive. Taken from a low angle, they seemed to show the machine flying well above the horizon, above the clouds, its propellers whirring along so fast that they photographed as a blur. Langley was overjoyed. After the aircraft had been returned to Washington and uncrated, he insisted that it be set up and photographed with huge markers showing the scale upon which it was built. He stopped all the Smithsonian publications in order to rush the printing of a report on the flights, complete with photographs. He brought it out as a special volume of the "Smithsonian Contributions to Knowledge" series.

The first newspaper reports had been factual and dry, noting the brevity of the flights and making allusions to the great expenses involved. As the story was picked up, however, by the Chicago and New York papers, it became exaggerated to suit the canons of yellow journalism. Within a month, Chanute had written them from Chicago congratulating them upon their great feat, and saying that the Wright brothers had been so encouraged by it that they were resuming their experiments.

Once the orgy of photography had finished, and Langley's guided tours had ceased to distract them, Jules and Francis were able to tear down the machine and begin to build new cylinders for it, machining them from steel tubing originally one-half-inch thick. Combustion chambers were then screwed on and brazed to the cylinders. The engine was tested, but failed. They took it apart, reconstructed it, and tested it again and again. Premature ignition caused by overheating was a recurring problem. When they did finally get it running smoothly and mounted, they found that the propeller and transmission shafts and their bearings could not stand the strain of the increased power. Newer and stronger shafts and bearings were constructed, and then it was found that the transverse frame which supported them was too weak also, and had to be strengthened by substituting newer and thicker tubing.

All of the work, delayed by summer vacations, trips to New York to observe unsatisfactory tests on the large engine, and finally by the excitement of the presidential campaign, extended through the summer and well into the fall. Jules would come home every evening exhausted, eat a light dinner, and then play with the baby for a short time before falling into bed, only to arise early the next day to start the routine again. Alicia nagged at him to spend more time with his family, but as long as he could avoid Langley's time-consuming demands, he worked on as one possessed.

Langley took the first boat back from Europe when his friend Governor Roosevelt was nominated to run for the Vice-Presidency on the Republican ticket. He was prepared to do business with whichever party might win, but he wanted to extend whatever discreet help he could to Roosevelt because the Vice-President was, by act of Congress, the titular head of the Smithsonian, even if its secretary was the de-facto executive, and Langley knew he could work well with Roosevelt. He had already discussed with him the possibility that the Smithsonian might pay for some "bully" hunting and exploring expeditions to Africa or South America under Roosevelt's intrepid leadership. Roosevelt was a great hunter, who gloried in the power of beautifully tooled guns. All of the discretionary funds that Langley could release without arousing the ire of the Democrats were poured into various Republication purses to finance critical congressional campaigns, and Manly and Huffaker were sent out on discreet missions, the nature of which eluded Jules.

The Democrats were dead set against the United States becoming a world power if it meant annexing land outside of the continental United States, and McKinley himself had consented to the annexation of Cuba, Guam, Puerto Rico, the Philippines, and Hawaii only under the press of events. With Roosevelt, however, he was teamed with a candidate who was a national hero, a man who could enlist the aid of all the jingoistic press, and wave the newly-bloodied flag of imperialism in a way sure to get them both elected.

Their silver-tongued opponent, William Jennings Bryan, was vicious—perhaps even treasonable in his attacks on McKinley and Roosevelt. When the tiny American army had taken over the Philippine Islands, the Spanish had surrendered meekly and sailed home gladly. The Philippine people, however, soon decided that they did not want to be dominated by yet another distant set of masters. They rebelled, and American troops soon learned how to wipe out whole villages and populations. They soon learned the vicious joys of torturing prisoners; the same tortures for which they had so roundly condemned the Spanish. The Democrats actually called upon American troops in the Philippines to refuse to continue fighting and to insist upon immediate discharge from the army.

When the bitter election campaign was over and the votes finally counted, McKinley and Roosevelt had won in a great sweep. The American people, in their wisdom, had made their choice. The American people had voted for imperialism.

The inaugural parade of the victors was buoyed by the winds of March. It was escorted by over five hundred former Rough Riders, including Francis on a rented horse, and wafted along on lively March winds reeking of horse manure.

As the newly elected Vice-President, Theodore Roosevelt presided over only one session of the Senate in 1901. By virtue of his office, he also presided over one meeting of the Board of Directors of the Smithsonian Institute before the summer doldrums set in. It was to be a largely formal affair, to be followed by high tea in the magnificent vaulted upstairs exhibition gallery of the main building. Jules was very conscious of the great honor of being the youngest member of the Board of Directors. His cutaway and striped trousers were brushed and pressed to perfection with all the care that Alicia could give them.

Except for Jules and a newly elected Republican representative from Vermont, Roosevelt was the youngest man there. He was all smiles, all teeth, and he called the meeting to order with a resounding crash of his cherry-wood gavel. The secretary, Langley, dispensed with the readings of the minutes of the previous meeting and began to give the directors a grandiloquent guided tour of the accountant's annual report and of the other expensively printed booklets that lay before them. He described the new zoological garden, the latest geological exhibits, and the newly-opened hall full of stuffed animals—"many of them contributed by our esteemed chairman, Vice-President Roosevelt." Roosevelt crinkled up his eyes and showed his teeth in a huge grin.

"And last but not least, my flights upon the Potomac of last summer with the largest heavier-than-air machine ever flown." Director Langley was a great and imposing man of science in the eyes of his Board of Directors. Unlike George Eastman, George Pullman, or Thomas Edison, he was handsome: well-tailored, well-barbered, and able to express himself in mellifluous phrases. Even Jules was impressed.

After the meeting, the ladies were milling about

in the great hall, majestic in their long silk gowns and wide-brimmed hats. Uniformed waiters from the Cosmos Club circulated with tea and champagne.

"How did it go, darling?" Alicia was beaming. "Did you speak to Colonel Roosevelt? What did he have to say?" Alicia was slim and tall and *soigné*, and she gestured with the little silk parasol that matched her dress.

"I didn't get a chance to open my mouth," Jules said as he smiled.

"Look who I found!" Francis walked over with a pretty young lady on his arm, a young lady elegantly dressed in a fashionable blue gown.

"I—uh . . ." Jules' mouth was open.

"Ho ho, you didn't recognize me, did you?" The girl broke into a buck-toothed smile and jabbed at Jules with her forefinger. "It's Alice Roosevelt!"

"Oh, Alice. It's nice to see you again," Alicia burbled. "Would you like some tea? Father tells me I'm supposed to be one of the hostesses here."

"How about some giggle-water?"

Alicia looked around, and then flashed a conspiratorial smile. "Come along, you two. We'll see what we can do."

Jules had gotten himself a cup of tea and a biscuit from the buffet table, and was gazing at the well-dressed crowd when Langley motioned him over to where he was standing with Vice-President Roosevelt and a group of awe-struck hangers-on.

"Mr. Vice-President, you remember my son-in-law, Jules Kincaid," Langley said as he presented him. Turning to Jules, he continued. "Mr. Roosevelt was asking about you."

"Ah, yes. I remember you now. A cracking good

scientist. Hasty Pudding. And you have that younger brother." Jules followed the Vice-President's gaze over toward the corner, where he could see Alicia, Francis, and Alice Roosevelt toasting each other with champagne.

"I don't approve of that young man," Roosevelt said.

"Ah—well." Jules smiled. "Your daughter is still very young, sir. Perhaps you should exert some parental authority."

"Mmm—that's not so easy." Roosevelt bounced up and down on his heels.

"Yes, I know. They're both without a mother to guide them. Francis is the one who ran away from home at the age of fourteen to join the Rough Riders."

"Theodore," Langley interrupted. "Have you seen the Cuban mountain lion we have on exhibition? It was brought down with a Marlin 30.-30, but we managed to patch it up pretty well."

"Really! We had one of those as our mascot in San Juan." Langley and Roosevelt guided their group into the newly furbished hall of stuffed animals. "We are putting up a great new museum in New York," Colonel Roosevelt said. "We'll have elephants and tigers—anything we can shoot. Jolly good sport on the Orinoco, so they say."

"The Smithsonian has already earmarked funds for your hunting trip to Africa, as soon as you can spare the time, Colonel," Langley purred smoothly. "It will be an honor to have you represent us on such an important expedition."

Jules let himself be elbowed to the outskirts of the meandering troop, and then looked around for Alicia. "Let's go," he said when he found her. "And let's get Francis out of here before he gets himself in trouble."

"Oh, they've already gone on to Senator Lodge's house. They're taking turkey-trot lessons. I wasn't invited," Alicia pouted. "Do we have to go? I was having such a good time."

"Let's get home before that baby-sitter discovers where we hid the wine bottle," Jules said.

The rest of that spring and summer seemed to be an endless series of tea parties in the upper hall of the Smithsonian, and receptions with Monsieur Cambon at the French Embassy. Too many of Jules' days were involved with writing up old experiments and translating them into French. Too many of his evenings were spent baby-sitting with Sam, for Alicia had rejoined Washington society, frequently acting as her father's hostess or accompanying him to important dinners. The Smithsonian horseless carriage would bring her home late—at eleven, or even twelve—and she would retail the evening's events to Jules as she took off her clothes and got ready for bed, being careful not to awaken Sam. Jules half-listened with a lassitude that was quite unlike him.

Francis had to some extent redeemed himself with Professor Langley by taking over the care and feeding of the Smithsonian limousine. He would assemble and disassemble the engine of the huge machine again and again, adjusting the spark and the carburetor and even machining new pistons to achieve greater speed. He often tested it on the smooth asphalt run of Connecticut Avenue late at night, and he was one of the first automobilists to be arrested by the district mounted police for speeding. He was re-

manded to the local hoosegow, and it fell upon Jules
to get him out.

Jules was looking forward to their summer reunion with Henry at Plymouth. It was becoming an almost annual affair. The Smithsonian was, as usual,
underwriting Professor Langley's trip to Europe. This
time, when they closed the offices and workshops for
the month of August, Jules, Alicia, and the two Sams
took a train together to Washington to see the professor off on the White Star liner he had chosen for his
annual jaunt. It was with great relief that they finally
arrived at Plymouth to find Henry already in residence. They were joined a few days later by Francis
on his chugging, spitting, odiferous five-cylinder
steed.

This year Jules was full of energy. His frustration
at their lack of progress in Washington had built up a
desire in him to do something positive, to create something with his hands. Immediately upon his arrival in
Plymouth, he ordered lumber from the town lumber-
yard, bought a post-hole digger and began to construct the new addition to the house. He paid for it
himself out of his accumulated savings. The house actually belonged to Henry and Francis, but Jules
wanted to feel that he was making a contribution.
When Alicia saw the plans, she said "Oh no, Jules. You
aren't going to have the outhouse *inside* the house, are
you?"

"Oh come on now, Alicia. It's perfectly sanitary.
Chamberpots and outdoor outhouses are going the
way of the eight-horse hitch. Don't be old-fashioned."

With the help of a local farm laborer, the three
Kincaid brothers put up the addition within two
weeks, working together almost every day. Alicia

would go shopping each morning in the one-horse shay they had rented, accompanied by Sam, shouting and bouncing beside her on the leather seat. She would return in the heat of the morning to cook huge midday dinners for her four workmen. At dusk they would often drive to the beach to take a quick swim, and then change into more formal clothes to have dinner at the club. The contrast between their days of hard work and their evenings of pleasant luxury was exhilarating.

Henry was still occupying Jules' old bachelor quarters in the haymow of the barn. After the addition to the house had been completed and painted, and the new-fangled flush toilet installed, Henry proposed that they should finish the glider which had been sitting there for years in the haymow.

Taking up where they had left off some two years before, they completed the construction and assembled the craft. The Penaud Tail was almost identical to the one they had been using in Washington. The adjustable wing-tips—Henry called them 'ailerons'—were to be repositioned for every flight, and were held in position with piano wire anchored by an adjustable turnbuckle. The three of them laid out their launching rail from the haymow door once again, but this time there were no haystacks around the barnyard in case of accident. They made seven flights with the glider on two brilliant, late-August days. The adjustable wing-tips seemed to work well in guiding the plane, although it was an intolerable bother to reposition them and lock them into place before each flight. On the eighth flight the glider crashed, was picked up by a gust of wind before they could get to it, and crashed again.

"Well, at least we don't have to go looking for driftwood to burn in the fireplace." Francis' smile was rather wan. But that night, as they sat around the hearth watching the last of their glider go up in smoke, Henry began to theorize.

"If we ran guy-wires to a central stick positioned at the aviator's seat in the center of gravity, he could control both ailerons with one hand, and the Penaud Tail with the other hand."

"He'd be like a juggler in the circus," Jules objected. "He'd have to have four hands. And what would he hold on to?"

"What do I do when I'm playing polo?" Francis asked. "I've got the mallet in one hand, four reins in the other hand, and I hold on with my legs."

"What is our aviator supposed to be?" Jules scratched his head. "A scientist, or an athlete?"

In later years, Henry would often remember that conversation, for Francis, as perfectly coordinated as a champion athlete, was to become one of the most skillful and daring pilots in the early annals of flight, while Jules would never become a truly great pilot, and he himself would never really learn to fly.

16

DURING the first week in September, Jules and Alicia returned to Washington by way of New York. Jules wired ahead for a carriage to meet Alicia. He wanted to spend some time in New York to finally settle the problem of the full-size gasoline engine intended for the Langley Flyer. The manufacturer, who had almost gone bankrupt in his attempts to build the engine—in spite of frequent advances from Washington to cover special expenses—was at his wits' end. They were no closer to a satisfactory bench test than they had been the year before, and deadline after deadline for delivery had passed. Hoping that Langley would not object too much, Jules cancelled the contract entirely and took all of the completed parts in exchange for their cash advances.

He had the parts shipped to Washington and was working with Francis to see what they could salvage from the costly mess, when Karr came bustling into his office, wringing his hands. "How could you possible cancel that contract without authorization? It ruins my whole financial plan. Couldn't you wait until Langley got back? He would never have authorized it."

"Mr. Karr, I've been specifically authorized to handle engine development, and that was my decision. It will actually save money for the Smithsonian."

"But Dr. Langley—"

"You can take it up with him when he returns. In the meantime, if you don't mind, we have work to do."

Langley came back from Europe, but the problems that Karr apparently had intended to introduce were forgotten in the excitement of the news that President McKinley had been shot. At first it seemed that the president would recover, but he lingered between life and death for days until, poisoned by septicemia, he died in agony. Theodore Roosevelt, the empire-builder, was the twenty-sixth President of the United States—and the youngest man ever to hold that office. Langley was quietly jubilant. He assembled Francis, Jules, Manly, and Alicia for a dinner in a private room at the Cosmos Club.

"Now we can really move ahead," he said when the table had been cleared and the last waiter was gone. "No more pettifoggery from General Shafter or Admiral Melville. They won't dare interfere with our budgets. We won't even have to go through Congress. The War Department will supply everything, including armed guards if necessary, and the Navy will have to supply ships. They'll have no choice. With Theodore in the White House and Graham Bell making publicity for us, we'll be miles ahead of anyone else."

"I'm going to be able to cannibalize that New York engine," Francis said. "All we need now is a new engine block."

"Now is the time to try an aluminum block, boring holes in it for the pistons."

"Don't bother me with details, boys. Just bring me the budgets, and I'll get the money for you." Langley leaned back in his chair, sipping on a rare vintage wine and gesturing with his cigar. "Your son will bear a famous name, Alicia," he said. "The name of the first flying machine."

"Let's have a toast to the Langley Flyer, and to its inventor," Manly raised his glass. "And to Sam Kincaid," Jules added.

The wine warmed them as they discussed their plans for the immediate future. Alicia's eyes glazed over with boredom and she began thinking of the new dresses she had ordered.

Sam had just turned three, and Jules found him a great pleasure to be with. While Alicia was more and more often in town acting as her father's hostess, or shopping, or visiting with her friends, Jules would sit with Sam, or take him out for walks on the rough brick sidewalks of Georgetown, or teach him little French nursery rhymes.

Sam's grandfather kept urging them to move back into Washington proper, but now it was Jules who valued his freedom; valued the chance to get away from the office and the workshops and away from the distraction of friends and relatives constantly dropping in. Jules' salary, plus his stipend as a director of the Smithsonian, left him in a position to put a little bit aside in savings again. Although Alicia seemed to spend more and more money on clothes, their living expenses were small, and Jules, on the days when he did not have to do any official entertaining for the Smithsonian, was more than satisfied to take his black lunch pail to work with him. He would pour out his hot tea and unwrap his waxed-paper covered sandwiches and eat while reading the foreign scientific papers that had regularly flooded his desk since he had been put in charge of keeping the Smithsonian apprised of foreign scientific events.

When Francis received an invitation to Alice Roosevelt's debut at the Executive Mansion, Alicia came to Jules asking him to obtain invitations. "But darling," he objected, "it's mostly for young folks, high society mucky-mucks and kids of college age. We would be just a pair of dowdy old married folks. It wouldn't be any fun."

"I don't care, it's *the* social event of the whole season, and I want to go." As much as she nagged him about it, it was the sort of thing that totally escaped Jules' mind once he had left the house. It was through her father that Alicia managed to obtain an invitation.

The great event was held during the depths of the winter. Jules had to obtain permission to rent a horse and carriage on the Smithsonian account. It was with great reluctance that he put on his old dress suit, and waited as Alicia gave last-minute instructions to the maid, who had come over from her father's house to take care of Sam for the night. For all the bother that Alicia had made about getting a new dress for the party, Jules might have been irritated with her, yet when she finally came down the stairs in her vel-

vet cloak, her honey-blond hair swept upward in a
fashionable pompadour, Jules was very proud of her.
Every year seemed to find her handsomer—not pretty
in a girlish way, but more beautiful and desirable.
The added lines around her eyes only served to set off
the sparkle of their blueness, and her regal air of self-
confidence was reinforced by a knowing smile as she
observed, from her cat-bird seat at her father's right
hand, the intricate ins-and-outs of Washington society.

"Oh, not that old hat again!" she scolded her husband. Jules took off his silk hat and looked at it.
"Here, let me see it." Alicia took the starched handkerchief from his breast pocket and tried to rub some of
the spots from his ancient silk hat and brush it to
make what little nap was left run all in one direction.

It was already ten o'clock when they drove up to
the Executive Mansion. Since the assassination there
had been a great deal of to-do about protecting the
president, and they had to wait while their invitation
was checked by the guards at the north gate. "Oh,
look how it's lit up," Alicia said enthusiastically. From
the windows of the dowdy old house, scores of flickering candles and dancing gas-lights cast a glow, and
two great electric lanterns lit the lines of white-gloved
Marine guards at the north portico. An occasional automobile would drive in past the line of carriages, and
the bangs and rattles of the engines made the horses
very nervous. "That contract," Jules muttered as he
handed Alicia out of the carriage, "I don't think we'll
ever get an engine out of those people. We'll—"

"Oh, don't talk shop tonight, Jules. This is going
to be the best night of the year." They paused as a
great Panhard racing phaeton drew up to the door,
and Francis stepped down from the high running-

board dressed in his fancy corporal's uniform with its gold fourragère. "Hello, hello," he said as he smiled and kissed Alicia on the cheek. "Where did you get that thing?" Jules asked. "Oh, I borrowed it from Cambon for the night. All the Foxcroft girls think I'm the highest-ranking corporal in the U. S. Army!"

They swept in the front door, and Edith Roosevelt started them through the receiving line. Potted palms and yards of festooned smilax and asparagus vine decorated the old mansion. Jules was looking forward to the champagne, but only a sickening red fruit punch was served. Alicia was tall and regal in her ball gown, and was soon surrounded by young embassy attachés and football players from Harvard. Jules knew some of the Harvard boys from Hasty Pudding, and they all seemed to know his brother Henry. He was able to get a complete report on Henry's very active social life.

When the Speaker of the House beckoned to him from behind a potted palm, Jules smiled and excused himself. He had a good idea what the old man had in store for him.

"Hello, Kincaid," Congressman Cannon said. "Come with me."

"Hello, Uncle Joe. What are you doing in this mausoleum?" Jules smiled as the old man led him past the marine guards, and up the stairs to a small bedroom overlooking Lafayette Square. It contained two brass beds and some clumsy walnut furniture in the style called "early General Grant". A sideboard with cut-glass bottles of liquor was set up, and Representative Cannon poured Jules a drink.

"How did you arrange this?" Jules asked.

"Teddy didn't like it, but he couldn't refuse me since I added to the re-decoration budget."

Jules was in a much better mood when he went downstairs to watch the dancing. Alice Roosevelt, looking radiant and demure in white chiffon and long white gloves, was jigging with Francis and a hundred others to the tempo of a turkey trot rather badly performed by the Marine Band. The carpet in the East Room was covered by waxed linen. The heat of a hundred bouncing bodies was tremendous. Alicia was nowhere to be seen, but when a Strauss waltz was played, Jules saw her emerging from behind a wall of flowers to dance with an elegant and bespurred cavalry officer from the German Embassy. Jules stood behind a table at the edge of the dance floor and watched the swirling, colorful dancers.

"You're Jules Kincaid, aren't you?" A tall and handsome fellow stood up from one of the tables and peered at Jules through pince-nez glasses. "Yes," Jules replied as he extended his hand.

"I'm Franklin Roosevelt. I'm Alice's cousin. Henry told me to make it a special point to say hello to you. Won't you sit down?" He pulled out a chair for Jules. "Henry and I had an English class together last year," the dapper young man said, "but it wasn't until last summer at Newport that I got to know him. He's quite a fellow."

"Yes, he is," Jules agreed. "He's making a good record for himself at Harvard. And he always knows the right people, including the President's cousin," Jules smiled.

"Oh, I'm just a poor relation. It's a huge family."

* * *

Edith Roosevelt led the way into the State Dining Room for the midnight buffet dinner. Jules loaded up two plates with the rather unappetizing-looking food, and looked around for a place to seat himself and Alicia. Francis was deep in conversation with an attractive girl at a corner table, and Jules took his wife over to join them.

"*Et voila.*" His brother stood up, smiling. "*Est-ce-que je peux presenter mon frère, M. Jules Kincaid, et Madame Kincaid. Mademoiselle la Comtesse Cassini.*"

"How do you do?" Jules answered with a smile, switching to English so that his wife could understand. "May we join you?"

"Marguerite is the daughter of the Russian Ambassador," Francis explained. "And she has the prettiest little red runabout you've ever seen."

"*Le p'tit François* is the only one who can keep it running about. And he's such a sweet boy." The dark-eyed countess tapped Francis on his head with her fan.

"How is it that you speak such good French?" Jules asked, toying with the cold roast beef on his plate.

"Oh, I grew up in Paris and Peking."

"Really? Did you know the old Russian Embassy in Paris? You must have. We used to go by there on our way . . ." Jules glanced over at Alicia, worried that she might feel left out of the conversation, but Alicia's eyes were sparkling. She was enjoying every moment.

Later, when the dancing resumed, Alicia and Jules were standing together at the edge of the dance floor. She whispered in his ear. "That one—that countess—they say she's illegitimate. But her father takes her everywhere."

"He's the one in the fancy white uniform, isn't he?" Jules asked.

"Yes. The president can't stand him. Among other things, he passes his wife off as his daughter's governess."

Jules blotted the perspiration from his forehead. "Let's go home. I'll get the carriage."

"No, not yet, Jules. There's another buffet dinner at three o'clock, and they'll probably be dancing all night. Let's stay for a while."

"Darling, I have to go to the office tomorrow, and I would like to be able to get something done. Let's go."

"Oh, all right. If we must."

In the spring of that year, Jules was finally forced to cancel the contract for the large engine of the Langley Flyer. The builder in New York had almost bankrupted himself, in spite of the extra funds supplied to him from time to time by Jules, who had to pry them out of Karr. The professor seemed to blame the entire fiasco on Francis. There had been a continuous series of changes on the engine, all of which were improvements. The actual mechanical construction of the more important parts had been well done, but the problem was that the engine would simply not furnish anything like the power expected of it. On bench tests it would hardly develop as much as three-horsepower. Even after several weeks of tinkering by Francis and Jules, they could never get it to the point where it would develop as much as four-horsepower for more than a few minutes. Jules cancelled the contract, causing another big fuss in Karr's accounting office, and took all of the parts with him back to the shops of the Smithsonian, where he could supervise the rebuilding himself.

Again, his work was interrupted by his projected trip to Boston for Henry's graduation, as well as by the summer vacation schedule and Langley's annual summer trip to Europe. Francis never seemed to be around when he was needed. "If he doesn't get that machine running by the end of the year," Langley snarled, "we'll have to let him go, Jules, brother or no brother. We can hire somebody from the automobile industry who is a real expert."

"We'll never get one at any decent salary," Jules said. "They're all getting rich with new patents. Look at Blériot. He's making a fortune on those automobile headlights he invented."

"Be warned, young man. Your brother is becoming nothing more than a social butterfly. It might even be better for *him* if we let him go."

When Jules passed this warning on to his brother, Francis laughed. "He can kiss my fetlock, the pompous old wind-bag!"

"What kind of language is that?" Jules was shocked.

They combined their trip to Boston for Henry's graduation with the annual family outing at Plymouth. They were all very proud of Henry, who received some of the top academic prizes. Tall and handsome in his black gown and mortarboard, Henry seemed to know everyone. Jules enjoyed introducing Alicia and showing off his young son to his grandfather's aged colleagues on the Harvard faculty, and to the Roosevelt boy and Henry's other friends.

Plymouth was cool and comfortable after their hot, brief sojourn in Cambridge. Francis was going to take a whole month off, but Jules was anxious to get back to Washington to work on the engine. "Why don't you let Alicia and Sam stay here with me for a couple more weeks?" Francis asked. "It would do them both a lot of good."

"What about you, Henry?" Jules asked. "You haven't said a word about your plans for the future. Are you going to crew on Commodore Vanderbilt's yacht again? Being chief oiler and wiper is a marvelous career for a Harvard graduate."

"I'm going on the *Corsair* this summer, and then I'm going to join Morgan and Company in New York. It's a wonderful job. I'll be working directly for the younger Mr. Morgan."

"Selling watered stock and worthless bonds?"

"Of course, that's part of it, but they want me for their technical analyses. They're still acquiring some of the smaller manufacturing companies for U. S. Steel. Each acquisition has to be preceded by a complete study and analysis of the company."

"What do you know about a profit-and-loss statement?"

"They'll teach me that, and the industrial engineering I already understand, but the important part is that I'm a gentleman. They can trust me."

"What has become of all your interest in flying?"

"I'll leave that to you and Francis for the present, Jules, but when the time comes when you have to organize a company to manufacture those crazy machines, I'll be ready."

Alicia was lithe and full of energy. She went to the beach every day with little Sam. She already had many friends at the Plymouth Beach Club, and she seemed to feel more comfortable with them, as a safely married woman and the sister-in-law of their local war hero, than she was in Washington, where everyone knew all about her—perhaps too much about her.

"Are you sure you'll be all right without me?" Jules asked.

"Don't worry about us, Jules," Alicia smiled. "I'm having a wonderful time. Francis is taking me to the polo match next week, and then there's a great big clambake."

"Whatever you say . . ."

Jules really enjoyed the unaccustomed luxury of solitude on his train trip south from Boston. On the spur of the moment, he got off in New York. He was able to get an inexpensive room at the Hoffman House, and took in a variety show at the Hammerstein Theater. He went downtown to Lüchow's for dinner, and enjoyed a solitary repast and a bottle of good French Bordeaux. New York was still suffering from the after-effects of the financial panic of 1893 and the ensuing years of uncertainty which had wiped out his grandfather's fortune, but Lüchow's and all the other good restaurants were filled with those hundreds of new young millionaires who had been created by the formation of U.S. Steel and the railroad amalgamations. They were all spending feverishly and conspicuously. When he returned to his hotel, Jules bought a Havana cigar and sat down in the lobby to watch the parade. Tammany politicians in silk top-hats, packing-house millionaires flushed with champagne, and showgirls in satin gowns swept across the tiled floor. Potted palms and shiny brass spittoons lined the corridors. Handsome women, always in pairs, eyed Jules boldly from behind flickering fans. Jules was tempted, but not for long. He stubbed out his cigar and trudged upstairs, huffing and puffing with the few extra pounds he had put on in the last several years, to his little room on the fourth floor. His mind was already occupied with the idea of adapting a dynamometer to make bench tests of his new engine.

The workshops of the Smithsonian were quiet and peaceful for a change. Jules arrived every day in the cool of the early morning, took a long lunch period and a nap, and left in the cool of the evening to go home to his silent house in Georgetown.

There was a separate sparking coil and a separate contact maker for each of the five cylinders of the engine. They were very heavy, and it suddenly occurred to Jules that it would be possible to devise a new multiple-sparking arrangement using only one battery, one coil, and one contact-maker to cause the spark for all five cylinders, using a small commutator to distribute sparks to each cylinder at the proper time. He designed the new arrangement, and when Francis returned to work they quickly made one. It worked well on the small engine of the quarter-size model, so they went on to apply the same principle to the full-size engine.

After that, they discovered another problem. The spark plugs would very quickly be covered with a coating of soot, resulting from the incomplete combustion of the gas and oil in the cylinder at the time of the explosion. It formed on the porcelain and caused a short circuit. Francis devised a way for getting around the problem by extending the metal portion of the plug for some distance into the cylinder, beyond the porcelain insulator. It worked very well, and Francis immediately adapted the same principles for the spark plugs of his motorcycle. "It's a great new invention," Francis said enthusiastically. "I'm going to take out a patent."

"You can't do that. All of our patents automatically belong to the Smithsonian."

"Well, you don't have to tell your revered father-in-law everything, do you?"

"Tell him. It'll help you keep your job."

Langley was back in town. The fall social season was beginning, and Alicia was looking prettier than ever. Francis kept disappearing for afternoon teas or all-night parties with Alice Roosevelt and the Cassini girl, but it all escaped Jules' attention. Jules attached their new engine to the propellers and was able to test it by using the water-absorption dynamometers he had devised. They made it impossible for the engine to run away with the propeller and cause serious damage. The longer running times for the engine, however, made the engine run very hot. They had been using wet rags to cool it for brief one- or two-minute tests, but now the construction of water jackets was imperative. The water jackets were made in halves, which had to be brazed together after they had been fitted carefully over the head of the cylinder. When they were finally seated, however, the new engine developed 21-horsepower at 825 revolutions per minute, and weighed only 120 pounds.

Jules was very enthusiastic when he invited Langley down to view a final test of the engine. "Let's take it down to Quantico and put a launching track on the river bank and test it."

"What about the boat? We have to use the boat."

"We can't stick this up sixty feet in the air and take a chance with it," Jules said.

"We figured that it would take twenty-four horse-power to fly the aeroplane," Langley objected. "You're not ready for a complete test."

"Then we'll have to build a duplicate engine and use two of them."

"Then do it. Where is your charming little brother?"

"Francis? I thought he was around here some-place."

When Francis finally showed up later that after-noon, he was driving a large purple Panhard limou-sine. "Look what I got," he laughed. "It's the one I captured in Cuba. General Shafter wants me to patch up the bullet holes."

"Professor Langley has been looking for you," Jules said. "He wants to see you right away."

"Wonderful. I want to see him, too. Come on along."

Jules was apprehensive as he went with Francis up to Langley's little hideaway office. "Hello, Profes-sor. I understand you want to see me," he said after he and Jules had been admitted to the sanctum. Langley was shrugging into his cutaway and wiping the sleep from his eyes. "Did you drive that automobile into the courtyard just now?" he asked testily.

"Yes, sir," Francis smiled. "It belongs to the War Department, but I've got a wonderful idea for you. Let's buy it and fix it up and give it to Alice Roosevelt. She's green with envy because her friend Marguerite has a car and she doesn't. It would be a feather in your cap."

"Really?"

"The Smithsonian could acquire it as an exhibit, or as a war souvenir, or even as a limousine."

"What would the president think?"

"What difference does that make? Alice does what she wants to anyway." They went on to discuss a proper price for the machine. Jules stood by fidgeting nervously.

When they had finished their discussion Francis said, "What did you want to see me about, Professor?"

"I just wanted to congratulate you on our new engine."

The construction and testing of the new engine had shown many places in which weight could be safely reduced. Jules decided to build an entirely new, and larger, single engine rather than a duplicate of the one they had with all its extra weight and synchronizing gears. The large aircraft, due to a number of small changes in design made over a period of years, was now scheduled to be much heavier than originally planned. Jules designed the new engine to give forty-horsepower when all five of the cylinders were working, and even twenty-eight when one of them was dead and acting as a dead load on the others. New pistons were designed, which actually weighed fifteen pounds less than the original set, and the various materials for the construction of the engine were ordered. It was a long time before all of these materials could be delivered, however, and Francis and Jules utilized the time by making new experiments with the carburetors and spark coils on the smaller experimental engine. Automobile engine carburetors had proved to be unsatisfactory when attached to the aeroplane frame, which was always shaking to a greater or lesser degree during tests of the engine. The carburetors would periodically flood, causing great injury to the transmission shafts and gears due to pounding. Francis developed a new type of carburetor, which eliminated this problem entirely.

Alice Roosevelt was very thrilled with her new Panhard automobile. When she was in Washington she drove it every day; and when she wasn't, it rested in the shops of the Smithsonian, where Francis worked on it. Once again, Francis was the cynosure of Washington society, but this time with the younger set: a fast and racy younger set that was looked on with frowns of disapproval by their elders, including Mrs. Roosevelt. Francis was but one of the many handsome and eligible young men who clustered around Alice and the Countess Cassini, and he seemed always to be running off to midnight champagne parties and fancy cotillions.

The President's hoyden daughter was rapidly becoming famous as "Princess Alice". The fashionable younger set dressed in Alice-blue gowns, and danced to the strains of "Where Are You, Sweet Alice?" The Countess and Alice wore enormous hats, so the world wore enormous hats. If Alice liked orchids, the world liked orchids, and their price doubled. At one party, George Westinghouse, newly rich from his invention of the air brake, decorated his new ballroom with forty thousand orchids.

President Roosevelt did not approve of Alice's friend, Marguerite Cassini. He despised the fortune-hunting Europeans who slithered through Washington

and New York society in search of American millionaires' daughters. He was disgusted with Jenny Jerome,
and with the Vanderbilt girl, who married the
Duke of Marlborough. He became violent when anyone mentioned the Duke of Abruzzi, who had contracted a Morganatic marriage with the daughter of a
Virginia senator; and he thought no better of Marguerite's father, who tucked his wife away on the second story of the Russian Embassy.

The President was under continual pressure to
condemn the Czar of Russia for his continuing po-
groms. He would turn red with rage when advised by
the State Department that a letter of protest wouldn't
even be accepted by the Russian court.

When Henry came down from New York to spend
Christmas with them, he was full of stories of his adventures with J.P. Morgan and Company. He was not
being paid very well, but he found the work fascinating. He would be sent out to Pittsburgh to inspect a
steel plant, and would stay with his college friends in
their new mansions. He had become an expert at ana-
lyzing a balance sheet, and could recognize watered
stock at one glance.

"The effrontery of some of those fellows is incredible," Henry said, dominating the conversation at
their Christmas dinner. "They will have a steam-
engine running a piddling little rolling mill operation,
and they'll have it listed on their inventory as worth a
hundred thousand dollars. They begin to bluster and
curse when I write off its value as less than than five
thousand dollars, but they quiet down right away
when I tell them exactly where they can replace it at
that sum."

"More, more!" Little Sam banged his spoon on his dish.

"He's the noisiest Kincaid of them all," Alicia said as she cut up some more turkey for the boy.

"And their stock always goes up as soon as there's any hint of a Morgan merger. They always claim they'll refuse to sell, but they always do."

After dinner, Francis took Sam upstairs to put him to bed, and Henry took Jules aside while Alicia was clearing the table.

"Confidentially, Jules," he said as he lighted their cigars, "If you've got any spare cash to invest, buy some McCormick Harvesting Machine Company stock. It's a secret, but we're putting together a group with McCormick, Deering, and three other companies. We're going to have a holding company that will manufacture eighty percent of the grain harvesters in the country. Almost a monopoly. The stock is bound to go up. I'm getting a good bonus on this if everything goes right. I only wish I had a little money of my own to invest."

"I wouldn't touch the stock market with a ten-foot pole," Jules said, lighting his cigar. "And you shouldn't either after what happened to Grandpa."

"Your friend Karr is certainly active. I see his purchase orders. He always seems to buy the wrong stocks."

"I wonder what a bookkeeper would be doing with an account at the House of Morgan. I thought you only handled the big boys."

"He's a big loser. But he keeps coming in with more cash. Why should we object? We get our fee on every transaction, win or lose."

"I wonder if Langley knows about this."

Henry shrugged. "I don't see how he couldn't." Seeing that Jules was upset, he decided to change the subject. "What's this I hear about Francis getting arrested for speeding?"

"Oh, that turned out all right. He got off. It's his racing that bothers me. He'll go as fast as forty miles an hour on those rutted country roads. He's a regular speed-demon."

"He's wild. He always was."

In January, Francis finally paid the price. Langley summoned him to his large office once again, and asked Jules to come along.

"Ahem." Professor Langley cleared his throat and tapped upon his desk with a slide rule. "I understand your—our new engine is all ready to go, as soon as we finish up the airframe."

"Yes, sir," Francis answered, mystified.

"Then I'm sure that you and Jules will agree that your period of service here in Washington should come to an end. The Smithsonian cannot afford to keep an expert on internal combustion engines on its payroll indefinitely, and surely Jules can do what has to be done now that the initial work is finished."

"Uh, what about the Panhard? And—is that the real reason, Professor?" Francis was stupefied at his sudden dismissal.

"Well actually." the professor was discomfited. "Actually, my friend Theodore summoned me to the White House yesterday. He's very annoyed with all the newspaper innuendos about you and Alice and that so-called countess running around in the middle of the night in high-powered automobiles. He may not be able to do much about Alice, but he can do some-

thing about you. Actually, Francis, it's all for your
own good. How old are you? Nineteen? All those parties and wild driving are not good for your character.
Surely you could find a much better position in private industry, with all your knowledge of gasoline engines."

"I'm sure I can." Francis stood up, obviously angry.
"Then if you don't mind, sir, I will start clearing out
my things and leave today."

"Now, Francis, don't take it personally. It's just
politics. Here, I've had a small bonus check made out
to you as a token of my appreciation for the work
you've done here."

"Thank you. I'll talk to you later, Jules." Francis
stalked out angrily.

Jules was dumbfounded. Francis had been of in-
valuable help in their work together, and his small salary had already been paid and repaid out of the prof-
its from the patents Langley had taken out on Francis'
new sparking plugs designs. Jules was tempted to resign then and there.

"I hope, Jules, that you don't take this too hard. It's
for his own good." The professor was lighting up a
cigar. "It's not good for a young fellow to run around
with that fast set. If he'd had an accident in that automobile with Miss Roosevelt riding with him—well, it
would've reflected very badly upon us."

Jules made an ineffectual gesture, and then they
both jumped as a great roar rattled the windows.
They looked out to see the Panhard racing down the
driveway of the Smithsonian, Francis at the wheel, his
blond hair streaming out behind him.

"See? Do you see what I mean?" The professor

stood beside Jules as they watched Francis disappear down the road toward the White House.

Jules was sorely tempted to quit, but he couldn't now; not when they were so close to finally completing the Langley Flyer. They had been working on it for five years, and it was at last ready to be assembled and flown. Jules had to see that project through.

It wasn't until that evening that he saw Francis. His brother shattered the night air of Georgetown by riding up on his motorcycle. He appeared elated.

"How are you? Did you hear the news, Alicia? I'm free. I haven't been so happy in years."

"What did you do with the car?" Jules asked, worried.

"I delivered it to Alice," his brother answered with a laugh. "A last gesture to the old Rough Rider. I bet he was mad."

"What are you going to do, Francis?" Alicia asked, holding Sam in her arms. The boy was getting so big that it was becoming difficult for her to carry him.

"I'm going to make motorcycles. I can buy all the components, and make what I can't buy. You'll see, I'll make the fastest motorcycles in the country. 'The Seven-cylinder Kincaid'."

"That'll take a lot of money."

"I've got a lot of money. My whole school and college fund has never been touched. Maybe I'll move out to Plymouth for the summer."

"How wonderful," Alicia said with a smile. "We're planning to go in August again, aren't we Jules? We'll all be together."

They discussed Francis' unsettled future for more than an hour, but Jules' mind kept going off on a different tangent. Finally he asked what he wanted to ask. "Seven cylinders? In-line, or radial?"

While Langley was away in Europe for the summer, Jules spent June and July supervising the installation of the superstructure on the great houseboat. The huge turntable had to be made to function smoothly enough so that a gang could operate it manually. Langley's pianola, furniture and rugs had to be taken out of the interior so that it could be used as a shop when they brought the machine out in the fall for tests, and the power launch had to be put back in shape. Jules hated to leave town for his vacation, but Alicia and Sam were looking forward to it so much, and there was nothing to be done there without Huffaker and Manly and the rest of the crew anyway.

Jules was full of excitement when he finally arrived at Plymouth and found Francis already in residence. The barn was filled with automotive parts, motorcycle things, and pneumatic tires. "What a mess," he said to Francis. "How can you get any work done?"

"I can't," Francis said. "I'm going to move into Boston as soon as the polo season is over. I've rented a little shop there, and I'm going to hire some assistants."

"How is your new engine coming along?" Jules asked.

"Expensively. I had no idea what it would cost to buy machine tools, tables, and everything else that goes with setting up a new shop. But that engine—it's going to develop eighty-five horsepower, or I'm a monkey's uncle."

"Don't talk about my son that way!"

*   *   *

Henry arrived at Plymouth in the greatest style imaginable. A 214-foot yacht steamed majestically over the horizon one day while Alicia and Francis and Jules were having lunch on the terrace of the Plymouth Beach Club. It stopped for a moment, and a steam launch was lowered. The launch came in to the club dock as the huge yacht steamed away. On board was Henry, immaculate in white ducks and hat and a yachting jacket that bore the crest of the New York Yacht Club. Francis ran down to greet him at the dock, but he could hardly get through the crowd of adoring young ladies who clustered around.

"What is all this?" Jules asked when Henry had finally made his way to their table. "Have you broken the bank at Monte Carlo?" Alicia smiled at her handsome, red-headed brother-in-law.

"They loaned me the launch for a few days. J.P. senior is over in France, and young J.P. took the boat to go up to Newport for a few days. I have to get back tomorrow."

"Henry, you're becoming a bloated plutocrat." Francis slapped him on the back.

"I'm slimmer than ever," Henry laughed. "It's Jules who's putting on the weight."

Little Sam crawled up onto Henry's lap and pulled at the great brass buttons on his blue jacket. "Uncle Henry," he said with a smile.

"Hello, Sam." Henry beamed and hugged the boy. "I'm going to take you on a boat ride today. Would you like that?"

"Boat! Boat ride!"

There was little Jules could do that summer. He finally learned how to swim. Francis laughed at his clumsy efforts, but he taught him well, as he taught little Sam.

Alicia was learning lawn tennis, hopping about on the green courts of the Plymouth Club, hobbled by her long, narrow skirts. Jules tried the game, but he could never get himself interested in winning. Alicia would more often find him sitting on the club veranda, reading the Boston newspapers.

Henry was elected to the Board of Directors of the beach club that year. To them, he represented a far-away world of great wealth; not only had his family owned property in the neighborhood for three generations, but he had the veneer of a solid Harvard background and the romance of the powerful corporations he dealt with. Neither quiet and moody, like Jules, nor flighty and unpredictable like Francis, he had an air of strength and self-confidence that was to develop into autocratic dogmatism with the passing years, as he became one of the great industrialists of his time.

17

SEPTEMBER and October found Jules, Langley and Manly back at their desks. Work was going forward with its usual agonizing slowness. Although things seemed to be almost ready for the crucial tests of the Langley Flyer, Jules' insistence on accelerating the work effort had no effect on the usual even tenor of mediocrity. There were the usual translations to be made, visiting firemen to be entertained, and a close relationship with the administration to be maintained. The motor for the aeroplane seemed to be all ready to go, and the launching apparatus was in as good a shape as it could be until the last minute preparations might reveal possible difficulties. The airframe, however, which was Manly's responsibility, still had to be altered to suit the various sets of wings and tails which they were planning to use in tests. To Langley and Manly, the crucial point was to get the center of gravity directly over the center of air pressure so that the machine would be in balance and capable of a horizontal flight.

One morning, when Jules was engaged in reading through the available literature on marine propellers—and the literature seemed to be totally devoid of any ideas as to why propellers propel—he received a special delivery letter from a subcontractor in New York. It was full of long and detailed complaints about the contractor's inability to get his cash advances as contracted from the Smithsonian. The letter infuriated Jules. He stomped over to the comptroller's office.

"Mr. Karr, have a look at this. How can it be? Why can we not pay this man promptly what is due him? There's a whole loft full of men on payroll who expect their pay-checks weekly, and he has his own suppliers who have to be paid. Are you short of cash? I want to look at the books."

Mr. Karr jumped up, flustered, and waved the one shirt-sleeved clerk out of the room. Jules took a Hodgkins Fund Ledger from the shelf and opened it up to try to compare the authorized payments and the dates of issued checks with the detailed list of complaints in the letter.

"You can't do that," Karr expostulated. "This is my department. No Smithsonian employee can come barging in here and create havoc wih our books."

"I am also a director of the Smithsonian, Mr. Karr, and all of the books should be open to me at any time. In fact, I think it is even my legal duty."

"But—but. . ." The old man was wringing his hands. "I'll tell Langley, and the books are supposed to be audited only at the request of at least two directors."

"Then I'll get Milburn."

Karr dashed from the office, and Jules could hear his boots clattering up the stairs to Langley's office, but he didn't care. He was able to trace authorizations and checks issued, but by comparing them with the letter from New York, he found that there were often delays of weeks and even months before the monies were received.

"What do you think you're doing, Jules?" Langley shouted as he stormed into the office, followed by Karr who was still wringing his hands. "Who told you to come in here and raise a ruckus?"

"Dr. Langley, I've complained and complained, but it doesn't seem to do any good. We're going to drive the contractor in New York to bankruptcy. And for no reason—unless you know something I don't. Perhaps we need an independent audit of our books. Is it a matter of gross inefficiency?"

"Jules, I absolutely forbid you to interfere with the bookkeeping department. You are far exceeding your authority. Mr. Karr has been running this department for years and years to my utmost satisfaction. I trust him implicitly. I will not tolerate insubordination—not even by my own son-in-law. You can be dismissed, you know. . ."

"Not as a director of the Institute. I have legal tenure."

"Now, Jules, we have let this thing go too far." Langley put his arm around Jules' shoulder and urged him toward the door. "I have told Mr. Karr that he must in the future get these checks out promptly, and I'm sure he will." Langley urged him through the glass-panelled door, outside of which the shirt-sleeved clerk waited with his little visor and steel pen still in hand. "I'm sure we don't want to make a big thing out of what amounts to a small family spat. I'll take care of Karr. Once we get our machine in the air, all our problems will be over. You don't realize, perhaps, how much money will be involved once we can demonstrate a flyable machine. All the governments in the world will be coming to us. There will be manufacturing, and all the patents will be in my name. It will all go to Alicia and to young Sam. Do you know what that means?" The old man had managed to mollify Jules and send him back to work, but he had raised nagging questions in Jules' mind—questions that were to haunt him.

Francis' disappearance from the Washington social scene had been widely, though briefly, mourned by bevies of debutantes. His absence from the workshops of the Smithsonian that autumn was unsettling for Jules. He missed having someone at the office in whom he could confide unreservedly. Jules was discontented, and he found no solace in Alicia, who always seemed to be involved with entertaining for her father or taking care of Sam. Also, there were no longer the brief overnight trips to New York on business to add variety to Jules' life.

When a letter came from Chanute inviting him to New York to hear an address he was making before the Society of Industrial Engineers, Jules decided to take a few days off. Ariel would be there, and besides, he had never seen Henry's new office at the House of Morgan. Langley and Alicia hardly seemed to notice when he said he'd be leaving for a few days.

It was with a sudden and surprising feeling of freedom that he packed up his Gladstone bag and took the trolley to Union Station. He hadn't even brought any technical papers to read. On the steam-cars to New York he simply riffled through the Washington Post, and had a leisurely second breakfast in the dining car.

Henry had reserved a room for him at the Plaza Hotel. When he had unpacked, he inquired about Professor Chanute at the hotel desk. A bellboy went up to the suite and returned to report that they were out, so Jules took the elevated steam railway downtown to Wall Street. Again he was impressed by the large white marble building in which the House of Morgan had its offices. He went through the massive doors and, before an usher could take him in hand, walked over to greet Mr. Bellamy.

"How are you, sir? Still at your post, I see."

"It's . . ." The older man stood up, extending his hand. "It's Mr. Kincaid, isn't it?"

"Yes, of course. I came to see my brother. Hasn't he taken over the ground floor yet?"

"Not quite yet," the old man said. "He certainly is making a good impression, though. I'll have someone take you up to his office." The smiling older man raised his hand to summon an usher.

"Isn't that old J. P. back there?" Jules pointed toward a glass-enclosed office at the back of the room. There, a massive old man with a bulbous red nose sat at a flat-topped desk, riffling through business papers with an imperial air.

"Yes," Mr. Bellamy said. "That's J. P. Senior, and over on the other side of the room is J. P. Junior."

Jules was awed to be in the presence of the

world's foremost industrialist. The spectacular ugliness of the old man seemed to be balanced by the spectacular handsomeness of all of the junior partners.

An usher came, and Jules thanked Mr. Bellamy before following the flashing white spats of the young usher up a marble staircase to the third floor. There, he found Henry in a corner office with several other young executives, each at his own roll-top desk.

"Hello, Jules." They shook hands with proper Bostonian reserve, and Jules sat down beside Henry's desk.

"How's your room? Was it all right?"

"Very luxurious. I hope I can afford it."

"They always give us the best." Henry closed a folder marked "International Harvester Company." "Analysing all those assets," Henry said. "It's tedious, but someone has to do it."

"Very impressive." Jules gestured at the large room full of industrious young bankers and clerks.

"Well, it's home—at least when I'm not out in Pittsburgh." Henry opened a humidor and chose a hand-rolled cigar. "You're looking very care-worn," he said. "How's Alicia? And Sam?"

"They're fine. Sam is getting so big I can hardly pick him up."

"And your charming father-in-law?"

"Getting worse in his old age," Jules said wryly.

"How can you speak that way about one of our nation's most esteemed scientists?" Henry said with a smile. "You need a little diversion. That fellow Blériot is in town with his niece again. I'm taking her out on the town tonight. Why don't you join us? You'd be bored stiff at that fancy dinner. How about it? Invite Ariel Chanute. We'll paint the town red."

"That sounds like a good idea, but I can't afford it."

"I'm paying. Here," Henry raised his finger to summon an office boy. "Let's send a telegram up to Ariel. We'll pick her up at the Plaza at eight. White tie and tails. My treat. Don't be the serious elder brother all your life, Jules. Let me show off a little bit."

Jules smiled wanly. "You know, Henry, something you mentioned last Christmas has been bothering me. You said that both Langley and Karr, the accountant, have been gambling on the stock market, and losing."

"An awful lot of people are getting wiped out these days, just like Grandpa did," Henry said. "I know. I'm the one who's wiping them out."

"What about Karr, and Langley, and all the Smithsonian funds? Are they safe? This could affect my work a lot." Jules sat up straight and his expression took on the usual serious intensity to which his brother was accustomed. "Could I look at the books? I'd like to know what is really happening."

"I'm not really close to it," Henry said, with equal seriousness. "It's not my department. But I guess I could have the ledgers brought up. I suppose I shouldn't let you see them, but after all, you are a director of the Smithsonian."

"Yes, that's right. I believe any director is entitled to examine the books at any time. But no one ever does."

Henry wrote a note requesting the records he wanted to examine, and sent it downstairs with another office boy. "We'll have a good time tonight. We'll go to Rector's," he said as he relaxed expansively and lighted his cigar. "You've never been to Rector's, have you? They have the best food in town. You need

a little change from your Georgetown diet. Here, I
didn't offer you a cigar, did I? We are getting the best
Havana has to offer since the occupation."

Jules used Henry's fancy gold implememt to clip
and pierce his cigar, and lighted it carefully with a
wooden match. It tasted wonderful. When the papers
came, Henry took Jules over to a side table by a window and spread out the ledgers before him so that he
could study them. "Take your time," Henry said.
"These stock transfers aren't easy to figure out. Do
you have everything you'll need? Here's an ashtray."

"Thank you. I'll be all right. You go ahead and do
what you have to do. If I have any questions, I'll come
over and ask."

Jules' cigar was burned down to a nubbin by the
time he had compared the various stock transactions
and the ups and downs of the bank accounts of the
Smithsonian. There was the account of the Hodgkins
Fund, a general account for the Smithsonian, and a
special fund which Jules presumed was the War Department fund. They showed huge and complicated
transactions which often seemed to cancel each other
out, with checks bounced back and forth between the
various accounts. Large checks were drawn in favor of
Karr, and then appeared to be deposited in his stock-
brokerage accounts, only to be wiped out by stock-
market losses. It was appalling.

"Henry, come over and look at this. It's unbeliev-
able." Henry came over and leafed expertly through
the papers to compare deposit dates with withdrawal
checks. "You're right," he said. "Your Mr. Karr has apparently been getting into the game with Smithsonian
marbles. Considering his relationship with Langley, I

would guess that your esteemed father-in-law is involved."

"It's fantastic!" Jules exclaimed. "What are we going to do about it?"

"I'm not going to do a thing. I shouldn't be poking my nose into these accounts, and God knows I should never have showed them to you. What the House of Morgan has done is perfectly legal. Officially, I don't want to know anything about it. It's your baseball game, and you'll have to decide for yourself what to do, if anything."

"Yes, I suppose I will." Jules stood up dazedly from the table and, after making an appointment with Henry to meet him at the Plaza that evening, left the bank and wandered all the way uptown on foot. He could hardly believe that his noble father-in-law, one of the most distinguished scientists in the country, might get caught with his fingers in the till. He was appalled at the thought that it could ruin the Smithsonian, wreck five years of concentrated aeronautical research, and perhaps even destroy his marriage. He tried to imagine how he could broach the subject to Langley, or to Alicia.

Jules was exhausted by the time he got up to the Plaza Hotel. Waiting for him at the desk was a scribbled note in French from Ariel Chanute. She said that her father was taking her for a shopping tour of New York, but that she could be ready and waiting for him in the lobby at eight o'clock. Jules went upstairs to his room and lay down, his mind in a turmoil. When it began to get dark in the room, he suddenly realized that he had to get bathed and dressed. His white vest was getting a little tight for him, but he still looked handsome as he tied his bow tie in front of the mirror. He only wished he felt as good as he looked.

Ariel Chanute was a vision in white as she stepped out from between the potted palms downstairs in the lobby. "Ariel, how you have grown!" Jules leaned over and kissed her cheek.

"I'm nineteen," said the little princess as she adjusted the bejeweled tiara that nestled in her golden coiffure. "I'm a grown-up lady now, and I'll thank you to remember that, Mr. Kincaid." Her eyes suddenly twinkled and she impulsively put her arms around Jules and kissed him on the lips. "It's so good to see you again, *mon cher.*"

"Here's my brother," Jules said, seeing Henry beckoning to them from the door. They joined him, and he rushed them outside to the carriage he had taken for the evening. "You remember Marie," he said. "Get in. We're off to Rector's."

The famous restaurant was crowded with fashionably dressed men and women, all gourmandizing merrily. Henry had reserved one of the best tables. He seemed to order one of everything from the menu, starting out with an Amontillado sherry, Cotuit oysters, Rhine wine, clams, and then a saddle of lamb acconpanied by a *Chateau Latour.* The two French girls chattered away, and Henry amused them with anecdotes of high life in New York and Pittsburgh, showing a new side of himself to his serious elder brother. Jules was rather quiet until the wine began to go to his head. A string orchestra was playing Viennese waltzes, and Ariel insisted that he dance with her. Much to his surprise, he found that he was enjoying it. He forgot his troubles, and Ariel was like a dream in white floating in his arms.

Henry had Moët-Chandon waiting for them when they got back to the table, and terrapin, grapefruit *au kirsch* and *Clos-Vougeot,* followed by canvasback ducks, cheese and fruit, and coffee and cognac. As Ariel lit one of Henry's Havana cigars for him, Jules undid a couple of his vest buttons and leaned back, full to the brim.

Henry had to leave early, since he had to go to work the next day, but the four of them decided to take a quick carriage ride around Central Park after dinner, and enjoy the fresh air and their Havana cigars. Ariel even took a couple of puffs on Jules' cigar, and made a funny face. Henry and Marie delivered them to the door of the Plaza and said good-night.

"Won't you come up, Jules?" Ariel smiled, her diamonds glinting in the gaslight. "Father said you would be my *beau chevalier* tonight." Jules offered his arm to escort her up the marble steps to her suite overlooking the park. She let herself in with a key and said "Come in. I won't be a moment."

The room was candlelit and almost intimate in spite of its tall ceilings and eight-foot windows. Jules gazed out the windows at the bobbing lanterns of the carriages on the drives of Central Park.

"There, that's better." Ariel had returned. Jules turned to her. She had changed into a devastating white negligee. "Come, sit with me," she said, perching on the edge of a tiny satin *fauteuil.*

"Where's your father tonight?" Jules asked.

"Oh, I'm all alone. He had to go to New Jersey for some silly meeting. Come sit down."

"And Mademoiselle?"

"Jules, I'm a grown-up woman now. I don't need a governess." Jules sat down beside her. The front of her diaphanous white dressing gown fell slightly open so that he could see the side of her breast. He was very distracted.

"What's the matter, Jules?" She asked. "You've been so distracted off and on all evening. What is it? Tell me." She took his hand in hers.

"I can't. It's—it's . . ."

"*Le pauvre Jules!* It must be that wife of yours." She reached out a tiny hand to stroke his blond hair, and her gown came open to reveal a silky white thigh. Ariel put her arms around him and pulled his head down on her shoulder. Hesitantly, Jules put his arms around her and breathed in the freshness of her youth. A moment later, hardly knowing what he was doing, he picked her up and carried her into the nearest bedroom.

Some time later, Jules opened his eyes to find Ariel lying nude beside him. "Oh, my God," he said, pulling up a sheet to cover their nakedness.

"What's the matter, Jules?" She kicked her legs free and lay there smiling happily. The little fringe of her pubic hair was blond and curly, and her limbs glowed like white marble. "You are wonderful. I always knew you would be."

"What have I done? I had no idea of . . ."

"I did, for years now. I always knew it would be like that, and I always knew it would happen. I love you as much as I love my father—in a different way, of course. Or perhaps not. Don't you love me?"

"Of course I do, Ariel, but . . ." Jules put his hands over his face as if to hide.

"Jules, come away with me. I have money of my own. We could go to Paris—London—Berlin. You could get an annulment in Rome. You could have your own laboratory . . ."

"Oh, my God." Jules got out of the bed, turning his back to hide his nakedness as he dressed. "What have we done?" he asked. "How can I ever face your father? I'm sorry."

"Don't be absurd, Jules. I wanted you. It doesn't mean anything, and it's made me very happy." She jumped up and ran to him as he started to go.

"Jules, don't go away. Come back. What is there to worry about? No one was hurt." She straightened his tie and smoothed down his hair. She was incredibly beautiful.

"Goodbye, Ariel. I'm sorry," he said, and left her hurriedly.

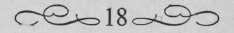

18

JULES awoke with the dawn, packed his bags, left hurried notes for Chanute and for Ariel, and took the first train to Washington without even contacting Henry. It was late in the afternoon by the time he got out to Georgetown, and he had begun to sort out his thoughts. He knew what he wanted to say to Langley and to Alicia, but as he tried to put together the phrases in his mind, visions of the tiny nude Ariel kept flashing before his eyes. Yet, as he walked up the brick sidewalk from the trolley to see his little house lit by the afternoon sun, he was glad to be home. "Hello, is that you, Jules?" Jules hung his hat on a peg and muttered "Yes," as he went upstairs. Alicia shouted after him, "Oh, good. I was just about to get supper ready."

He undressed quickly and took a sponge bath with cold water, almost enjoying the cold shock of the water on his naked body, perfumed as it was with the odor of Ariel. Alicia poked her head around the corner of the door as he was getting dressed again. "I didn't expect you until Sunday, so there's not a lot of food."

"That's all right. Where's Sam?"

"He's out in the backyard. He's having such fun with that little cart you made him. He doesn't know you're home yet." Jules nodded, and turned his back on her as he leaned over to put on his slippers. Alicia hesitated a moment and then went downstairs. After a few minutes, Jules went down too, silently got a glass of wine from the bottle beneath the icebox, and went out to sit in the backyard and watch Sam play. Sam just looked up and said, "Oh, hello, Daddy."

Jules was silent, seemingly almost sullen and morose as he watched the boy play. Alicia came out to sit with him, but she sensed his mood and said very little, speaking mostly to Sam.

After a time, Jules turned to her. "I had some pretty astounding experiences in New York yesterday," Jules said.

"Yes, I can see you did," Alicia agreed seriously. She seemed to be worried.

"You know that all of the Smithsonian accounts go through the Morgan Bank in New York, don't you?"

Alicia seemed suddenly relieved. "Yes," she said, paying careful attention.

"Well, Henry let me examine them. That's confidential, of course. He could be fired if it got out. But I found out some very interesting things. As far as I could tell from an examination of their books, Karr has been gambling on the stock market with Smithsonian money—and losing. Losing heavily. I don't see how he could get away with it without your father's cooperation."

"So that's it. That must be what's been bothering him so much lately," Alicia said. She stood up and went to lean on the bannister of the tiny back porch. Sam looked up at her anxiously. "That's where all the money's been coming from. All these years. That sly old fox!"

"You're not shocked? I was afraid of what it might do to you. I was really worried, Alicia."

"Shocked? I'm the one person in this world who could not be shocked by anything he might do. I know him better than anyone—you know that. The whole world has always been so impressed with the great Dr. Langley, but I have always known the kind of man he really is."

"What are we going to do?" Jules stood up and began to pace. "Sometimes I'm tempted to just chuck it all." A sudden poignant picture of Ariel leaning over him, nude and lovely, came to his mind, and he quickly rejected it. "How can I handle it? It could be the end of all our research at the Smithsonian. It could be the end of the Smithsonian. Five years of work down the drain."

"Jules." Alicia stepped close to him and took his hand. "Jules, whatever you decide to do, I'm on your side. Don't ever forget that for a minute. If you want to leave and get a job in New York, maybe that would be just as well. Let *them* take all the blame for whatever may happen. Why should you ruin your reputation? There's going to be more scandal . . ."

"And leave five years of hard work to be dumped into the Potomac? I don't know."

"Whatever you decide to do, Jules, Sam and I are with you." Alicia looked him in the eye, and then went inside to put their dinner on the table.

After dinner, Jules stared out the front window, his thoughts in a jumble. After Sam fell asleep in his little trundle-bed in the living room, Jules and Alicia went upstairs to get ready for bed. He told her of all the complicated transactions he had seen between the Hodgkins Fund and Karr's personal account—a history of chicanery. Alicia listened carefully, and let him speak his piece.

"Mama." Sam was calling from downstairs. Alicia got up, gave Jules a glance, and then went down to take care of her son.

Jules and Alicia lay together that night in their wide bed, and the cool moonlight streamed in upon them. Jules felt that he could almost hear Sam breathing in his little bed downstairs. Jules was holding Alicia's hand. Silently he turned to her, and they made love.

Afterwards, he fell into a deep sleep. But Alicia lay awake in the moonlight, staring at the cracks in the ceiling.

Jules had no sooner arrived at the Smithsonian the next day and gone down to his office, when Langley's old biddy of a secretary bustled in. "Dr. Langley would like to see you immediately, Mr. Kincaid," she said in stentorian tones.

"Good. I want to see him, too." Jules hung his coat on the coat tree and put his bowler hat on the corner of his deak.

"*At once*, Mr. Kincaid. It's something important. There's a *man* here. Mr. Langley doesn't want to *see* him."

Jules glanced up. The old biddy's face was flushed, her usual forbidding demeanor ruffled. "All right, all right. I'm coming." He followed her up the stairs to Langley's outer offices. A sunburned, hatchet-faced man was sitting there, hat in hand, fidgeting. Jules knocked and walked right in to Langley's office. The old man was pacing up and down behind the desk.

"Oh, there you are. Is that door closed?"

"Yes, of course. What is it?"

"This man outside," Langley said, flustered, "he says he comes from the Wright brothers' camp down at Kitty Hawk. Do you know him?"

"No. I've never seen him before in my life."

"He says that the Wright brothers are ready to begin manned, powered flying. They have a big new machine, with the motor already installed. He wants to tell us how they're going to do it."

"Well?"

"That's all we need," Langley snorted. "Then the Wright brothers could claim that we stole their ideas. They could start their own lobby in Congress. They could get their own grants and we would lose ours."

"So you simply refuse to see him."

"Exactly." The old man clapped his hands together, but then a sly look came over his features. "On the other hand, I would certainly like to know what they are doing. Unofficially, that is."

"Well, I'll get rid of him for you if you don't want to see him. That's no problem."

"Excellent. You're turning into a diplomat. Of

course, if you were to invite him down to your office, just to ask about your old friends at Kitty Hawk . . ."

Jules gave a sharp glance at the old man's fox-like features, but they were inscrutable. "I'll get rid of him for you, sir. Right now. Then we have some talking to do ourselves. I was in New York, you know, and I found out some very interesting things about your stock market manipulations." A quick look of fear came over Langley's face, to be immediately superceded by an icy look of disdain. Jules opened the door and went out without saying anything more. He closed the door behind him and spoke to Langley's secretary. "Please make a note of this in your office calendar," he said, and, turning to the hawk-faced man, he extended a hand.

"I'm Jules Kincaid," he said. The man stood up, shifting his hat nervously from one hand to the other. "Fred Harris." He put out his hand.

"Secretary Langley has asked me to say that he refuses to see you. He cannot accept any information about the Wright brothers or their camp unless it is submitted to him officially in writing. I'm afraid your trip has been in vain, Mr. Harris."

"Well, I . . ." The man moved hesitantly toward the door, and Jules walked along with him. "How is my friend Bubbo?" he asked. "And Dr. Spratt? Is he still down there?" Jules walked down the corridor with Harris speaking of his friends at Kitty Hawk, and then he invited him—unofficially of course—to join him in his office for a cup of tea.

Jules offered the man a seat and closed the glass-panelled door. "How do you like your tea?" he asked, pouring some from his thermos into a battered mug. "Sugar?" Jules sat down at his desk and stirred his own tea. "And how is Wilbur? Still as full of cracker-barrel wisdom as ever?"

"He's fine. Had a shot at a bear the other day. But Mr. Kincaid, this is important business. Those boys are going to fly an aeroplane. Very soon. I know how it's made, I know how they do it. I've seen their tests."

"I was down there a couple of years ago, but they wouldn't let me see their glider."

"Well, I've seen it, and the new big one too, and I know how they're made. I'll give you the information if you cut me in on the patents. I know you've got lots of money. Just a little in advance . . ."

"We couldn't do that. We have our own machine, which we are planning to fly shortly. We don't want any conflicting stories about where we got our ideas."

"But you don't understand, it's a matter of who's going to fly first and get the experience and the fame—and the money. The information is already public knowledge. The Penaud Tail, the Mouillard patents on wing-warping . . ."

Jules stood up. "Really, Mr. Harris, I cannot listen to any more of this. The Wright brothers are friends of mine, and I don't want to hear any of their professional secrets." He ushered the man out angrily, and stood at the front door of the building until he saw him out of sight.

Jules returned to his office and paced up and down, fiddling with a pencil. Then he stopped in front of a shelf and leafed through some papers until he found a copy of the Mouillard patents of 1901. He had glanced at them before, but now they had new meaning. They showed a practical way to control the flight of a flying machine by bending the outer tips of the wings up and down. Jules filed them away again, paced a few minutes more and then went upstairs to Langley's office. He hardly paused to knock as he went in and closed the door behind himself. "Very illuminating," Jules said to Langley. "I didn't want to listen to too much . . ." Langley gave him a sharp glance. "But they've got a big new machine, motor and all, and they're about ready to fly it. They've got a method for turning in flight which is apparently based on the Mouillard patents, and Harris thinks they're a step ahead of us there."

"We don't have to turn. All I want is a straight flight. How soon can you get our machine ready?"

"It depends upon Manly. You know how many last minute hitches there can be."

"Get it started, Jules. Drop everything else. Tell Manly the same thing. We've got to beat them. Give me an estimated date as soon as possible."

Jules sat down on the corner of Langley's desk. The old man peered up at him through beetled brows and fiddled with a pencil. "Yes?" he said.

"I had a good look at the bank records and stock transaction records at the Smithsonian while I was in Washington. As a director, I felt I was entitled to do so." Jules stopped and let Langley stew in his juices for a moment, hoping that he wouldn't put two and two together and remember that Henry was an officer at the Morgan Bank. "No wonder Karr has been kiting checks," he said. "You fellows are in a lot of trouble. He's been transferring Smithsonian funds into his own accounts, and they went down the hole. And I'm not so simple-minded that I can't see your involvement in all of this."

"I'm completely innocent, Jules. I know how it looks—but I swear I didn't know about Karr's doings until very recently. But I know people will think I'm involved." Langley looked at Jules intensely. "That's exactly why we've got to get that aeroplane in the air as soon as possible. That will settle all our problems. The money will start flowing in, and we'll be able to avoid all the trouble that a situation like this could create. I'm innocent Jules, and you have to help me."

"I don't believe you, and I don't want any part of it. Alicia and I have already talked it over. We'd leave tomorrow if it weren't for the plane."

"That's it exactly." The old man seized at a straw. "If you leave now, it will look suspicious. People might start snooping. But if you get that aeroplane in the air, then all our troubles will be over."

Jules stood up. "I'll do that," he said fiercely. "But then Alicia and I will get out of this town so fast that you won't even see the dust settle." He went out, slamming the door behind him.

Jules stomped down the stairs, put his luncheon sandwiches in his pocket, and went to find Manly in the workshops. "Mr. Manly, we have some new marching orders. We are to drop everything and get this machine into the air as soon as possible. How soon can the airframe be ready?"

Manly stood up, wringing his hands. "I've been waiting for some parts from New York," he said.

"Let's send them a telegram, or go up in person to see if they're ready. Or make do without the parts. Let me look at the plans and the airframe." As Manly bustled out, Jules stared unseeing at the plans for the airframe. So much had happened to him in the last few days that he could hardly concentrate. He knew that the longer he stayed around, the more likely it would be that Langley's defalcations would be uncovered, and that he, Jules, could suffer severe consequences. It could be the end of his career in aeronautical research, even the end of the Smithsonian. It would be five years of concentrated research lost.

He also realized that, since no patents had been applied for, he would probably be able to form a company and build a machine of his own, with Henry supplying the financing and Francis designing the motor. More than that, he felt he had to see the Langley tests. He had to find out if the machine he had worked on for so long would fly.

Jules studied the plans and the partly-assembled airframe closely. He inspected the wings and tail which were suspended from the ceiling of the workshop. Cutting through Manly's forest of excuses, explanations, figures, and estimates, he decided that the aeroplane could be assembled within a week or two, and he left Manly, after repeating Langley's orders to drop everything else and concentrate on the aeroplane.

That afternoon, after sending a message to Alicia, he took the train down to Quantico where the large houseboat was moored in the Potomac River. There were a number of small repairs and tests to be made on the launching apparatus. Jules made lists of what had to be done, spent the night on the boat, and returned the next morning to Washington.

"I would say two to three weeks, Professor Langley," Jules said when he showed his notes to the older man. "Middle of November, perhaps. Then we'll have to try at least five or six flights in perfect weather with a simulated pilot weight before we can try a manned flight."

"Simulated pilot weights? We cannot risk this incredibly expensive machine without an aeronaut on board. What if it crashed? It would take us a year to build a new one."

"Surely you aren't thinking of risking a man's life in an untested machine at forty miles an hour, sixty feet in the air? Lilienthal died doing that, and it wasn't even a powered flight."

The professor had a foxy smile on his face. "We will see, Jules. In the meanwhile, get that machine ready as quickly as possible."

The next several weeks were a blur of work and fatigue for Jules. Sometimes he would forget to go home for days at a time, and Alicia would show up at the Smithsonian with or without Sam, ready to complain bitterly. But, seeing his preoccupation, and knowing the importance of his work, she would wait for a while and make sure that he ate his sandwiches, or sit in the corner of the room where he was working, trying to keep Sam quiet. When one group of men would be assembling and disassembling the machine in the workshops or the courtyards of the Smithsonian, making last minute changes and cursing with frustration as they found one or another part of the complicated machine did not fit as planned and would have to be redone, another large group was down at Quantico testing out the great turntable and adjusting the springs of the launching device. Jules tested out the launch and the ramp, and rented a tugboat for the tests which they had scheduled for November fifteenth. Just before everything was ready, he had another interview with Langley in the secretary's office of the Smithsonian.

"Everything is ready for the test on Wednesday, Professor. It will be just a matter of waiting for wind and weather. I've taken down two hundred pounds of chains to use as a simulated pilot weight, and we can add them in increments of fifty pounds as we make our tests. We have extra sets of wings and tails in case of damage. I feel sure that the frame and the motor components will be waterproof, and not likely to be severely damaged in a crash."

"Jules, I've told you before. We cannot take any risks. I refuse to send this expensive machine up without a man on board to make adjustments in flight. You're very fortunate, Jules. You'll be the first man in the history of the world to make a powered flight in a heavier-than-air machine."

"Surely you're not thinking of sending me up in that thing without tests? It's extremely dangerous, and absurd."

"What's the matter, Jules? Have you lost your nerve?"

Jules sprang to his feet. "This is not a question of nerve or of courage. I have already flown in gliders, and I have every intention of making a flight. But it would be foolhardy to do it without proper testing."

Langley took a long Havana cigar from the humidor on his desk, crinkled it between his fingers appreciatively, clipped and punctured the ends, and lighted it carefully with a wooden match. "The Wrights will beat us," he said with an insidious edge to his voice.

"This is not a horse race, Professor Langley. If either we or the Wrights have a bad accident and someone is killed, it will set back aeronautics by another five years."

"Jules, we cannot waste any more time. I insist that you make that flight on Wednesday. And if not, then perhaps Manly—"

"I wouldn't let you send that poor little fellow up. He'd be so scared he couldn't move, but he might just be foolish enough to let you talk him into it."

"Jules, you are not indispensable. Son-in-law or not, that flight will be made on Wednesday." He stood up, obviously anxious to terminate the conversation.

"And if I were to expose your recklessness and your embezzling?"

"You wouldn't do that, not as long as you are not *certain* of my guilt, would you Jules? I know you wouldn't. You're too interested in seeing if the machine will fly."

Jules let himself be shown out. Langley was right. For all his faults, he had a shrewd understanding of Jules' mentality. Jules couldn't possibly miss the flight.

19

"Hello. Is that you, Jules?" Jules hung his hat on a peg and merely muttered "Yes," as he went up the stairs. "Good!" Alicia shouted after him. "Supper will be ready in half an hour."

Jules was silent as they had their dinner, only smiling occasionally at Sam's innocent chatter. Afterwards, he stood gazing out the front window, his thoughts in a jumble, until Alicia finished washing the dishes and came to join him. Sam was upstairs, playing quietly.

"What is it?" Alicia sat down in her usual chair. "You're very quiet tonight."

Jules turned and looked at her, and he thought of Ariel. For him, Ariel represented young love, and

325

beauty, and freedom. Alicia was duty, and home,—and yes, love. Love of a different kind.

"It's your father. That flight." He wanted to reach out to Alicia, to touch her, but he couldn't. "He wants me to fly the aeroplane on Wednesday."

"Is it very dangerous?" she asked cooly.

"Perhaps. But I'll have to do it if I can't talk him out of it. It's my responsibility."

Alicia twisted a strand of her hair and stared into the cold fireplace. "I suppose that's a decision you'll have to make all by yourself," she said softly. "Whatever happens, I'm your wife. Not Langley's daughter." She came over to stand next to him. "But may I go out with you for the day? I'd be miserable here, just worrying about you."

"You might as well. Everybody else in all creation will be there. Newspapers, Army officers, photographers—every Tom, Dick, and Harry in Washington."

"Like a Roman circus. They want to see blood."

"We'll try to disappoint them." Jules smiled. He turned to her and took both of her hands in his. "I do love you, Lish," he said. But visions of Ariel danced through his head, and he thought of how easy it would be just to walk away from it all and go to Paris or Berlin.

 20

THE cool afternoon light settled upon the Potomac. The water was freezing cold, and sheets of ice floated on its surface. Photographers were stationed along the shoreline and in the tugboat, directly downwind. The Langley Flyer was positioned and ready on the catapult of the houseboat. Manly had been secretive and full of sly smiles in the last few days as they prepared for the flight. Langley was on hand. Ostentatiously, but without saying a word, he went to the pile of chains next to the aeroplane, picked them up one by one, and threw them over the side. Jules ran his hand through his hair, and said. "Well, are we ready?"

He took off his coat and then took his watch and watch-chain from his vest pockets and put them on top of his coat.

"All right," he said, and climbed into the aviator's box in the center of the Flyer. He glanced around, touched the control for the Penaud Tail, and gave Manly a nod. Manly gave one of the propellers a downward pull and the fifty-horsepower engine exploded into action. Jules watched as the r.p.m.'s climbed to above four hundred, and then nodded at Manly again. The catapult clanged open and the aeroplane lurched forward, suddenly going at a speed of nearly forty miles an hour down the monorail of the turntable. It gave a sudden lurch as it left the catapult, and Jules' heart stood still. The machine began to point upwards, its propellers whirling madly. Jules quickly spun the control wheel for the Penaud Tail to straighten the machine out, but the Flyer continued until it was pointing directly upwards and seemed to hang there for a moment, suspended in the air. Then it fell, tail first, into the Potomac, and Jules was thrown against the side of the airframe. His arm broke with an audible snap, and he felt incredible pain as the machine turned over on its back, pushing him down beneath the icy water. He turned himself upside down, trying to kick his way free from the aviator's box, but he seemed to be held in by the network of guy wires. Finally he found a way out. His lungs were bursting and his arm was a torture. He kicked toward the surface, and finally emerged, gasping for air.

"Jules—Jules! Where are you?" He could hear Alicia screaming from her place on the afterdeck of the boat. Jules turned on his side and tried to float motionlessly.

The steam launch soon came chugging up. Huffaker tried to fish Jules out of the icy water. Jules screamed with pain. "My arm—it's broken!" They pulled him on board the launch and Jules screamed again as the two ends of bone ground together. They piled blankets and coats on top of him at the bottom of the boat as it steamed off toward the houseboat. The doctor who Langley had asked to stand by came down into the launch and administered laudanum to Jules before they rolled him onto a cot and lifted him gently on board the boat. Even as the doctor pulled his arm to straighten it and put it into a splint, the others were cutting the icy clothing off Jules' body and rubbing his limbs with towels.

"Jules—Jules. Are you all right?" Alicia had finally been let into the cabin and she came and knelt beside Jules, holding on to his one good hand. Jules tried to smile, but the laudanum was already fogging his mind. Yet when Professor Langley came into the room, Jules was jolted out of his stupor. "You son of a bitch," he began, and Langley herded them all out of the room.

Jules had no memory of the carriage trip back from Quantico or of the doctor who had put on his plaster cast. When he regained his consciousness, he was at home in his own bed with Alicia sitting beside him.

"Are you feeling better now, darling?" Alicia was holding up a bowl of soup. Jules suddenly felt very hungry.

"Help me sit up," he said to Alicia. She put down the bowl and came around to the other side of the bed and helped Jules, putting pillows behind his back and his head. Sam was peering wide-eyed over the end of the bed. "Samuel, come give your father a kiss—no, not on that side. Climb up on the other side of the bed, that's right."

"Daddy all right?" Sam climbed up and kissed Jules on the cheek, then sat on the edge of the bed, watching his father with interest and, it seemed, concern.

Alicia fed Jules some soup, and then he took the pewter spoon himself, but the effort of finishing the bowl seemed to exhaust him.

"I'm glad you're feeling better. You've been muttering and talking French ever since yesterday."

"Is the aeroplane all right?" Jules asked.

"Yes. Mr. Manly said the motor is fine, and the frame isn't even bent. The wings and the tail were ruined, but apparently they have replacements. What I don't understand is . . ." She looked at Sam. "Samuel, you go downstairs and play now. I want to talk to your father."

When the boy had left, Alicia turned back to Jules with a serious look in her eyes. "What I don't understand is, why did father have a doctor standing by?"

"He knew there was a risk."

"And you got in that contraption anyway?"

"He insisted on it. I think he was ready to try and fly it himself."

"And he let *you* take the risk? He let *my husband* risk his life just so he could grab the glory?"

Jules leaned back and closed his eyes. "I wonder what happened," he muttered.

"Manly issued a statement. He said the aeroplane was hit by a gust of wind just at the end of the launch. Jules, we've got to get away from here. How about New York? Or Boston? You could get a job somewhere. Let's get away from the great Professor Langley and Washington society and the whole thing. You could still do your research at home and on weekends. You've always said that those Wright brothers managed to do very well with practically no money."

"We'll have to find out what happened."

Langley didn't come to call. Manly didn't come to call. Nor did Huffaker show up in Georgetown. The newspapers, in the next few days, had passing mentions of a failed experiment in which a Mr. Kincaid had suffered a broken arm. They also quoted a statement from Professor Langley to the effect that the failure of the attempted flight was not due to any error in the design of the Langley Flyer, and that it was in perfect condition and would be tested again within two weeks. Telegrams came from Henry and Francis inquiring how Jules was and whether they should come down to see him. Jules sent back word that he was coming along fine, and that there was no need to go to any trouble on his account.

After three days of restlessness and returning strength, Jules decided to go down to the office. "Well, if you must go, let's at least get a carriage to take you," Alicia said.

"No, I'll take the trolley car as usual," Jules answered. "Where is that old tweed cape of mine? I could just throw it over myself, cast and all. Is it in the trunk down in the root cellar?"

Jules cut a strange figure as he walked down to the trolley stop in his moth-eaten old cape and his bowler hat. It was good to be out in the fresh air again. Alicia and Sam walked with him and waited for the trolley at the corner. He tried not to show how much the brief walk had tired him out.

"Now don't do too much, Jules. And take a carriage home if you're tired." Jules waved to her as the trolley pulled out.

He went first to the workshops, and found Manly with the Langley Flyer, its new wings and tail already attached, suspended from the ceiling for tests.

"Hello, Mr. Kincaid." The little man was beaming as he bustled around giving the workmen their orders in preparation for an engine test. "How are you feeling? We didn't expect you back so soon."

"What happened, Manly? You were watching. What happened?"

"Well, we had to issue a statement."

"Yes, but what really happened? You must have seen something. Was there really a gust of wind?"

"You'd better ask your father-in-law about that."

Jules questioned Huffaker, but Huffaker had been making signals to the tugboat. The workmen were of no help. They wouldn't have recognized a malfunction if they had seen it. Jules trudged upstairs to Langley's office. The battle-axe of a secretary announced him. Langley ushered him in and closed the door. He didn't offer to take Jules' cloak, or offer him a chair. Jules put his hat down on the desk and sat down heavily in a chair.

"What happened? Did you see anything? What was the cause of the crash?"

A fleeting half-smile crossed Langley's features, usually so inscrutable or jovial in public. "Who knows? Maybe it was the wind. Or perhaps you spun the control wheel the wrong way. Some experiments fail, some succeed."

"What do you mean? Did you see that happen? Did anyone see that happen? What's this about new tests?"

"Of course we'll have new tests. The newspapers have already been invited. We must have a new test."

"You're not going to risk anyone's life in that thing after what happened to me. You can't."

"Don't tell me what I can't do." Langley's eyes were blazing. "The attention of the whole world is focused on us, and we must prove that this machine will fly, just as the little ones flew. There's going to be a test next Thursday, and it will succeed!"

"If you let anybody risk his life in that damn machine—even yourself—I'll resign from both of my offices and take Alicia and Sam with me. I'll issue my own press release, telling them exactly how reckless you are, and what a champion embezzler you've been."

"You have no proof, and furthermore, you wouldn't have the courage if you did. You hardly had the courage to get in . . ."

"Merde!" Jules jumped to his feet, and winced at the pain it caused him. "Damn it, I do resign. Here and now. Alicia and I, nom de Dieu, we're getting out of this damned place." Jules jammed his bowler down on his head and strode to the door. Turning, he said, "And don't believe I won't do what I said. I'll issue a statement that will blast you right out of Washington."

Langley laughed. Jules opened the door and slammed it shut behind him. Going down the stairs he was suddenly exhausted. He had to grab the banister and stop until he quit trembling.

Manly was still bustling about the workshops, pouring gasoline into the tiny tanks of the aeroplane engine. Jules spoke to him quietly. "Manly, you're not going to let him talk you into flying this thing, are you?"

Manly stopped what he was doing and looked up apprehensively. "I really don't want to, although the professor says it is quite safe."

"Don't let him talk you into it, Manly. I tell you as a friend. You could get yourself killed. I'm washing my hands of the whole thing. I'm resigning and leaving town."

Jules stalked away with more energy than he really felt. Manly stared after him, dumbfounded.

The trolley ride home to Georgetown seemed to be even rougher and more jolting than usual. Jules held on to the seat in front of him with his one good hand. He could hardly make it off the trolley and drag himself home. He entered at the front door and sank down into the nearest chair. Alicia came in from the kitchen.

"What happened? Oh, you look so exhausted. Let me take your cloak." Jules brushed her hands away. "We're leaving. I quit my job. We'll sell the house and . . ."

"Yes, Jules." She unbuttoned his cloak and drew it back carefully from his shoulders, and hung up his hat.

"We'll sell the house. That'll give us a little money, and a little time to look around. Maybe we'll go up to Plymouth. It's terribly cold in the winter, but . . ."

"Whatever you want to do, Jules. Whatever you decide, Sam and I are with you." She walked to the kitchen door and paused, her hands on the molding of the door frame. "It'll be nice to get out of Washington," she said, looking back at him pensively.

The next day, Jules went downtown to a real-estate broker to put his house on the market. The bank that held the mortgage could handle the transaction for him, and the broker assured him that it would be no great problem to sell the house, although they probably wouldn't get much. On his way home, Jules sent a telegram to the Smithsonian officially confirming his resignation from both his job and from the Board of Directors, effective immediately.

As they began packing up their few belongings, having decided to go to Plymouth at least until after the holidays, Jules discussed it with Alicia. "I can't believe the old bastard is going to go through with it. According to the *Star*, he's going to attempt another manned flight on December 8th."

"I tell you, he's reckless. He'd sacrifice anything for fame and fortune. He's always been that way. Look what he did to Mother." She packed Jules' battered top hat carefully in its leather hat box, and filled the box up with union suits and stockings.

"Now he's going to risk the whole thing on one more throw of the dice! He could even lose his job."

"Not father. He's too smart for that. He'll probably even figure out a way to blame everything on you and Karr."

When Jules and Alicia went over to the Smithsonian the next day to clean out his office and pack up his papers, they didn't go up to the director's office. The workmen, with whom Jules had worked so closely for so many years, were peculiarly distant. They smiled and doffed their hats, but they didn't venture to start up any conversations. Jules left it that way. He saw Manly once, and merely waved his hand to him. Manly didn't stop to talk. He seemed quietly exuberant.

For dinner that night they had the last scrapings of their Virginia ham. "I'll make some good soup with this bone tomorrow," Alicia said.

"The tests are scheduled for Thursday. I'd like to stay around until after that, if you don't mind. We could leave on the tenth."

"Whatever you say, Jules." Alicia patted his hand and turned to her son. "Sam, stop banging your plate."

The afternoon of December eighth found Jules, bundled up in his cape, an old felt hat on his head and a pair of heavy binoculars around his neck, on the train to Virginia. Jules knew that without his help, they wouldn't be able to get ready in time for a dawn launch. It was no secret where the tests were to be made. Jules knew exactly where he could find a hilltop near Clifton Point, right on the railroad line, so that he would be able to look down on the entire thing.

It was a barren hilltop, cold with winter. Here and there were small groups of interested people out for the same purpose he was. As he swept the river and the opposite bank with his heavy binoculars, Jules could spot vantage points where official photographers were stationed with telescopic lenses, and he could see the rowboats full of reporters and photographers. He could see the Langley Flyer mounted on the turntable. Even at this distance, it looked large and impressive. He could make out Manly rushing

around, and even Langley on the covered afterdeck.
Jules put his binoculars down. They were hard to hold
up for long periods of time with only one hand. Clumsily, he fished a packet of Fatimas from his pocket. It
took him almost a half a box of wooden matches before he could manage to light a cigarette. Nervously,
he walked around, not approaching any of the small
knots of men who stood together stamping their feet.

Two men in tweed coats and bowler hats attracted his attention. "Hello!" Jules said. It was the
Wright brothers. "Gentlemen! What a surprise!"

"Hello, Jules. We didn't expect to see you here.
We thought you had left town."

"I didn't expect to see you here, either." Jules
said.

"We were down at Kitty Hawk. We weren't invited, but it's no secret where the tests are being
held."

"That's right." Jules raised his binoculars to his
eyes again. He saw signal flags being waved on the
tugboat, downwind from the houseboat. Manly was in
the aviator's box.

"It ain't gonna fly," Wilbur said. "You know that,
don't you Jules?"

"What do you mean? How do you know?" Jules
asked.

"We knew last month. Not with those wings." A
rocket went up from the houseboat. The Wright
brothers were each peering through telescopes. Jules'
one arm ached from holding up the binoculars. In the
distance they could hear the gasoline engine start up
and rapidly increase its r.p.m.'s. Its echo banged and
sputtered from the Potomac shores.

"What do you mean?" Jules asked, his eyes glued to the eye-pieces.

The Langley Flyer sprang forward and Jules fancied that he could even hear the springs of the catapult. It rapidly rolled down the launching rail, its propellers whirling. It reached the end and went out over the water and seemed to pause for a moment; then it nosed down into the river, its wings splintering, and its engine noise suddenly stopping as it went under water.

"God!" Jules' arm trembled. Exclamations came from the other groups nearby on the hill, but the Wright brothers were silent, peering through their telescopes. Bits of wing and tail surfaces were coming to the surface of the river. Jules scanned the wreckage. It seemed forever before Manly surfaced and began waving his arms at the nearest rowboat full of reporters. Wilbur Wright broke in a huge guffaw and slapped his leg.

"I knew it, *I knew it*!" Wilbur laughed and slapped his leg again. "There weren't no way them wings could hold up five hundred pounds."

"What do you mean by that?" Jules asked, incensed.

"We ran wind-tunnel tests on all them wings," Wilbur said, smiling exuberantly. "We knew they were going to crumble. There weren't no way they could hold up that weight."

"And you let us go ahead? And risk our lives?" Jules could barely control his anger.

"Now Wilbur." Orville Wright gestured at his brother. "You've said too much. Don't tell Mr. Kincaid how to run his business."

"He could have been killed. I could have been

killed. If you were so sure, why didn't you say something?"

"Well, now," Orville Wright tried to mollify Jules. "We're running our own tests next week. Then we'll know for certain."

"Then we'll all know for certain."

"At least Manly is all right," Jules said.

"Thank the good Lord for that."

Jules got away from them as quickly as he could, and on the way home to Georgetown his mind was in a turmoil. He remembered every word of their conversation, and heard Wilbur's scornful laugh over and over again in his memory. He believed them. They would fly. They would be the first to fly.

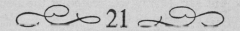

21

THEIR little house was empty and cold. The trunks had been sent on ahead. Alicia and Jules and little Sam stood on the brick sidewalk looking back at their first home; Alicia's first home of her own. A tear came to her eye, and Alicia brushed it away with her glove. The coachman fidgeted nervously and cleared his throat. "Ah, well," Jules sighed, "let's go." He helped Alicia and little Sam into the carriage, and then grunted as he maneuvered himself into position with his one good arm.

There was little to say as they rolled smoothly down Pennsylvania Avenue. Alicia was suddenly alert. "Where are we going? This isn't the way to the station."

"I thought we should say good-bye to your father," Jules said softly. They stopped in front of the main building of the Smithsonian. "You wait here," Jules said. "I'll see if he's in his office."

As Jules swung out of the carriage and went up the stairs of the Smithsonian, Alicia was embarrassed to see him in the shabby, moth-eaten old cloak that covered up his arm, still in a sling. As he went through the doors he took off his bowler hat, and Alicia could see the crease it left in his blond hair.

Jules went up the stairs for the last time to the director's office. The outer office had been changed around. Now there were two desks. The forbidding old secretary with her typewriting machine was not at her desk, but Mr. Manly was seated at the new desk, writing up an experiment.

"Good morning," Jules said as he gave a little half-bow. "Is Professor Langley in?"

"No, he isn't. He's spending the day at home. He was feeling rather tired."

Jules paused. There was one thing he wanted to know. "I'm glad you didn't get hurt, Manly," Jules said. Manly stood up, clearing his throat and tapping his pencil on the desk. "What made you do it? How did he get you to do it?" Jules asked.

"Well . . . I've been made a member of the Board of Directors." Mr. Manley raised his chin, and a smug, self-satisfied smile came over his face. "There was an opening," he said.

"Well, I wish you the best. Good-bye, Mr. Manly." Jules offered his good hand and Manly shook it. "Good-bye, Mr. Kincaid, and I wish you well in your new endeavors, whatever they may be."

Jules went downstairs and got into the carriage. "He wasn't there," he explained, and told the driver how to get to Mr. Langley's house. "We can catch a later train, Alicia. We should at least give him a chance to say good-bye to his grandson."

The gray stone mansion was lit by winter sunshine, but its dark windows, veiled by dusty white lace curtains, were like empty black eye-sockets; no life behind them. Alicia, Sam and Jules went up the stairs, and Alicia knocked on the door for the first time in her life. They stood there alone in the December silence, and only the stamping of their carriage horse behind them broke the stillness, until a maid's quick steps echoed in the hall of the house.

"Oh, hello, Miss Lang—uh—Mrs. Kincaid."

"Hello, Sally. Is my father in? We came to say goodbye."

"I—uh—I'll find out if he's in."

Uncomfortable in their heavy coats, they waited in the corridor until the maid came back. With a sly little smile, she ushered them down the familiar hall and opened the sliding doors to the study. Immaculate in cutaway and striped trousers, Langley was sitting at his desk, and affected to be immersed in some papers in front of him until the door had been closed behind them.

"Oh, good morning," he said as he looked up and smiled weakly.

"We came to say goodbye," Alicia said. "Sam, shake hands with your grandfather."

"Ah, that's a little man." The professor came around his desk and shook hands with his grandson. "Will you miss me, sonny?"

Sam just looked up at him in silence. He hardly knew his grandfather.

"It's too bad you're leaving just now, Jules. I have

just received the welcome news that we are going to receive the body of James Smithson. He was a descendant of Henry the VII, you know. It's his first trip to the great institution that bears his name. It will be the finest occasion since the cortège of President Lincoln."

"Good God," Jules muttered. "Well, goodbye, Professor. You'll always be welcome to come up and visit us at Plymouth." They shook hands. Alicia offered her gloved hand, but then broke into tears and threw herself into her father's arms. Good-bye, Father."

"Mama, Mama. What's the matter with you?" Little Sam tugged at her skirt.

"It's nothing, Sam. Come along now." Professor Langley showed them to the front door.

Once they were settled in their railway carriage, Alicia was quiet and pensive. Little Sam stared, fascinated, at the snow-covered countryside that seemed to roll past the train windows. Jules opened up a copy of *The Washington Star* which he had picked up in Union Station, and propped it against his crossed legs. It was still full of stories about the failure of Langley's flying machine, and suggesting that there might be a Congressional investigation into the expenditure of War Department funds on such a crazy project. Lord Kelvin and Sir Hiram Maxim were quoted again and again, *ad nauseam*, to the effect that heavier-than-air machines were physically impossible to fly due to the rule of the cube relating to supporting surfaces. On an inside page there was a little story picked up by the Associated Press from the *Norfolk Virginian-Pilot*. It stated that the Wright brothers, two bicycle manufacturers from Dayton, Ohio, claimed to have made four flights in a heavier-than-air machine that they had constructed. The longest had been a flight of 59 seconds and had covered 852 feet. They said the machine had been shortly thereafter destroyed by a sudden gust of wind, and that they were unable to supply pictures of it in flight at this time. Jules put the paper down and stared out the window.

22

"MERRY Christmas, Merry Christmas, Jules!" Henry bounded off the inter-urban trolley at Plymouth, and the brothers pounded each other on the back, Jules taking care to protect his bad arm. Henry was the very picture of the successful young Wall Street tycoon, as indeed any Morgan employee was expected to be.

"Where did you get that old trap?" he asked, pointing at the dessicated horse-and-buggy into which his brother was loading his packages and valise.

"Just bought it," Jules said proudly. "Cheap, too. It's the off-season for the livery stable." As the old horse set out at a lively trot over the frozen, rutted road to the house, Henry and Jules exchanged friendly banter. "What's that?" Henry asked when they arrived.

"A coal-bin. I bought a whole load of cannel coal.

It burns much cleaner and I don't have to spend hours gathering driftwood. But we have a wood fire today!"

"That's wonderful, Jules. How's the old house holding up? Does the wind still howl through at night?"

"Cozy as a bug in a rug. We're having a wonderful time. Sam loves it."

"Hello Henry. Merry Christmas!" Alicia stood at the open door. Sam was beside her holding on to her skirt. "Uncle Henry," Sam said uncertainly.

"Hello, Alicia. Merry Christmas, dear." Henry hugged her and gave her a big kiss before leaning over to pick Sam up. "Oh, do I have some nice toys for you," he said.

The fire was crackling merrily in the fireplace, salt-soaked driftwood giving out blue and red sparks. A wide and handsome Christmas tree completely filled one corner of the room, and reached right to the ceiling. Alicia and Sam had decorated it gaily with strings of multi-colored popcorn and bits of red and green paper.

"When is Francis coming out? I stopped and looked around at his shop, but some kid there said that he was entered in some sort of motorcycle race."

"Oh, he'll be out in time for dinner. We're having a huge roast goose. Can't you smell it?" Alicia smiled.

"I get the drumstick," Sam said, jumping up and down.

Late in the afternoon Francis roared up on the loudest motorcycle they had ever heard. They all went out to greet him, shivering in the cold.

"Merry Christmas, everybody. Merry Christmas, Henry." The three brothers drew together, laughing and putting their arms around each other. Sam kept pulling at their legs and Alicia stood to one side, smiling. "You must have been doing fifty miles an hour on that thing," Jules said. "You're going to kill yourself."

"I did seventy-two on the Post Road last week," Francis said with enthusiasm. "We're going to have a regular race on New Year's day, and the winner gets a hundred dollar prize. Where could I park this thing so it doesn't freeze up? Can I leave it just inside the door, Alicia?"

"Oh, no you don't. I won't have that oil and grease dripping on my clean floor."

"You'll just have to build a fire under it tomorrow morning," Jules said. "Put it in the barn, out of the wind."

"Let's get inside," Alicia said. "I'm freezing."

Christmas dinner was enlivened by their traditional hot, spiced wine. Francis was raving about his motorcycle races. "Wait until I get my new seven-cylinder job into action. I bet I'll be able to do ninety."

"What does it weigh?" Henry asked.

"Oh, it weighs a ton, but that will help me hold the road. Even the little one is so fast that I have to skid around the corners. Some day all of these roads will have to be banked, like race-courses."

"Like turning an aeroplane in mid-flight. I think the same principles will apply," Jules said.

"How are things on Wall Street, Henry?" Alicia asked.

"Just marvelous." Henry was suddenly pontifical. "We pulled off the International Harvester offering beautifully. We control eighty percent of the industry. The stock is badly watered right now, but we keep the market churning. They put me on the Board of

Directors." Henry examined his beautiful manicured nails. "Now that fellow Blériot wants to incorporate a company to sell his automobile headlamps. He's making a fortune with them in Europe. I'm thinking about quitting my job and making the offering myself."

"Oh, you wouldn't do that, would you, Henry?" Alicia asked. "Quit a good job with all that security and prestige to start up a new company in such a competitive business?"

"This is the age of entrepreneurs, Alicia. Look at my little brother. He has his own business and he's getting rich."

"I'm losing my shirt," Francis laughed. "Everything I've got is invested in parts, and I've hardly sold any machines yet. But winning these races will help me to become known. Don't worry about little Francis." He tossed his blond hair and smiled his winning smile.

"What about you, Jules?" They sat around the fireplace, smoking great Havana cigars that Henry had brought up from New York, and toasting their feet on the brass fender. Alicia, still drying the dishes, listened carefully.

"Oh, I don't know," Jules answered. "We've got a little money from the sale of the house to tide us over until I find something. But—did you fellows see that news report?" Jules took out his wallet and handed them the clipping from the Washington Star. "The Wright brothers really did it. The press hasn't said much about it yet, for some reason, but I'm sure they flew. And I know how. We could do the same thing if only we had a little money. You see . . ." Jules became very intense, his brothers leaning forward to hear his every word. "You see, it involves wing-warping—

controlling the flight pattern by bending the wing-
tips up and down, not unlike your old aileron idea,
Henry. And the other thing is that they have been using a wind tunnel. It's simply an old box with a fan
blowing air through it, but you can test miniature
wing surfaces in it, and measure lift. We could easily
rig one up . . . "

From upstairs, where she was tucking Sam into
his bed with visions of sugarplums dancing before his
eyes, Alicia could hear the low mutters of conversation from the Kincaid brothers down below. She
couldn't help wondering what the future would bring.
She could only trust in Jules. He was a man of
strength and character, and there was a burning core
of determination there inside him. She could only
trust in Jules.

Later that night, after Alicia had gone to bed,
and after he had heard his brothers, lying together in
the broad bed in which Prudence Kincaid had died,
quiet down, Jules lighted up the fag end of a Havana
cigar that Henry had discarded and stood looking out
the window at the snowy meadow beyond the road.

"We'll do it," he said to himself. "We'll fly. Right
off that meadow. And not just ten feet above the
ground, either. A hundred feet, a thousand feet."

It was man's ancient dream, and the Kincaid
brothers would make it come true. Jules knew it, and
soon the world would know it. They would fly.

**FIRST IN THE DRAMATIC NEW
SKYMASTER SERIES:**

TO SOAR
WITH EAGLES

Richard Hale Curtis

Carl Kincaid was a young American with a dream. In it, he soared through the air, over rooftops, across oceans. But Carl was not content merely to dream—his was a burning ambition to be among the pioneers who would build the first heavier-than-air flying machines, and conquer the final element.

Caught up in the tumultuous events of revolt-torn France of the latter nineteenth century, driven by the idealism of the beautiful French girl, Louise Barrault, and haunted by failure and scandal in his work with Europe's foremost inventors, Carl was sworn to realize his dream—and forge a dynasty that would fight through the generations for mastery of the perilous sky. . . .